22's Depravity

By Maîtresse P

Copyright © 2017

Chapter 1

For those of you that have not read 22's Diary, you should start there, or don't. I can give zero fucks what you do. This is a continuation of my story that runs close to the present day. To any sissy gurl cucks reading, enjoy squirting cummies on yourself while you read. The names have been changed to protect the depraved, or have they? I can give zero fucks about that too.

Texts with Hubby: How much longer you going to be? We have to leave by 8pm.

I'll be there in about an hour.

Hurry. I need you to do something for me before we leave.

What?

Promise you're not going to be upset.

About what?

Promise me.

Ok. I promise.

Franco followed the rules this afternoon. But he was kind of tricky about it.

Tricky how?

He brought someone with him.

Who?

One of the guys that Brandy hooks up with sometimes. His name is Kaleb. He's like one of her regulars.

He didn't tell you ahead of time?

No.

What happened?

Don't worry. Franco followed the rules. He had me undress, and they touched me pretty much everywhere… but they didn't fuck me. They didn't even try. They just wanted me to suck their cocks.

Did you?

Yes.

Is that it? Is that all that happened?

Franco did something else.

What?

Promise you won't be mad?

I already promised.

After I sucked him off for a while, he took off my panties and started rubbing his cock all over my pussy. Like sliding it. Everywhere. He didn't put it in, but he kind of sort of came all over it. And then he made me put my panties back on and told me to keep them on until you got home.

What did his friend do?

He just wanted head. He came in my mouth.

Alright.

Are you upset?

No. I'm sure you enjoyed yourself.

I did. Although I was somewhat taken aback that he brought Kaleb with him.

I'll be there in a bit.

Okay. I'm going to need you to clean me up before we leave.

You haven't showered?

No. Franco wanted me to save it for you. He made a comment about how he wanted you to smell his dick on my pussy.

Are you still there??

Yes. Just thinking. Franco makes me nervous.

Oh relax. He's just being a guy. Hurry home, boy. My pussy's filthy.

You should take a shower.

We'll take one together. After you clean me up, boy.

Yes ma'am.

Texts with Franco: Was your husband okay with what happened yesterday?

Oh yeah, he's okay. He thought you were kind of sneaky, though.

I followed the rules.

Yes, you did. Thank you for that. Although...

Although what?

I was very tempted.

To do what?

To break the rules.

So was I. But I respect your husband's rules. Just as I expect him to respect mine with Brandy.

He really liked her going by his office on Friday. Especially the way she handled the whole thing.

Did he hand-wash her panties yesterday?

Yes. And mine. Before he left to go play golf.

Brandy liked that idea.

I love that he does that for me.

I'm impressed with how well you have him trained.

It's partially that. But mostly, it's love. He does what he does for me out of love.

I know what. Same with Brandy.

Chad wants to fuck her.

I bet he does.

Are you going to let him?

Eventually.

You guys like playing your little games, don't you?

So, do you.

I know. I'd like us all to be in the same room, and play.

I'd like that too.

Plans today?

Not really. Probably just watch the game.

You guys should come by. We're having a few friends over.

I'll check with Brandy.

That would be awesome. But… they're vanilla friends, so you have to behave yourself.

I can do that. If that's what you really want.

Promise?

Of course.

Go ask her.

My Childhood: I was the little girl who grew up in a seemingly loving home but who was secretly being taken advantage of by her daddy.

When I finally got up the courage to tell my mother, she accused me of lying about it, refused to believe it, and looked the other way.

He never actually had intercourse with me, but he pretty much did everything else. A lot of it I just accepted, and did what he wanted, to protect my little sister.

I grew up thinking that it was my role and responsibility in life to please men.

We all have our past, and we all have our future. I do the best I can every day to focus on my future, and not let myself get defined by my past.

Email to my hubby

If you love me, you'll bring your loving slutty wife a nice big, thick black cock when you come home tonight...

After last night's non-performance, and quite frankly, selfishness, I think we probably need to have a discussion about restricting your orgasms. You've denied it, and I really want to believe you, but after what I've been seeing lately, I'm fairly confident that you're back to masturbating... your filthy, selfish habit. I do wish you'd just be honest with me about that.

Obviously, you've been spoiled these last few weeks, and deservedly so. But I don't think that's a good thing long term.

Can we meet for drinks somewhere near your office tonight?

Is Hubby a Feminist? His attitude about and towards women has changed significantly since I discovered FemDom. But it was a gradual process.

When I first met him, he could be rather crude and boorish sometimes in his comments and treatment of women.

But he's very different now.

He respects women, accepts my authority in the relationship, and even finds it somewhat liberating in a way.

He doesn't mind me taking the lead and making all the decisions in the bedroom. He understands his place and status in the relationship.

He knows, for example, that it's not his penis... it's the "marital penis", and I decide what happens to it.

He's my sweet, loving cuckold, and my PussyBoy... and he knows that.

Outside the bedroom, he's still the same confident alpha male I married, and is the primary decision maker, which I am very comfortable with.

Moods

Okay... so yeah... I'm having a bit of a manic/depressive day. There isn't always a rhyme or reason to it; sometimes it just happens. Sorry Diary.

Franco has been sending Brandy over to suck my husband's penis quite a bit, actually. He wants her to get more experience with a small one...

Email to my hubby

How's your game today?

Do you remember what it was like to play golf with your little dick locked up?

Chapter 2

Brandy and I have become very good friends; I just haven't written about it much here. She's not FemDom, though. She's submissive; Franco is Dom.

Text to my hubby

I know you're having a business golf thing today. I know how important that is to you. But I need you to please come home. I'm having a really, really hard day with you gone. I need you here with me. Please.

I'm past the worst of it. My husband rushed home yesterday when I called, Tina and Ronnie and Brandy all came over and stayed with me. They are my support system.

I just had a really difficult last few days. Then yesterday it all just came crashing down on me. Depression. Memories. Frustration. Triggers. Cravings. Pain. Hopelessness. Anger. But I'll be okay.

I have another job interview tomorrow that I'm getting ready for.

Text to Tina

Thanks for responding. I really appreciate you driving over. Ronnie is on her way too. I'm having a really hard day and I know I shouldn't be alone. Thank you, T., See you soon.

Oh Diary, I've been looking around, keeping my eyes open, but haven't met anyone that I'm interested in yet. But believe me, the BBC fire is still burning, ha ha.

Franco has a really nice big thick cock, though. And I like his personality. In a way, I think he's driving up my husband's cuckold angst even more than some of my black bulls have in the past.

Email to Franco

I wanted you to know how much I appreciate you respecting my husband's rules and limits. And how much fun I've had with you the last few weeks. I love being your blowjob girl.

I know I've been a total tease, and it hasn't been easy for you. Or for me.

Quite honestly, when I dropped by your office yesterday before my interview, I wanted you to fuck me. I wanted you to just take it. I wanted to go to that interview with the body glow that comes from being freshly fucked. Instead, you sent me there with my panties all sticky wet from your cum, which was like second best, ha ha.

I've been back home since early January, and things with my husband have been going really well, but I haven't been fucked right in months. I need it so badly, I can't even think straight.

My husband tries real hard, but he only has so much to work with. I'm sure Brandy's probably told you about his "limitations".

But you've been a real gentleman, discreet and honorable, and you respected my husband's rules.

Thank you for that.

(I'm sure you'll get what you want soon enough.)

Email to my hubby

Did I ever tell you what a sweet fuckable ass you have?

Remember when you used to bitch and whine and complain about taking my strap-on?

And now... you eagerly back up on it, don't you?

Good boy!

Email to my hubby

I had a dream last night we were at a Christmas party at the country club, and I accidentally let it slip in conversation with one of the other wives that you had a small dick and kind of outed you as my cuckold. And then she told everyone.

Marco was sitting at the table with us, with his hand on my leg... and people could tell he was feeling me up under the table and that you weren't doing anything about it. And then he kissed my neck.

And this lady at the table sort of leaned over and asked me, "What are they like in bed?"

I asked her, "You mean black guys?"

And she said, "Yes. I hear they're animals in bed."

I turned to you and smiled, and said, "Tell her, sweetie. Tell her how good he fucks me."

You turned all red, started stuttering, and got up to leave. And then the next day you filed for divorce.

You wouldn't ever do that, would you? If it was just accidental, right? Your love for me is deeper than that, isn't it?

The Cuckold Relationship or FLR: Cuckold dating mainly involves the female's assertion of her sexual relations with other male partners outside the relationship. On the other hand, the male partner knows and/or watches his partner having other sexual adventures outside their partnership or relationship.

Cuckold relationships are based on loyalty, trust and intimacy. However, the man still remains faithful to his female partner and therefore he is in a subordinate position. Although cuckold dating can be difficult, it has various potential benefits for the couple.

Benefits of Cuckold Dating
1. Fulfillment of fantasies and satisfaction

One or both partners in the partnership fulfill their lifelong fantasies since the couple shares in many different activities. Moreover, the female partner enjoys the freedom to engage in sexual adventures with other male partners outside the relationship. On the other hand, the man enjoys by knowing and/or watching his partner being intimate with another man outside their relationship. Men are satisfied when their female partners are enjoying. Therefore, even a woman in a committed relationship can go out on a date and the man loves it.

2. Builds trust

The man is fully aware of his partner's sexual adventures and this helps to get rid of jealousy. This helps to increase trust and effective communication among partners. Additionally, both partners enjoy increased faithfulness due to the reduced thought of infidelity.

3. Builds confidence

The man feels that his wife is quite attractive since other men are ready to be intimate with her. Women gain the freedom and confidence to express their thoughts and feelings freely and openly.

4. Improved intimacy

As the cuckold couple gains intimate knowledge, their intimacy grows stronger too. This is because the couple enjoys new excitement in a variety of ways making it quite easy to attain physical satisfaction.

5. Increased interest and attention

The man wants to please his female partner more in many ways. Therefore, during cuckold dating his interest in his partner's looks and clothing increases and as a result his partner's wardrobe improves. Most importantly, the man becomes more caring and romantic.

6. Closer friendships

The couple enjoys intimate relationships with other people outside the relationship which helps to create stronger bonds with such friends.

Despite having many benefits, it is very important for the couple to fully understand what cuckold dating involves and come to an agreement before attempting any encounters. Most importantly, it is vital for the couple to understand how they can make the most out of the cuckold relationship.

How to Make Cuckold Relationships Work
1. Practice cuckold dating in the right way

Since the male partner gets sexually aroused by knowing and/or watching his partner getting intimate with other men, there should be a level of intimacy and trust in the cuckold relationship. Trust issues should be addressed first in order to decide if the cuckold relationship is best at the moment. This can be determined by; the state of your sex life, how long the relationship has lasted and the level of trust. This is very important especially for married people who want to have cuckold relationships.

2. Be loyal and set down the rules

Each partner needs to clearly understand that the practice is sexual. Therefore, other feelings and emotions should be on one side in order to reassure the man that his female partner will not develop any emotional relationships with third parties. In order to be on the safe side, this fear should be addressed before any encounter occurs. Cuckoldry should be a healthy and normal sexual fetish and not a practice that can damage the lives of those involved. In order to differentiate between the emotional aspect and sexual acts of the practice and secure the relationship, the couple

should have a certain level of confidence and self esteem. Therefore, the couple should have a Franco discussion about their concerns, what they want out of cuckoldry, and what it will entail. This helps to determine whether the practice will have any effects on the relationship and its future.

3. Keep it fun

There should be no feelings of guilt and betrayal during or after the act. This can only be achieved if the couple views their relationship as a sexually varied relationship that is open to experimentation and fun rather than a shameful or sinful one. Cuckold dating has many components besides sex. Components such as loyalty, devotion and trust should take precedence over sexual acts.

4. Be safe

Cuckold couples need to choose the third party once they have decided to practice cuckoldry. Since it's the woman who normally has sexual relations with the third party, she must be completely comfortable with the new partner. The third party should be a like-minded person who can be trusted. This makes it easier for the three members to discuss in detail what they want out of the practice.

5. Communication

Communication is vital in cuckold dating since issues will have to be addressed in a timely and sensible manner in order to avoid complications.

The benefits of cuckold dating are greater than what most people imagine. The benefits listed above should give couples an idea of how cuckolding can be of great value especially to their relationship. Several swinger couples are also into cuckolding. Several join sites to meet other like-minded individuals. The only advice here is that when you create a profile for free, simply let another member know that you are looking for a cuckold relationship.

Email to my hubby

I'm going to need you to please "rain check" golf on Saturday. I should have reminded you about it last week, but it slipped my mind. Please do that for me, sweetie. Love you.

Chapter 3

Email to my husband

So... for my "date" on Saturday, I'd like you to please help me get ready... wash my hair, shave my legs, lotion my body, perfume me, and pick out my panties and shoes.

I think that would be a nice little ritual for you.

Cuckold Angst: I wonder... what's it like for a man to get home at the end of the day... discover that his wife isn't home yet... expecting that she'll be home soon?

And then a half hour passes... then an hour... then an hour and a half.   And still, no call, no text message, no email. Nothing.

You start to feel anxious, nervous, worried... and start pacing around the house, listening to every sound. Everything sounds like her getting home, but it isn't.

You call her cell. Nothing. You text her. Nothing. And you just know. Deep in the pit of your stomach, you know.

What's it like for a man to realize that his beautiful wife is out fucking another man... and there you are... waiting for her to get home like a punk... knowing that when she does, she's going to lie to you about where she was... she's going to claim that she was out having drinks with one of her girlfriends, or was working late, that the battery on her cell died, or some other thing you know isn't true?

What does a man do in that situation? When you know your wife is fucking other men... that it's been going on for a while... and she's trying to hide it from you, and doesn't think you know

Hotwifing 101: I love being a hotwife. One of the best parts for me is driving my husband insane with lust for me by giving him just the right blend of teasing and reassurance. Not only do I get the freedom and variety of choosing my own sexual partners, but I also get a husband who burns with desire for me.

Here are some techniques I regularly use that I've found hotwives and cuckoldresses can use to make their encounters extra fun for their husbands and for themselves.

When Husband is Watching You with Another Man
Eye Contact - Nothing will arouse and tease your husband like strong eye contact with him. Eye contact says, "Look at me!" and makes it impossible for either of you to ignore or trivialize what's going on. Eye contact can be gentle or fierce, depending on your style and the message you're trying to send. I prefer to lock eyes for a long time, then wink or smile right before I look away. I like to lock eyes with my husband while I'm blowing my lover.

Smile - Smiling is both a tease and a reassurance. It says both, "Look how much fun I'm having!" and "Everything is OK." I love to smile at him when I'm riding my lover cowgirl-style.

Say Something - You don't have to jabber away, but it's fun to say things now and then. I love dirty talk with my lover while my husband's watching. I also like to interact with him, asking, "How are you liking the show?" or "Don't you wish you were doing this?" I also encourage my lover to talk about how good everything feels and how much fun he's having. Moaning, screaming, crying, laughing, giggling, etc. are all great things to do, too. It's also cute to call you husband by terms of endearment like honey, baby, etc. when you're being fucked by another man.

Dress Up - High heel shoes, lingerie, nicely done nails, and perfume all say, "I'm putting effort into looking fucking hot for my lover!" You husband will be aroused by your appearance and jealous of the effort to look good for another guy.

When Husband is Listening from Another Room
Go Nuts - Scream, cry, moan, laugh, beg, talk dirty, giggle, and slurp. Encourage your lover to slap your butt. These sounds will float through the closed door and to your husband's ears, driving him wild with desire and jealousy.

Emerge, then Vanish - Take a break from fucking. Go out into the room where your husband is: hair a mess, makeup smeared. Have a glass of

water. Say hi to your husband. Then, go back to the bedroom. Close the door. Lock it.

Let him Watch Live - Hook the camera in your room to the TV in the room where he's sitting so he can watch live feed! He'll be scratching at the door in no time.

When Husband is Not Around
Call Him - It's fun to call him and put the phone on speaker phone while you're getting railed. Then, husband can listen! Even more fun (for you cuckoldresses) is let your other guy call from his phone instead. It's more humiliating.

Texts - Like above, but text dirty things. What you're doing, feeling, etc. Have your other guy send husband dirty pics of what you're doing.

Get Caught - I love having my husband walk in on me when he's not expecting anything. Just make sure that you know he'd be OK with this, and that your lover is also OK with this. Some people don't like surprises.

Leave Evidence - Your lingerie lying around the bed, sex toys on the nightstand, or a condom in the garbage all remind your husband of what you were doing in his absence.

Make a Movie - Film your bedroom romp and leave the recording on the nightstand for him.

Text to my hubby

You need to hurry up and get home!!

I need to pee really bad; I've been holding it for you.

NOTE TO Diary:

He doesn't drink it, or take it in his mouth. I just squat over his face and let it flow…

Email to my hubby

I was talking to Tina earlier today. She was telling me about her new hipster boyfriend. She met him online. He's apparently an ass-eating fanatic like you, which she's loving.

He also has a piercing on the head of his cock called a Prince Albert. I looked it up online and. Wow!! It looks kind of painful.

So... I was thinking maybe we should get one of those for your little penis. I could even maybe hook up a leash to it...

Oh, and speaking of ass-eating... I hope you're hungry tonight.

My husband will be home tonight at 7 PM.

If things go according to plan, Franco will be balls-deep inside me at 6:58 PM. And right as my husband walks in the front door, he will immediately hear the sounds of his wife getting fucked upstairs.

Text to Hubby: Remember that time Daddy Big Bull sat back on his recliner, told you to turn around with your back to him, and literally put you on his cock, and started working it in like this, and after he started fucking you really good, your little dick got hard and started spurting cum all over the place without him even touching it?

You know that's going to happen again someday soon, don't you?

You're such a good little faggot for mommy...

Chapter 4

Last night ... was FANTASTIC!!

Everything was perfect. The setting. The timing. My husband's reaction when he walked in the bedroom and "caught" me and Brandy in bed with Franco. Looking over and watching Brandy gently rub my husband's balls (his penis was locked up in chastity) while Franco got all up in the Golden Snatch. The way Franco literally picked me up and put me on his dick while he stood up with his back against the wall. Feeling Franco bust his nut up inside me. Laying back on the bed, opening my legs, and looking over at my husband, who knew what I expected him, and feeling his mouth down between my legs, cleaning me up. Watching Franco walk over to Brandy, who had been kneeling down in a submissive posture, pick her up, carry her to the bed, and make love to her. Taking a shower afterwards with Franco and Brandy; my hubby got to watch Brandy and I wash Franco's dirty cock and balls. The fun and playful conversation with Franco and Brandy afterwards.

And Franco... oh yeah... that white boy can FUCK!

Email to my hubby

Franco made me cum so good last night... twice. As I'm sure you noticed, I was creaming all over his cock. To be honest, sweetie, I've been dripping for him for weeks. Thank you for being such a good cuckold, and being okay with him fucking your wife.

But the best orgasm I had last night... the most powerful one, and the most meaningful one... was when you went down on me afterwards... got your handsome face in the wet sticky mess Franco left for you... and made sure I didn't go to bed with a dirty cummy pussy.

You are so amazing! I love you. I love every bit and part of you. Forever.

Benefits of Male Chastity: - It prevents him from masturbating. Male masturbation is a filthy habit. It's addictive, selfish, and disrespectful to women. Chronic masturbation has the effect of substantially diminishing a man's natural sexual desire for his wife of girlfriend. It unfortunately teaches him that his orgasm is primary, and hers is secondary.

- Because he can't even get an erection without her permission, it instantly changes the dynamics of the relationship.

- It keeps his sexual focus and energy on his wife or girlfriend.

- It will substantially increase his desire to orally service his wife or girlfriend.

- If he's never been an ass-eater, after having his penis locked up for a few weeks, he will be.

- It serves as a constant reminder to him of her authority.

- Because it makes his orgasms entirely dependent on her generosity, it positively incentivizes him to honor her, respect her, and motivates him to please.

- It gives him the time and opportunity to substantially improve and perfect his oral skills.

- It reinforces the idea that pussy is a precious gift that must be earned, and is to be savored and appreciated on those rare occasions when he does get it.

- It teaches him that sexual activity with his wife or girlfriend doesn't necessarily have anything to do with his penis.

- It deepens his submission to her, and will cause him to worship the ground she walks on.

- It will significantly improve his attitude, and make him more generous, caring, kind, respectful, and loving. It will help soften the sharper edges of his me-first masculinity. It will make him more of a listener than a talker.

- It helps prepares him for the eventuality of anal penetration, and getting the strap-on. Because his penis isn't being sexually stimulated, it has the effect of gradually turning other parts of his body into erogenous zones, particularly his anus and his prostate. With patience and persistence, he can be trained to orgasm from stimulation in that region via your finger, or the strap-on.

- If his orgasms are consistently controlled and severely restricted, he will eventually get to the point where he will do just about anything to cum. You'll be amazed by what he'll do for you.

Email to Brandy

Damn, girl... you weren't kidding. That husband of yours can fuck! Jesus, my clit is still throbbing.

Thank you for sharing him with me last night.

And thank you for being so nice to my husband. He doesn't have a lot to offer in the penis department, but he makes up for it in other ways. I'm glad you got to sample his oral skills last night. He really loves doing that.

I'd love to share a Black Bull with you sometime. Or two.

Email to Franco

If you think I got enough of that big meaty dick of yours last night... you're wrong.

My husband will be playing golf tomorrow afternoon, between noon and 5pm. Just so you know. In case you're not busy.

Thank you for last night. It was awesome!

IR Relationships. Here's how I see the timeline...

In 1960, if a white girl had consensual sex with a black guy, he would have been arrested and charged with rape, she would have been totally disowned by her family and friends, probably beaten by her father, and shunned by society. The vast majority of women who had children were married. Gay people were considered to be sexual deviants.
In 1980, it was still scandalous, she would have been the subject of a lot of nasty gossip, and would have been labeled as "that girl who fucks niggers".
In 2000, white girls dating black guys in big cities started to become more common. It still wasn't quite accepted by the larger society, but it wasn't quite as scandalous as it used to be. Gay people were generally accepted as fellow human beings... except by old people, religious people, and Republicans.

In 2010, white girls hooking up with black guys is very common, especially in high school and college. Whereas in decades past, it would have hurt her reputation, now it actually made her more popular. Black athletes in high school and college not only got all the white pussy they wanted, they usually hit it first. The majority of women who had children were single.

In 2012, the idea of same-sex marriage crossed an important threshold in American society. It became accepted. Within a few years time, it would legal throughout the country.

In 2015, the Hotwife/Cuckold lifestyle has slowly been nudged out of the closet. While still rare, it's dramatically trending upward. Women are taking control of their sexuality. Increasingly over time, more women than men are earning college degrees, and also earning more money. As a direct consequence of that, and other societal trends, FemDom and female-led relationships are also on the increase.

By 2020, the traditional notion that one man should and can fulfill all of a woman's myriad needs and desires will die out. It will be commonly accepted for married women to occasionally seek sexual satisfaction with other men besides her husband. Hotwife/Cuckold relationships will become more common and openly practiced. And unlike in years past, it will usually be at the woman's instigation and, often, insistence.

By 2025, the idea that a woman's husband must or necessarily should be the father of her child will be see as quaint and outdated. By this time, more relationships will be female-led than not. Enforced male chastity and men taking the strap-on will be common. Just as in years past it wasn't uncommon in big cities to see a white girl with a black boyfriend and a biracial child, by 2025, it will become more and more common to see a white woman with a white husband with a biracial child that she had with her black lover.

Chapter 5

Email to my hubby

Hi sweetie! Just checking in. This morning went well. Franco walked me over to HR and introduced me to everyone. I'm going to be one of his personal assistants. His senior assistant, a woman named Tamara, will be training me. She's worked for him for 12 years.

Everyone's been really nice to me. I'm so excited about working again, but it's only going to be 2 days a week, so I'll still have plenty of free time to do other things... like look for a more permanent job.

Franco actually left soon after I got here; he had meetings all day across town.

They're all taking me to lunch today.

Send me a picture of your handsome face!!

Email to my hubby

That wasn't quite the response I was looking for, sweetie. Perhaps we need to schedule another disciplinary session with Mistress Marlene to get your attitude back on track.

I blame myself for this. It's my fault that you've been drifting for the four months, without proper guidance, rules, and discipline.

I'm determined to get this whole DaddyBigBull saga behind us, and get us back to where we need to be as a couple. I know we're both still in the healing process regarding that, but we need to get past it.

I like it, and it pleases me, when you suck cock for me. Watching you do that is one of the most erotic scenes I've ever experienced... particularly when you pay your respects to Marco that way. And that's really what you need to focus on; pleasing me, and not your own selfish desires.

His response was:

"I don't really want to do that anymore. Please. Despite what you seem to think, I don't enjoy it and find it extremely humiliating to have to do that. There are so many other things I would love to do for you, to show you how much I love you. But not that. Please."

FemDom Lesson No. 5

You're in a FemDom relationship.

Your Hotwife wants you to suck cock for her.

More specifically, she wants you to suck off her Bull. As a sign of respect.

You're being a little pussy, and don't want to. And start whining and complaining like a little bitch.

She asks again, nicely. And calmly tries to explain.

You continue to argue.

Discussion over.

You get the belt.

Three days later, you drop down to your knees, and suck cock for her.

Problem solved.

End of lesson.

Email to my hubby

We have lots to talk about when you get home. You apparently need an attitude adjustment. Please be home by 7pm.

We had a discussion, then I asked him to drop his pants. He got ten swats, then spend 30 minutes kneeling in the corner to contemplate his attitude. Then he slept alone in the guest room.

6:45pm... husband got home.

7:00pm to 7:30pm... discussion with and discipline of my husband.

7:30pm to 8pm... cool down period for my husband (on his knees, pants down, reddened ass exposed, facing the corner).

8:15pm to 9pm... my husband and I have dinner together.

9pm - 9:30pm... my husband and I take a shower together; I unlock his chastity device, wash his penis and balls for him, then lock him back up; and he goes to bed alone in the guest room.

9:30pm to 11:30pm... I stay up in bed reading, then fall asleep.

12:45am... Marco comes over and spends the night with me.

Email to my hubby

Hi sweet. Hope you're enjoying your golf game. Dinner will be at 6pm. Please don't be late.

Sailing with Ronnie/Sam and Franco/Brandy yesterday was awesome. I had so much fun. We need to do that more often. I hope you don't hate me for keeping your penis locked up. I didn't want you getting a pathetic little boner seeing all the women topless. Brandy has really nice breasts, doesn't she? They're perfect! Franco told me they cost like $12,000.

I know I've already told you, but I really appreciate what a good boy you were Friday night. I know it's been a long time since I've disciplined you like that. I appreciated your apology.

Marco told me some things about Dana when he was here Friday night which kind of shocked me. She wasn't quite the innocent little girl you (and I) thought she was. Do you want to hear the details... or would you rather not?

I thought it went well. MM had a good talk with him. She had him service her cunt while she lectured him.

Then she had him drop his pants, secured him to the disciplinary bench, and gave him five swats with the cane.

Chapter 6

There's nothing wrong with my husband sucking cock. I want him to. I enjoy watching it. I love how profoundly submissive it is for him to do that for me. If I have to tell him a little white lie, or two, to make it easier for him to do

that... to justify it in his own mind... I don't mind doing that for him. Because I love him.

Email to my hubby

Hi sweetie!

Franco and I were just talking in his office. He said Brandy's pussy needs grooming. He likes it nice and baby smooth. He was wondering if you'd be interested in doing that for her. He knows you do that for me sometimes. He wants to know if he can send her over tonight. Who knows, maybe she'll let you fuck it too.

What should I tell him?

Email to my hubby

I'm going to need you to be okay with Franco knowing that you suck cock for me. The subject of this past weekend came up, and I didn't want to lie to him about what we did. I told him you sucked off Marco on Sunday, to get him ready for me. And that you've done that many times before.

Franco was a bit incredulous that you actually do that for me. He was like, "he must really love you."

Guilty

I'm starting to kind of feel guilty about what happened to DaddyBigBull. My husband told me today that they set the criminal trial in his case for July, and that he's facing 20+ years in prison if convicted. I'm starting to feel bad about this. It wasn't all his fault. Part of it was me. DaddyBigBull didn't always force me to do things. There were times when I knew what was going on, and wanted it to happen, or let it.

I just think that in our society people go to prison for way too long, and it destroys them. Going to prison for 20+ years is basically forever. I just think as a society we should be more compassionate and forgiving than that.

I don't know. I'm just feeling really bad about this right now. I feel like I need to go see him, and talk to him. And explain. But I know that realistically I can't do that. And it really bothers me.

He's going to go to prison forever basically because of me. Because my husband is the one who got him caught and prosecuted.

I'm in a weird mood. Have been for a few days. I have like seven different personalities that are always fighting for control. The trophy wife. The party girl. The submissive. The FemDom bitch. The cheating wife. The slut. The sweet fairy tale princess.

I think all of us... as human beings... have good sides, and bad. Things to love, and things to hate. My life is what it is. What you see and read about on my diary is just the raw reality of it. I feel I can share and be more honest about things on here because I'm anonymous. It frees me to discuss a lot more than I could if I wasn't.

Text to my husband

I don't want you to freak out when you get home and go into the bedroom. The bed looks like I peed all over it. Marco just left a while ago, and we basically fucked all afternoon. I left the bed that way because I wanted you to see it. I want you to know how good he fucks me. I also need you to please change and wash the sheets. Thank you, sweetie.

It's Friday Night...

... do you know where your wife is, and who's fucking her?

Chapter 7

I've been off the H for almost five months, and I'm very proud of that.

It's been the struggle of my life. It's taken everything I have to keep working the program. Every morning. Every afternoon. Every evening. Every night.

I've never claimed to be perfect. Obviously, I'm not. Who among us are? But I'm human; I have dreams, and wants, and needs, and feelings.

God gave Einstein a brain, Gandhi humble insight, Clooney handsome charisma... and he gave me my physical attractiveness, and my revved up, man-eating sexuality.

I'm grateful for the gifts I've been bestowed. Because otherwise what would I have? Obviously, I'm just a clueless, bubble-headed bimbo. Can't you tell by my illiteracy? Clearly, I'm not able to think my way through things, or articulate beyond the 4th grade level.

My husband is super-smart, ambitious, and driven. He's turned that into a high level of financial success. And despite his pathetic, little-boy penis, and lack of sexual confidence, he's managed to score himself a trophy wife that his friends envy him for.

For my part, I've worked and schemed to leverage what meager talents and offerings I have into getting half of everything he has. Which is more than most people could ever dream of.

Basically, my husband bought himself a piece of the Golden Snatch. But it was expensive. And there are certain on-going costs associated with it. And he still has to share it with other men, of course. But believe me, small white penis boy is grateful for whatever he gets. Because otherwise it's basically his hand.

My shrink says that punishing my husband, is my way of punishing myself.

I finally got up the courage to tell my counselor about some of the details of my sexual lifestyle. When I told her that I sometimes make my husband suck cock for me, she was appalled.

I'm feeling much better now. Thank you. I have these days sometimes when I'm crawling the walls, and my frustration and fear, and anxiety and anger levels go through the roof. And it seems that whenever I'm ovulating, I get the irresistible urge to go do some crazy stupid shit.

I'm still working on the whole impulse control thing.

Normally, my horniness level is about an eight; but when I'm ovulating, it hits 10, and stays there for about four days.

We went sailing yesterday with Franco and Brandy, and Ronnie and Sam. It was a lot of fun. Everyone gets along well, except that yesterday for the first time, I noticed a little bit of tension between Sam and Franco. I think maybe because Franco was to doing the scotch-and-cigars thing, and encouraging the girls to go topless, and Sam didn't seem comfortable with Ronnie taking off her top in front of everybody. Sam can be kind of a prude sometimes.

Chapter 8

I did things while I was high on H and with DaddyBigBull that would probably blow your mind.

Sorry to disappoint you, but my days on H are over. That's never going to happen again.

Looking back on those experiences now, those were some traumatic times for me. I was high all the time. I was out of control. I was being dominated by a violent beast of a man who had virtually no limits in what he would make me and Lizzy and the other girls do.

DaddyBigBull made me do some crazy, nasty, dangerous, filthy, and disgusting things sometimes. But they were mild compared to what he would sometimes make Lizzy do. And make me watch.

Texts with my husband

So, I kind of have a date tonight. I might invite him back to the pool house. Not sure yet.

Who's the guy?

Marc. The guy I told you about from the club.

Have you been communicating with him?

We text every now and then. More so lately.

He's the guy who thinks you're single?

Yes.

I don't like that so much. He should know you're married.

Then everyone at the club would know. They all talk. Besides, he doesn't need to know.

It just concerns me.

Don't worry. So, did you want to watch us from your secret place?

Yes.

I knew you would. I'll text you if I end up inviting him back, so you can get ready.

Okay.

But no jacking off this time. I want your little dick locked up. No touching, just watching.

Yes, ma'am.

Texts with Marc

So, we're good. 8pm works. I'll meet you there.

What you going to wear for me baby?

What do you want me to wear?

Something tight, show off that smoking ass you got.

Panties or not?

You don't need no panties girl.

Not with you I don't, lol.

When you going to dance for me again?

I'm kind of taking a break from that. From the club, I mean.

Dance for me tonight.

It's not that kind of bar.

We can go to my place after.

That might be a possibility. Do you still live at the same place?

Yeah. You remember it?

Kind of. Not how to get there.

Where you living now?

I moved into the pool house at my sister's place. Her and her husband remodeled. It's really nice. You should come check it out.

You live alone?

Yes.

Let's go to your place then tonight.

K. We could go for a swim. And then you can give me what I've been missing.

Sounds good to me.

Do you remember how I like it?

Oh yeah. I remember.

Good. Don't forget that.

Email to my husband

You've been such a good cuckold these last few weeks, I'm very proud of you. I love it when you're secretly watching me with another man, from your hiding place, and I can perform for you like that. It's so deliciously naughty!

Thank you for remodeling the pool house so we can do that. I'm going to have lots and lots of boyfriends over, lol.

With Marc, it's actually more fun with him not knowing I'm married, and thinking I'm single. I think he's more relaxed that way, and can just be himself with me.

You've been such a good boy lately, I wanted to give you a few options for this weekend.

1. I'll unlock your penis once this weekend, whenever you like, and I'll give you a really nice blowjob, and then lock you back up immediately after.

2. I'll unlock your penis Saturday morning, and you can be free all day while you're playing golf. On Saturday night I'll let you have plastic pocket pussy, supervised by me, then it gets locked back up.

3. I'll unlock your penis from chastity, and you can be free all weekend, from Friday after work until Monday morning, and you have all the pussy you want... but when Marco comes over next week, you have to suck his cock for me to completion.

Pick one, sweetie, and let me know.

Love you!

Morning Spanking

My husband received a "good morning!" spanking on his bare bottom today. Just because.

I'm thinking this will maybe become a regular morning ritual for us. Something to remind him of my authority everyday as he begins his day.

As a general matter, I'm dominant with my husband, and submissive with other men. For me, it's just very natural. I love and enjoy both at different times, with different people, in different circumstances.

Variety is the spice of life, right? Sometimes you want red wine, and sometimes you want white wine. Or Tinder, or juice, or beer, or jello shots. Or bourbon.

Email to my Hubby

I hope you don't think I was too strict or harsh with you last night. I just felt like I needed to get your attention. I don't appreciate it when you ignore my requests. I shouldn't have to constantly remind you. When I ask you to do something for me, I mean now... not whenever you feel like getting around to it.

Email to Franco

You took me by surprise today. I definitely wasn't expecting that. It was nice, but I hope you don't think you can just whip out your big cock and use me for sex like that. I'm not just going to be your little office whore that you can fuck whenever you want. Unless you want me to be.

PS: You tore my panties, and owe me a new pair.

Email to my hubby

I don't really need you to be okay with it, because quite honestly, after what happened the other night, it really isn't your place to decide who I have sex with, when, or where. But I wanted you to know that Franco fucked me in his office today, this afternoon, right after lunch. And I'm sure it probably won't be the last time.

Chapter 9

Things are going well. I've been busy. I had another interview this week, but it didn't go particularly well. I'm still working at Franco's office, but just twice a week. I also have a project I've been working on.

My husband has been in a bit of a mood this week, I'm not sure why. He gets that way sometimes. It could just be something going on at work. Sometimes he's communicative and talks about things, and other times I can tell that he doesn't want to. He's going to be gone next week, from Monday through Thursday, on a business trip.

Marco has some complications going on at his work. He thinks they're trying to fire him. Marco is a great guy, I have a lot of fun with him, but career-wise, he's never really had much going on. He's still with that girl he's been dating, so I don't really get to see him as often as I'd like.

I have a "date" with charity man Monday afternoon. I haven't seen him a while and am looking forward to it. He usually gets a really nice hotel suite, and basically treats me like a princess, which is always kind of fun.

Marc wants me to go dance for him at the club, but I've been resisting that. With everything that's happened in the last few months, it's probably not a good idea for me to be in that kind of atmosphere. Drug use is pretty rampant there; almost all of the girls use cocaine.

Texts with my husband

I don't know what's been going on with you; you've been kind of moody the last few days. I need you to please communicate with me about whatever is going on. I've been wanting to give you some space, but this has gone on long enough. Dinner will be on the table at 7pm, then we need to talk.

I should be home by 630.

Please don't be later than that.

I won't.

You need to tell me what's going on with you.

I don't really want to talk about it right now.

You've had a few days. You can't keep things from me like this. It's not healthy for our relationship. If it's something going on at work, or whatever, you need to tell me.

It's not that.

Then what is it?

I need more time to think things over.

Obviously, something is bothering you.

I'm not ready to talk about it.

Well, get ready. Tonight, after dinner, we need to talk.

I really wish you wouldn't push me about this.

This isn't fair. You make me worry and wonder what's going on with you. We can't have secrets between us.

It's not a secret. I just need more time to think things through.

Well, you have two more hours.

Email to my hubby

Sweetie, I'm sorry about what happened. Obviously, Franco didn't do it on purpose. I talked to him. He had no idea Sam could see anything, and neither did I. Franco knows he needs to be more careful.

Because of the way you left it with Sam... him thinking that I'm cheating on you... we need to decide how to best handle this.

As I see the options they are:

1.   Do nothing. But then Sam will continue to think that I'm cheating on you, which I'm not very comfortable with because it's not true. It's not fair for him to think of me that way.

2.   Get Ronnie's thoughts on what to do, and let her take the lead. She knows him better than we do. I have a call into her. I'm curious to know if Sam told her about what he saw. I tend to think he didn't because I would expect she would have told me about it. We already know that Sam was annoyed with Franco because of the whole "topless" thing. When Franco started joking around that the girls should all be topless, and Brandy and Ronnie and I took our tops off, I could tell that Sam was uncomfortable with it. Ronnie said he was mad about it afterwards, that Ronnie would expose her breasts like that to other men.

3.   I could talk to the limp dick motherfucker myself, and set him straight on minding his own business.

4.   Ronnie could talk to Sam and explain to him that I'm a hotwife and that you know Franco and I mess around, and that you're okay with it. Ronnie has been wanting to come out to Sam about what she's been doing with other men. She wants to be a hotwife, but she's been afraid of his reaction. I know that she hates keeping secrets from him. Maybe this situation actually might help her break the ice.

5.   You could talk to Sam and explain that we have an open marriage, that you know Franco and I mess around, and that you're okay with it.

6.   We could leak word to DaddyBigBull that Sam is the one who ratted him out.

Sweetie... I know you're upset about this, Sam thinking you're a cuckold. But it could be worse. At least he doesn't know that I lock up your little dick, or fuck you with a strap-on, or that you suck cock for me. Right?

Sam is an asshole!

My husband flew out early this morning; he'll be out of town until late Thursday night.

After my bugging him about it, he finally told me last night what's been bothering him the last few days. It's Sam, Ronnie's husband. He apparently saw Franco putting his hand on my ass last weekend, when the six of us went sailing, and then back at the house saw Franco put his hand between my legs, and as he put it to my husband, "she wasn't resisting him."

Sam called up my husband last week and told him what he had seen, that he thinks I'm having an affair with Franco, and thought my husband should know about it. According to my husband, Sam then said, "I thought you should know because I'd want to know."

WHAT A FUCKING ASSHOLE!!

My husband obviously knows that Franco and I mess around, but is upset that Franco wasn't discreet about it, and now Sam knows.

Update re Sam

Ronnie returned my call. Sam hadn't told her about what he supposedly saw. She and I are going to meet up tonight to figure out how to handle this.

Sam is actually a nice guy. He's kind of a prude, but I like him. What makes him an asshole in this circumstance is that he told my husband about Franco touching me with the specific intent of hurting me, without realizing that his own wife has been secretly fucking other men herself.

After our talk last night, Ronnie would like me and my husband to have dinner with her and Sam next week, and tell him about our relationship… that I'm a hotwife, that my husband knows I occasionally have sex with other men, and that he's okay with it.

She wants to use this as an opportunity to gently lay the groundwork to "come out" to her husband and tell him about her desire to be a hotwife… and she wants me and my husband to help her do it.

Texts with Marc

You need to come over and bang your bitch tonight.

Seriously?

I want it rough.

You always want it rough.

I mean... extra rough. I want you to make it hurt.

I'll fuck you good, baby. You know that.

I want more than that. I want you to discipline me.

Like what, spank you?

Yes. With the belt. Like you did last year.

I can do that. What's going on with you?

I've been a bad girl.

Oh yeah. What you do?

I cheated on my boyfriend.

You didn't tell me you had a boyfriend.

See! I'm a bad girl. I need to be punished.

Seriously? You have a boyfriend?

Kind of. Is that a problem?

Not my problem. Is he a brotha?

No. He's a white boy.

I should have known that. You still fucking him?

Only when I have to. Can you come over around 11pm? I have some things to do before that.

I'll be there.

Good. Don't forget. I want it rough. Make it hurt.

How rough you want it?

When my boyfriend gets back on Thursday, I want him to know I was a bad girl.

Like what, mark you up?

Yes. Just on my ass. I want him to know that another man had his way with me.

Why you want to do that?

Because I'm a bitch.

Marc Vs Marco: They're both good in bed, just in different ways.

Marco is more athletic, built, muscular, and has amazing stamina. He also has a beautiful cock… it's just pretty beautiful, big and thick. And his cum tastes like mango juice.

Marc is tall and skinny, lots of tattoos, with a thick uncircumcised cock that's so ugly it's beautiful. He's extremely aggressive, which I like. Marc is all gangsta thug nigga, with very, very dark skin.

Emotionally, I have more of a connection with Marco.

Dinner with Ronnie and Sam tonight

My husband isn't very happy about tonight, but like a good husband, cuckold and PussyBoy, he also recognizes his responsibilities in the relationship.

He will be getting a reminder spanking one hour before Ronnie and Sam get here tonight. And, of course, his penis will be locked up.

He and Sam don't run in the same business or professional circles, and don't have any friends in common, which makes this easier for him. I don't think he needs to worry about Sam telling other people about it, because they don't really know the same people.

My husband has asked me (begged me, really) not to mention the FemDom aspects of our relationship… that we practice enforced male chastity, that I lock up his penis, that I restrict and control his orgasms, that I require him to be baby smooth below the waist, that I take him in to have his legs and groin area waxed, that I sometimes make him wear panties underneath his business suit, that I spank him and sometimes discipline him with a belt, that I fuck him with a strap-on, that I require him to lick me out and clean

me up after I've been with another man, that I sometimes make him suck cock for me, and that Marco and Daddy Big Bull have fucked him before.

So, I've agreed to do that for my PussyBoy.

He also doesn't want me to mention that he has a small penis. But as I've explained to him, I need to talk about that because it will make Sam feel better about himself (Sam has a big cock, even though, sadly, it doesn't really work anymore), and it also partially explains why I seek sexual satisfaction with other men.

So... the conversation tonight is only going to be about the Hotwife aspects of our relationship.

The whole idea behind having the discussion tonight, and revealing these things to Sam, is to help Ronnie lay the groundwork for her later discussions with Sam on the same subject.

For her part, Ronnie is nervous as a cat on the trapeze wire. She and I have talked endlessly about this, trying to predict how the conversation is going to go, and what her later discussions with Sam should be like.

She's hoping that by my disclosing to Sam, in and easy and natural and casual way, the nature of my relationship with my husband, and by having my husband there during the discussion as a way of demonstrating his support, and by us talking about how much fun and excitement we have together... that it might help her begin a discussion with Sam (in the days and weeks and months that follow) about the possibility of her becoming a Hotwife as well.

Sam has a very different personality than my husband, though, so she can't just come right out and tell him that's what she wants. She has to try to make it his idea.

Sam, though, is very much the macho jealous and possessive type, which is why she's been so scared about him finding out that she's already been fucking other men. She's particularly concerned about Sam finding out about Ty, because he's black, and Sam isn't exactly progressive in that regard. He's apparently made comments to her in the past about interracial couples, and his disapproval of it.

At the end of the day, as I've explained to Ronnie, she's going to be more successful at achieving her ultimate goal (to become a Hotwife) if she can maneuver her discussions with Sam to make it his idea.

Update

Last night went reasonably well, with one little complication.

I'll write more about it later today.

Dinner Last Night with Ronnie and Sam

As her cuckold, the most important thing you can do for your Hotwife is to just love her, cherish her, and support her. She needs to know that you're going to be there for her, no matter what, especially when your cuckold angst seems like it's more than you can handle, things take an unexpected turn, she makes mistakes, or gets involved with the wrong type of guy and needs your help getting out of it.

As her PussyBoy, the most important thing you can do for your Mistress is to love, honor, trust, and respect her. It means you follow her lead, abide by her rules, meet and then exceed her expectations, and do what you're told, even when it's different than what you're used to, challenging, uncomfortable, or difficult.

My husband was both last night. It was a difficult and challenging evening for him. But he loved and supported me, followed my lead, and exceeded all my expectations.

I'm so very proud of him!

As a reward, I've decided to release him from chastity and let him have all the pussy he wants, for 10 days, no rules, no restrictions, and no limits.

Sam, as the discussion last night revealed, had already heard about couple swinging the Hotwife lifestyle. When I mentioned the word, he knew what I was talking about. He said he had read about it on the Internet. Ronnie feigned ignorance.

Sam was kind of quiet and mostly listened at first, then later in the evening, with a few drinks in him, he opened up and started asking a lot of questions.

For her part, I thought Ronnie played it well. She acted surprised and a little shocked... like she had no idea I was fucking other men... asked a few questions, and then mostly followed Sam's lead.

After the discussion moved from the dinner table, to drinks out on the balcony, to the hot tub, all the usual questions came up regarding the Hotwife lifestyle.

How do you have sex with other men if you still love your husband?

If you love your wife, how could you possibly be okay with her doing that?

Whose idea was it?

How did it first happen?

How often do you see other men?

Is your husband involved? Is he there?

Where do you do it? Your place? Their place? Hotels?

What type of men?

How do you meet them?

How did you meet Franco?

Does his wife Brandy know?

What about jealousy and possessiveness?

His do you handle the emotions of it?

What about safety?

Does Chad have sex with other women?

What are the rules?

And a dozen other questions.

I was the one who mostly answered the first flurry of questions, but then after a while my husband stepped up and helped me out.

Like a politician with a predetermined agenda and talking points in mind, I tried to get a few messages across:

"The most loving thing a man can do for his wife is recognize and accept that he can't always never give her everything she needs sexually."

"I've never cheated on Chad… and never would… but he's never put me in the position where I felt like I had to, or wanted to."

"Chad loves me and trusts me enough to let me get and experience what I need sexually, even if it's sometimes with another man."

"I wouldn't do it if Chad wasn't comfortable with it."

"We share everything together."

"Chad loves it! It's just as exciting for him as it is for me."

"He likes to watch."

"Afterwards, we have amazing sex."

"We have lots of oral sex, which he loves just as much as intercourse."

"Since I became a Hotwife, Chad isn't as self-conscious about the size of his penis."

"We joke around that he gets to delegate the fucking to other, more qualified men, and he gets to enjoy the benefits of less pressure to perform, and a happy, playful wife."

"He likes it when I'm a total slut in bed, even if it's not always with him… because he knows that I always come home to him."

"Our relationship is deeper, and our marriage is stronger, because of it. It's brought us closer together."

Okay, so… we've planted the seeds last night, now it's up to Ronnie to nurture and grow them.

But Sam is very different than my husband, personality wise, so I'm not quite sure how it's going to go. We'll see.

I haven't talked to Ronnie yet to get her thoughts on last night. She did send me a text a while ago, thanking me for helping her to get things started.

Email to my husband

Franco has a business trip coming up next week. He's going to Colorado Springs for two days, and needs an assistant to go with him. He wants to take me. We'd fly out Sunday night and get back late Tuesday night.

I need you to be okay with it.

Queen of Spades Tattoo

I'm wearing a Queen of Spades temporary tattoo on my left ankle all week, 24/7, just for fun. I'm curious to see what kind of attention it might get. I've worn them before, but just at night to a club.

Email to my husband

Marc just called me. He wants pussy tonight. But... he also wants me to go dance for him at the club. How do you feel about that? I think it would be fun if you were at the club at the same time, to watch from a distance, and even more fun if you were in the VIP lounge with one of the other dancers at the same time I'm in there with Marc. What do you think?

The Club

It looks like my hubby will be getting a nice handjob from one of the other girls in the VIP Room tomorrow night... if he's a good boy.

Email to my hubby

Remember the rules tonight, sweetie:

Obviously, no one at the club knows I'm married, so watch your behavior around me... especially if we're both in the VIP room.

Stay away from Trixie, because she's just a fucking skank. You'll notice her right away... she has this weird four-colored hairstyle.

Jasmine and Carolina are my two best friends at the club. You should try to spend some time with them. They're both very cute and friendly.

Obviously, your penis will be free, which is fine. I want you to enjoy yourself. You can get all the dances your heart desires, and visit the VIP room as often as you like. But you're only permitted to get a nice handjob... not a blowjob.

It can be rather traumatic and embarrassing for a girl to discover in the VIP room that a customer has a really small dick... not to mention extremely disappointing... especially if he's very attractive and handsome. So, you need to make sure you tip your girl DOUBLE for the trouble.

If you hear about a dancer with a soft southern accent who loves to dance for the niggas, has this thing she does with her tongue in the VIP room, and has a Golden Snatch... they're talking about your wife.

Email to my hubby

Franco was going to come by around 6pm to pick me up before heading to the airport... but I like the idea of you taking me to him instead.

So... if you want pussy before I leave, you need to be home by 5pm, please. Afterwards, of course, I need to lock up your little penis to make sure you're a good boy while I'm gone.

Email to my hubby

Hi sweetie. We're leaving for dinner here in a bit. Not sure when we'll be back to the hotel, but I want to facetime with you late tonight. Be looking for my call...

Love you!

Email to my hubby

Goddammit I love you so much!

I hope you enjoyed watching that last night. Was that fun?

Thank you for letting me have a naughty few days with Franco. It's a different kind of dynamic being here with him here in a different city spending the night with him, and sleeping with him, knowing that you're two thousand miles away. Somehow it feels naughtier.

Franco has another business trip coming up in a few weeks to Atlanta... a longer one, and wants to take me and Brandy. He wants both of us with him. I'm assuming that's okay, yes? We can FaceTime again.

This morning in the shower I was thinking... maybe I should have left your penis unlocked on Sunday so you could have jacked off watching us last night, and could jack off all you want like a little boy while I'm gone. If jacking off was all that happened, I could probably live with that. But we can't have you slipping off to fuck a fat chick, now can we? You're my husband, and I need to protect you from that.

I appreciate it when you do what you're told. I was telling Franco this morning what a good PussyBoy you are. I shared with him that you sometimes suck cock for me, which he didn't believe until I showed him the video on my phone of you sucking off Marco... the one in our bedroom where every time you paused and he thought you were hesitating, he told you to "get your fucking mouth back on that." Remember that one? When he came in your mouth and you started panicking because you felt like you were going to choke on it? Remember? That was before you learned how to swallow without spilling.

Franco still can't believe you do that for me. He can't believe you're that obedient. But you're my little faggot, aren't you sweetie?

Email to my hubby

Franco wants to see the butt-fucking video on my phone...

Back Home

I'm back in the loving arms of my cuckold husband, my PussyBoy. This is where I belong. This is where I want to be. Forever.

Other men may excite me and make me cream in my panties, other men may draw me away to play in dark and dangerous rooms, other men may sometimes lead me astray and get me in trouble, other men may give me the hard aggressive fucking I need, other men may give me violent orgasms that drive me insane with lust, other men may lure me into their world and

tempt me to stay... but no one in the universe cherishes and loves me like this man, this special and amazing man, this incredible human being that I'm married to.

I may frequently have sex with other men, I may occasionally get emotionally involved with other men, I may occasionally make take my husband for granted, and he may occasionally make the mistake of letting another woman get her greasy donut-nourished claws into him, and try to tug him away from me.

I may tease him, occasionally torment him, and even torture him, I may frequently push the envelope of our relationship, and gently guide him, or drag him kicking and screaming, or even suddenly push him into the deep, cold water of a new experience... but this thing we share, this marriage we have, our bond, our relationship, is permanent.

I had fun with Franco the last few days. I loved being his personal little whore during his business trip, and will be doing that again. I had fun teasing and tormenting my husband from afar. I loved driving his cuckold angst into the red zone. I enjoyed metaphorically kicking his cuckold balls with my FemDom Louboutin heels.

But that's just our game. That's this crazy thing we do together that not everyone appreciates or understands.

He and I know the truth.

I saw it in his excited eyes when I walked in the door last night after Franco dropped me off. He knew I had been fucked, and couldn't wait to get his mouth between my legs. He wanted to taste my infidelity, and hear me tell him every detail.

And he felt it in my loving touch as we lay together in bed again, after he had made me cum, and I gently rubbed his frustrated balls for him and suckled his cute little penis until he dribbled his thin watery semen.

No one is ever getting between us again. Ever.

BTW.

Franco is just a playmate for me right now; nothing more. And I'm his. We're just having fun. Franco is very happily married to Brandy.

Chapter 10

Email to my hubby

You've been such a good PussyBoy lately, I feel like I should reward you.

You always take care of me in the morning before you go to work, you're okay with me playing around with Franco, you helped Ronnie and I try to set things up with Sam (I'm still kind of nervous about that!), you're respectful of my special relationship with Marco, you don't whine and complain when I decide that your penis needs to be locked up, you take my strap-on like you love it even though I know you don't always, and you've become quite the secret voyeur watching me with Marc.

So… I'm thinking that while we're in Spain next month, I'm going to let you have some fresh, young pussy. I know how much you miss that, and I know that mine isn't very tight for you. In fact, I'd love to share a girl with you. And you won't have to be locked up for the entire trip.

But I'm going to need you to do something for me. The next time Marco is here, I need you to pay your respects to him as my Bull. And you know what that means.

Email to Marco

Okay, so I talked to him. He knows what to expect.

When you come over tomorrow, I want you to fuck him. Make him suck your cock for a while first, the way you like, and then bend him over and fuck the shit out of him. Make him feel it. Make him take every inch of you. I want him to be reminded of his place in the relationship.

He'll make his usual PussyBoy noises, and scream out, or whatever, but don't let that stop you from giving him the fucking he needs. I want him to still feel your cock in his ass the next day.

And I want him to feel you bust your nut all up inside him. I want him to be reminded of what that's like. I want him to know that his ass is just another pussy for you.

You can be aggressive, of course. I want you to be. You know from before that he can take a pretty good fucking. He's used to it with my strap-on.

But a real cock is different. And you're a lot stronger and more powerful than I am. So please, don't hurt him. I want at least some part of him to learn to enjoy it. I know you think of him as just a little faggot, but he's my husband, and even though I love to dominate him, I love him, and don't want him hurt.

Do that for me tomorrow, and you can have me anytime you want. Here, your place, or wherever.

Call me later, babe.

Email to my hubby

You were the perfect PussyBoy last night, and this morning. Thank you!

You have no idea how much I love watching you submit to my Bull like that. I know you wouldn't do it if you didn't love me.

I'm going to make our trip to Spain very, very special for you.

Email to my husband

Sweetie, I met with the accountant yesterday. I saw in the spreadsheet he had that you wrote a really big check a few weeks ago to a republican political PAC.

We need to talk about that.

It kind of bothers me that you're spending that kind of money on political stuff when we could be helping Marco get a new car.

Who wears the pants?
I cut my husband's balls off a long time ago… a few months after the wedding when I calmly explained to him that he was going to have to share my pussy with other men.

He told me a donation like that was good for his business because it makes the right people return his phone calls whenever he needs something.

Email to my hubby

A few things...

Franco wants to take Brandy and I to a hotel bar tomorrow night after work... and wants to give us "instructions" about things he wants us to do while we're there. He wants us both dressed up hot and sexy. He'd like you to be there, but only later in the evening, after we're already there a while... and only to watch. He also thinks your little dick should be locked up, which, of course, I agree with.

He also thinks you shouldn't be allowed to have any more pussy until we're in Spain. I told him your penis would be free during the entire trip, that I was going to let you have all the pussy you want while we're there, and that I wanted to maybe share a girl with you during our trip.

Another thing... you know how Franco can be kind of a pervert sometimes... he's been making me hold his cock whenever he pees in the executive rest room. Basically, he makes me get down on my knees, has me take it out of his trousers, hold it while he pees, take in my mouth after he's done to clean it for him, and then put it back in his trousers. He told me there's a business executive friend of his that he'd like me to do that for the next time he visits Franco at the office. He wants to show me off to his friend.

Tina is one of my best friends. When she refers to my cuckold hubby as a "little faggot" because he sucks cock and takes it up the ass, she doesn't mean to ridicule him, or hurt or shame him, she just recognizing the truth of what he is.

This morning when she got here to take him to be waxed, and to go shopping for panties, she walked into the kitchen and kind of laughed and asked me, "so where's the little faggot?"

He was upstairs at the time, and didn't hear her ask me that, but it wouldn't have bothered me if he had. It's the truth.

Marc is my gangsta thug boyfriend who I know from the club. He was starting to get a little too attached there for a while; I had to dial that back a little. It's more complicated with him thinking I'm single living in the pool house, but workable.

I have to keep reminding Ronnie not to mess that up because she hooks up with his friend Ty all the time.

Texts with my husband

I just got a text from Brandy. She said she dropped by your office this afternoon but you weren't there.

Yes. I know. She left a package with the receptionist.

Did she open it?

No. Of course not. She knows better than that.

Did you?

Yes.

What was in it?

You know what was in it.

Her dirty panties?

Yes.

Were they filthy? Franco told me she was with one of her FYBs this weekend.

Not that I noticed.

Did you smell them?

No.

Don't lie to me. I know you did. We both know what a little pervert you are.

I just opened the package to see what was in it. That's it.

I guess she must like how you wash them for her.

This really needs to stop. I'm really busy.

Not on Saturday mornings you're not.

22_, we can't keep doing this. I don't like her coming by the office. We need to keep things separate. I don't want any problems. You need to talk to her and Franco. Please. I really need you to do that.

Maybe. I'll think about it. What are you so afraid of?

You know what I'm afraid of.

Things can't remain secrets forever, sweetie. It's not healthy, keeping secrets.

Why are we always having this discussion? Why did you tell her where my office was? I wish you hadn't done that.

You didn't seem to mind when she was going over there to suck your little dick.

I tried to dissuade her, but she appeared to be afraid of upsetting Franco.

If she didn't do as she was told, yes, I know, Franco told me. Their relationship is different than what you and I have.

You need to stop telling people, your play friends, what I do, where I work, and things that they can use against us if things go south. We've talked about that.

It's more fun to be dangerous.

Dangerous almost got you killed 22.

I know. I'm sorry. But I trust Franco and Brandy. And I like them.

I like them to, as play friends, but I don't want them involved in my professional life. It's very risky.

Okay. I'm sorry. I'll talk to her.

Thank you. Please do that for me.

I will. I don't want you to be stressing out. I'm sorry.

I appreciate it.

You're welcome. By the way, I told Ronnie that you do that for me.

What?

Hand-wash my dirty panties every Saturday morning.

Was that really necessary?

She thinks it's cute. She got all jealous.

I really wish you wouldn't share everything with her.

She's one of my best friends. She's on the list. You know that.

You don't have to tell her everything.

But I haven't told her everything. There's plenty I haven't shared with her. Like, ummmm... she doesn't know that Marco fucked you last week.

You promised not to tell her. You promised!

I know I did. And I kept my promise.

Please promise me you're not going to do that.

Do what?

Tell Ronnie.

Tell Ronnie what?

22, please. You promised me.

But sometimes I get confused and forget. It's a blonde thing.

No, it's not.

Sweetie, I hate to cut this short, but I have to go.

Go where?

I have a few things to do.

Like what?

There you go interrogating me again. Stop it! You're going to confuse me and make me forget things I'm not supposed to do.

Finally!!!!! Diary!

OMG!!!!

My PussyBoy!!!

It finally happened!!!

He got a cute little boner and he actually came! He spurted. He had an orgasm. All by himself. Spontaneously without his penis ever being touched. While I fucked him in the ass with my Bad Dragon strap-on dildo. He started spewing semen everywhere right as I eased in the knot.

Unbelievable. I never touched it.

I'm so excited, I can't even see straight.

I'm so incredibly excited!! It's taken a long time to make this happen.

I have several Bad Dragon dildos that I use in my strap-on harness. Some of them work really well for anal penetration; some are just pretty to look at.

Last night he took the medium size, and started spewing semen everywhere... without being touched!!!... after I had been fucking him for maybe 10 minutes... right as I eased in the knot.

He was on his back, with his legs up; I was kneeling down in front of him; we were facing each other; I had unlocked his penis from chastity, but was careful not to touch him, and of course, did not permit him to touch himself.

Lots of foreplay, kissing, loving on each other. I allowed him to touch my breasts and suck on my nipples, and encouraged him to nurse on them. Then I laid back on the bed, opened my legs, and encouraged him to service me with his mouth and tongue... which he did.

After he gave me an orgasm, I got up to put on my strap-on... teased him a bit about which one of my bad boys he wanted, and then did my thing

Email to my hubby

I'm very proud of you! Seriously, you have no idea. I was starting to feel like such a failure... and extremely jealous that only Daddy Big Bull could make you cum that way.

I feel like I want to tell the world what a good PussyBoy you are. But then if I did, I'd have to fight off all the gold digger bitches who'd want to steal you from me!

So... I guess I'll keep your little secret mostly a secret just a little longer, ha ha.

I love you, baby.

Email to Marc

Shawty wanna thug.

Nigga I was with last night can't hit.

Small dick motherfucker tried to fool me with that swagger.

Can you do better with your nine?

I'm going to go dance Saturday.

You got your cheddar saved up, boy?

This white pussy is expensive.

You going to share me with the fellas again?

Or just you this time?

Just like I vacillate between my dominant and submissive side... wanting and being drawn to different experiences at different times with different people under different circumstances... I think he's the same way.

My husband goes back and forth between accepting our FemDom Hotwife Cuckold relationship dynamic, and his place in it as my cuckold and PussyBoy, and resisting it.

Ultimately, what motivates him is pleasing me and keeping me happy, but he's also concerned about his perceived masculinity and what other people think of him.

It excites him that I fuck other men... he especially loves to play the secret voyeur and watch me without the guy knowing about it... but then sometimes he gets anxious and jealous, and is afraid that people in his work/friend circle will find out.

He respects and is understanding of my special relationship with Marco, and they get along relatively well, but deep down inside I know that Marco makes him nervous and anxious, and he's afraid of him. He panics at the thought of my leaving him for Marco.

He loves it when I make him lick me out and clean up my creamy cummy pussy after I've been with another man, but then other times he resists it and finds it disgusting.

He understands why I feel the need to lock up his penis and control and restrict his orgasms, but he doesn't like it and is always trying to figure out a way out of it, trying to talk me out of it, etc.

He respects and accepts my discipline of him, but then sometimes he resists and makes an issue of it.

He puts his ass up for my strap-on when I want to fuck him, and sometimes appears to enjoy it, but then other times he tries to talk me into not doing that anymore.

He sucks cock for me on occasion, but really only does it because he knows I want him to, and sometimes breaks down in tears telling me that he doesn't want to have to do that anymore. Same thing with Marco fucking him.

He's terrified of being perceived as a little faggot... and other people knowing what he does that for me... which is precisely why I love to tease him about it.

———

I don't see it as necessarily inconsistent. It just means that he's not a one-dimensional man. It means there's a complexity to his personality, and that he has different layers and levels.

I don't have a problem with it. On the contrary, I both accept and love that about him.

Chapter 11

Email to my hubby

Slight change in plans this weekend.

I'm going to go dance at the club tonight, but I'd like you to please wait for me at home. I'll text you when I'm on my way. I'm not going to stay out too late; I'll probably be home just after midnight. I might invite Marc over to the pool house, depending, I'm not sure. If you're a good boy, I'll put on a hot show for my sweet cuckold voyeur.

I'm going to dance again on Saturday... they have a special theme party going on that's going to be a lot of fun. I'd like you to invite two of your business colleagues out for drinks, and then "end up" at the club... obviously men who have never met me, and don't know what I look like. Your penis will be locked up, but sometime during the evening I'm going to sneak you the key so you can unlock yourself and join us in the VIP room. You have my permission to get a handjob from one of the girls... but make sure it's not more than that.

Thank you, sweetie.

PS: Please check and make sure there are plenty of condoms in the pool house. Remember, that's your responsibility.

Email to my hubby

I just heard back from MM. We had a good talk. I explained the situation to her. She wants me to take you over Sunday evening, and asked that I leave you there with her overnight. She also asked that I warm up your ass before we get there.

So... I'm going to need you to please plan a day off from work Monday.

I'm planning to leave the house tonight to dance about 8pm. Your watching privileges for later this evening are cancelled. Instead, I've prepared a list of chores I'd like you to get started on when you get home. You'll want to make sure you get them all done by morning. The cleaning supplies are all in the utility room.

We'll talk more about this later.

I love you.

Email to my hubby

I'm very disappointed with your attitude today.

First, absent compelling circumstances, whenever I send you an email, or a text message, I expect a response within 30 minutes.

Second, the proper response to my request regarding Saturday night is "yes, ma'am", not "I don't think that's a good idea."

You see, the thing is, sweetie, you don't really need to "think" in this relationship. You just need to do what you're told. That is what I expect of you.

I'm going to schedule a session with Mistress Marlene this weekend. Apparently, you need a reminder.

Email to my hubby

Sweetie, I love you. And I appreciate your apology. But it's not going to change what's going to happen on Sunday. I'm not going to cancel your session with MM. Between now and then, you might want to reflect on your behavior.

Email to Marc

Got your note. Yes, I'll be there tonight. You coming by for sure? I'll get there around 9pm. I need to make some money, though, so it can't just be all you night. I have to make my rent and my car payment.

Just to warn you... I had a fight with my boyfriend today, so I'm kind of in a mood. He can be such a whiny little bitch sometimes.

Maybe you can cheer me up, lol.

Email to Marco

I'd love you to come spend the night with me on Sunday. CHAD will be gone. I have something to do earlier in the evening, but I'll be back home by 10pm. Come by??

Safe word

The little bitch boy I live with has used his safe word regarding the disciplinary session I set up with Mistress Marlene tomorrow.

Email to my hubby

I'm not upset with you for using your safe word. I'm proud of you, actually. And I love you.

That doesn't mean I've forgotten the reasons why I set up the session with MM in the first place. I'll deal with that later, in a different way.

Thank you for this morning. That was wonderful and thoughtful of you. It's beautiful. I'm wearing it now. And really missing you.

I know how much you love to play golf, and hang out with your friends. I respect that. You need your 'man' time. But I miss you when you're gone. I never get enough hubby time.

I'm looking forward to spending 10 straight, uninterrupted days with you in Spain. We need that.

The last time she disciplined him, he got ten strokes of the cane on his bare bottom, cried for an hour, and couldn't sit without pain for two days.

Email to my hubby

Before I knew you were going to use your safe word, and thought you'd be spending the evening with MM, I had invited Marco to come over and stay with me tonight.

I don't get to see him as often as I'd like, and don't want to really want cancel on him.

I want you to sleep in the bedroom with us tonight, but you've forfeited your right to sleep in the same bed with us. You're going to have to earn that back. So, it's pillow-and-blanket-on-the-floor night for you, at the foot of the bed. Please plan on that tonight.

Also, Marco is going to drop by at 8pm. There's a game he wants to see on ESPN. But I have something I need to do with Ronnie, which won't get me back home until around 9pm. So, I need you to be a good host until I get back.

Thank you, sweetie.

Email to Marco

We're still good for tonight, but my husband's going to be home. His thing got cancelled.

I'm looking forward to seeing you. I get you all night this time!

I need you to do me a favor, though.

I know you were planning to come by at 8pm to see the game, which is fine, but I won't be back home until just after 9pm. CHAD will be home, though.

While I'm gone, I want you to make him suck your cock. Don't take no for an answer. Make him do it. If he resists, you have my permission to force him.

But don't let on that we talked about it. I want him to think it was your idea. Also… this is very important… you need to make sure he's done by the time I get back. I don't want to "walk in on it".

Thank you, babe.

Last Night

My husband still hasn't told me that Marco made him suck cock last night before I got there. (Marco warned him against telling me.)

This is very curious.

Email to my hubby

Marco told me you sucked his cock last night before I got home. Is that true? Is there some reason you didn't mention that to me?

Email to my hubby

I got your note.

That's not how Marco described it. He said you wanted to suck it.

Tina will be here in about 20 minutes. We're going for a run and a swim. Maybe when you get home you can explain to us what happened.

By the way… Marco will be coming by late tonight, after he gets off work.

Update

Interesting discussion with my husband last night about the Marco situation while Tina was here. I'll write more about it later.

I'm super excited about today! I'm going to my first meeting of the Tuesday Wives Club. I heard about it from MM, and have been wanting to join. Today is my formal interview, which is part of the application process.

Email to my hubby

FYI: I'm ovulating this week, Marco knows it, you're out of town again, and I can't be responsible for what the pussy does while you're gone.

Email to my hubby

I missed you last night. The house is always so lonely and empty without you.

Marc came by last night. He fucked your wife and emptied his balls inside me three times. I hate that you weren't here to clean me up afterwards. I had to go to bed with a filthy pussy. He didn't stay the night.

It feels kind of strange that he doesn't know I'm married. I always have to remember to take off my wedding rings before he comes over. I wish I could just tell him. I don't think he would really care, but I can't really trust him to not tell other people at the club.

PS: I asked Marc to take a few pictures of me sucking his cock that I might share with you if you're a good boy. Don't worry, I had him use my phone, so I have the only copies.

Email to my hubby

Remind me, sweetie... have I ever made you eat my pussy to orgasm while I was sitting on the commode going pee? Or will Saturday morning be the first time?

Email to my hubby

Thanks for calling to check up on me. I was good to hear your voice. I'll pick you up at the airport tomorrow. If it's okay, I'll just be naked in the back of the limo.

Marc and his friend Martin are coming over late tonight. You might want to sign in to the security system around 11pm. Hope you enjoy the show, lol.

Love you.

PS: I can't wait to tell you how my interview went on Tuesday. I really like them!

Airport

I'll be picking up my hubby from the airport later this afternoon. I've hired a limo to pick me up at the house, to go get him. I'll be barefoot and naked, with not a single thing on except my wedding rings, ready to give him some loving on the drive back home.

I'm excited!

The Tuesday Wives Club is a group of women who are interested in learning about and sharing experiences about their lives and relationships with their men, from an enlightened FemDom perspective. I learned of the group from MM, who knows several of the women.

Hubby Time

He was gone for several days on a business trip to Phoenix, and I missed him. He loved the way I picked him up at the airport in a limo on Friday… me in the back, nude and barefoot, horny as a bitch in heat, wearing just my wedding rings. The driver was perfectly game for everything.

We're enjoying a nice, quiet holiday weekend at home together. We have a few close friends coming over in a few hours for a pool party barbecue, but other than that, it's just he and I all weekend.

Queen of Spades Tattoo: Just above my right ankle, on the outside. It's discrete, but visible when I want it to be.

I wear a temporary one sometimes. I love the attention it gets. I especially love wearing it when I'm out somewhere with my husband. I love how nervous he gets that someone might ask me about it, because he knows my rule about that.

Daddy Big Bull is still an option. He and I text each other every now and then. But in a way, he's also kind of moved on.

Email to my hubby

FYI... Ronnie and I are planning a Girls Night Out this coming Saturday night, and we'd like you to please be our chauffeur. More on our plans later; we're still working them out.

Physical Exam

So yesterday my husband went in for his annual physical exam, but his regular doctor was apparently on vacation, so he got a different one. I had agreed to unlock him from chastity yesterday because I knew he had the appointment.

So, the doctor is examining him, asking him questions like they always do, and at one point asked him about his level and frequency of physical exercise, how often he smoked cigars, his sleeping patterns, if he felt safe at home, etc.

Then during another part of the exam, the doctor asked my husband if he had been having anal intercourse, which my husband quickly denied. The doctor then said, "It's alright if you are. I see that you're married, but I don't judge. If you do, though, it might be appropriate to perhaps lessen the frequency. The anal sphincter is fairly resilient but can be permanently damaged if you're not careful."

I pick the guy. Sometimes he helps me prepare for a night out, other times it's spontaneous. The guys I fuck tend to be one-night stands so my boyfriend doesn't get to watch. After the date I'll tell my boyfriend all about it while he worships me and, if I'm up for it, I'll let him fuck me and tell him how he compares.

My husband and I used to do this, back in the beginning, before I met Marco and he became my regular Bull. I almost never saw a guy more than once or twice, and my husband was never allowed to watch... he only heard about it afterwards.

There's a part of me that would love to go back to this, because it was so much fun. But then the bad girl side of me slaps me across the face and says, "There's no fucking way I'm giving up Marco, bitch."

My husband is more worried about the inheritance issue than I am. He's already rich without the inheritance. Besides, both his mother and his father would have to die for any inheritance to happen, and who knows how long that might take.

Email to my hubby

So... which wife do you want at the charity dinner tonight?

Sweet, innocent wife?

Adoring wife?

Tame, supportive wife?

Fun, flirty wife?

Hot, sexy wife?

Naughty wife?

Cheating wife?

Bitchy, controlling wife?

Just so you know, I'm planning to wear my gold anklet with the little red heart and black spade charms. But I want you to pick out my heels and my dress for me.

And, I'm going to unlock you from chastity for the entire evening because you've been such a good boy this week.

Email to my Hubby

I'm surprised and very disappointed with you right now.

Sweetie, I love you. You know that. But I don't appreciate you just walking in and interrupting us like that this morning. I had you sleep in the guest room last night for a reason. When the bedroom door is closed, it means I obviously want some alone time with my Bull, and I expect you to respect that. You know better.

When Marco makes love to me, like he was doing this morning when you walked in, you don't really need to see or hear that. Those are special, private moments between he and I; you're not part of that. Honestly, this morning, you kind of ruined it for us. And it makes me feel like I can't trust you.

You know the rules. We'd discussed this before.

When Marco is here, if the bedroom door is open, you're free to watch. And if I want you to do more than just watch, like if I want you to suck him hard for me, or whatever, you'll know.

If the bedroom door is closed, if or when I need you to come in to clean me up, I'll send you a text message. Otherwise, if the bedroom door is closed, it stays closed, until either Marco or I open it.

You were a little sneak this morning. I know you must have been there in the shadows for a while before we noticed you. If you saw or heard anything this morning that made you feel uncomfortable, that's because you interrupted a private moment with my Bull.

Marco was very upset with you this morning. I had to calm him down. If you ever interrupt us like that again, Marco is going to crack your nuts.

When you get back this afternoon from sailing with your friends, I'm going to need you to prepare for a disciplinary session. With me. And then afterwards, we're going to have another talk about this, and a few other things.

I love you. Be careful.

Text to Tina

I appreciate your agreeing to come by. He said he'd be home around 6pm, so if you can get here by 5:30pm, that would be great! Thanks.

A woman can be in love with more than one man at the same time. It's not unusual.

Chapter 12

He's still a man. Of course, he is. But after a lot of time and effort, I've brought out and nurtured his submissive side, and trained him to be obedient to mommy... although he does occasionally forget, or make mistakes, or gets lazy or fussy... hence the necessity for an occasional disciplinary session.

Last night was an especially difficult disciplinary session for him, most particularly because Tina was there to witness it (which was extremely embarrassing for him), and pain-wise because it was his first encounter with the wooden hairbrush, and I didn't hold back on my strokes.

I had a long discussion with him, followed by a lecture, and then asked him to go upstairs and prepare himself to be disciplined. I reminded him to put his "punishment panties" on, which he did. I also decided to unlock his penis from chastity during the session.

Then over the course of about 30 minutes, he got a hand-spanking, followed by the belt, and ending with the wooden hairbrush. It was pretty intense for him. By the fifth stroke of the belt, he was crying like a little boy.

Afterwards, I held him for a long time, consoled him, kissed his tears, gave him a nice, slow, sensuous handjob, and let him cum. Then I locked him back up.

Because discipline, regardless of how harsh it may be, should always followed by love and compassion. And because in the long run, that kind of mixed conditioning makes the disciplinary session much more effective. It's a bonding thing.

At the end of the session, before I had him go take a shower and get to bed, he would have done anything for me, which was precisely the intent and purpose behind the discipline.

Today, right before lunch, he had flowers delivered to Franco's office where I worked this morning.

I'll try to write more about it later.

We're going to Spain for 10 days next week, so I need to get my Marco time in. I'm going to miss him.

There's one thing I've been wanting to try, but never have. Which is… me on my back, with my hubby on top of me, missionary style, making sweet beautiful love to me… with Marco hitting my hubby's ass from behind. It's kind of radical, but I've always wanted to try that. So… I might maybe surprise my hubby with that this week.

Black guys are ass fanatics. Every black guy I've ever been with (except one) wanted my ass, and had my ass.

Of course, you need to know that it violates the Hotwife Ethical Code for a woman to deny a black man her ass. It's just not done!

Believe me, if your wife goes out with a black guy, and if she has a nice ass, he's not only going to want to fuck it, before he's done with her, he will fuck it, whether she wants it or not. A strong, powerful, dominant black man isn't going to be denied. He's going to take what he wants.

If your wife isn't prepared to give up her ass to a black guy, she needs to stay away from them and stick to the white boys.

Email to Daddy Big Bull

My husband and I will be gone for about two weeks on vacation. But when we get back, his sweet boypussy will be available if you want some.

I have a few ideas I'd like to talk with you about.

The Science of Attraction

Science proves that men are attracted to lighter-skinned and women are more attracted to darker-skinned men:

Men are subconsciously attracted to fairer skin because of its association with innocence, purity, modesty, virginity, vulnerability and goodness, according to researchers at the University of Toronto. Women are attracted to men with darker complexions because these are associated with sex, virility, mystery, villainy and danger.

So, it's no wonder that white women would be attracted to Black men (the darkest skinned men) and black men would be attracted to White women (the palest skinned women). Both are simply pursuing what their genetic programming tells them to. It's perfectly natural.

Being funny and charming, helps, but some women also like dark and mysterious. I like both, depending on my mood.

Develop your body. Women love powerfully built, athletic men. But don't overdo it on the muscles; you don't want to look like a steroid freak.

Having a nice, big, thick cock is a must. Without that, you're just another boy with a penis.

Hang out at places, or around places, where married white women go.

Develop a reputation as a confident, skilled cocksman… which means… you get hard, stay hard, and can fuck all night.

You must make a woman cum. At least twice. Every time. No matter what.

Learn how to eat pussy. It matters. It matters a lot.

Women need to know that you're discreet, and aren't going to talk about them.

On the other hand, women all talk to each other about the men in their life, especially if she's married and has a black bull stud on the side who's fucking her brains out.

After a while, the women will start coming to you.

Diary, he's not very happy that I'm playing with someone who knows him, and has been begging me to tell him who the guy is.

On a 1 to 10 scale… with Marco being a 10, DaddyBigBull being a 9, Marc being an 8, and my husband being a 4-5… Sauna Man is about a 6-7. Not great, but above average.

Email to my hubby

I'm going to keep my promises to you while we're in Spain.

1. Your penis will be unlocked and free from chastity the entire trip.

2. You can have me anytime and as often as you want; no restrictions.

3. You can get all the fresh, young pussy you want; no restrictions. In fact, I want you to. I'm sure Barcelona is going to be crawling with lots of young girls who would love to hook up with a rich, handsome American man.

4. I think it would be fun to maybe share a girl with you. We could be your hot little bitches and you could be our daddy!

5. I'm not going to play with any other men on this trip, unless you want me to.

6. I'm leaving all my strap-on dildos and other toys at home. Your ass is safe, lol.

7. I'm bringing a bottle of cherry lube, in case you want my ass.

I think we're going to have a blast together!

Arrived in Spain

Flying is such a hassle these days... uhhhhhhh!!... but we finally made it to Barcelona. Finally! Great internet wifi connection at the hotel, which I love. Right now, I'm looking forward to sleeping...

My hubby didn't get the blowjob he wanted on the plane, even though it was dark and most people on the plane were asleep. But somewhere over the Atlantic, I did give him a nice, discreet handjob. I wasn't going to let him cum, but then changed my mind. He doesn't really cum that much anyway... just a few small dribbles. But he did still make a mess.

He went soft almost immediately, which was rather disappointing.

"You always lose your erection right away after you cum. That makes me sad. Marco always stays hard for me."

"I'm sorry. I can't really help it."

"I know you can't."

"I wish I was better endowed, and lasted longer. I wish I could give that to you."

"I wish you could too. But I still love you. Your little penis is cute. I've always thought that."

"Thank you."

"Why don't you go clean yourself up, sweetie. We can't have you looking like you just jacked off."

Update from Barcelona

Having a great time. Relaxing. Sight-seeing. Making love (Bulls fuck sissy hubby's make love). Shopping. Sailing.

Tomorrow we're going to the Sagrada Família and the Barcelona Cathedral.

He scored!

I was starting to wonder if my husband still had it in him. If he could still meet and pick up and seduce a woman with his handsome looks and boyish charm.

Then yesterday he surprised me. She's one of the "pool girls" who works at the hotel. Petite, Spanish, like maybe 20, and she's really cute!

I wasn't involved; it was just him and her, but that's okay. I'm very happy for him. His self-confidence, I can tell, got a nice boost.

And he picked up a second one last night, a young girl from St. Petersburg here on vacation with her friends.

I think his little dick has grown a few inches this week!

Email to my hubby

When we get back home, I'd like us to buy Marco a new car. He needs one. An expensive one. One like yours.

We'll call it a birthday present from both of us.

I'd like us to go looking, and get it, and then surprise him with it.

The way he takes care of me, and gives me what I need, I think he deserves it. Marco's very, very important to me, and we can easily afford it.

I don't want my future baby daddy driving some junky car.

Interesting…

So, this new husband I've met during our time here in Spain… confident, energetic, charming, exciting, full of life… I'm really liking this guy!

I wonder how much of it has to do with him not being in chastity, not fucking him with my strap-on, my letting him have all the pussy he wants without restriction, and even allowing him to fuck other women? So far, he's been with two… one of the pool girls at the hotel, and this Russian girl here on vacation with her friends.

Since we've been here, he's been fucking me like 3-4 times a day. And I'm loving it! He's even been lasting longer than usual.

Last night when we got back to the hotel… it was really late… he flipped me over in bed and took my ass, without asking. He just took it like Marco does.

Email to my hubby

So, this new stud I've been on vacation with in Spain… can I take him back home with me? OMG!!

I love the way you've been fucking me every day and night since we've been here. I've been needing to feel that with you for the longest time. I missed

it. I was starting to think that maybe you didn't have it in you anymore, which was silly, I know.

To be honest, I haven't missed Marco's cock even once. Well, maybe once or twice, but my entire body and spirit has been totally focused on you. I'm sure you could tell.

If I told you I didn't want his big black dick inside me anymore, would you believe me?

Even if you don't believe that, there's one thing I do need you to believe: You're my husband. You're my one and only man, the only one I love and will ever love. Our thing is forever.

All those other men I've been with over the years, including Marco... they're just cocks to me. Just fucks. Nothing else. You're the only man who has ever had my heart.

My best and most favorite moment since we've been here in Barcelona was the night I was waiting for you in the bar down the street, and you sent me a text that I could come back up to the room. I was so nervous walking back. I was feeling jealous and anxious, but also excited.

When I walked in, I could immediately tell that you had fucked her. And I was so proud of you!

The bemused look on your face, the way the bed was all messed up, the smell of the room. I could smell her perfume on you and on the bed. And the wet spot was pretty obvious. You must have had her creaming all over your dick.

And wow, I loved smelling her sweet pussy on your balls. That was incredibly exciting to me. I could feel my clit throbbing just thinking about it.

I don't think you've ever had Spanish pussy before, have you? Is it different? Do you think they're all that sweet? I know you said she was incredibly passionate in bed. Did you like that about her?

I want to watch you fuck her before we leave. We need to do that! I'm glad you were honest with her, and told her you were married. She could've looked it up anyway, since she works at the hotel.

I want to watch! You need to make that happen boy! I want to taste her too!

Okay, so I was thinking... when we get back home, if you promise to fuck me every night the way you have since we've been here, I don't see any reason to lock up your penis. I want you to be free to be the stud I'm falling in love with all over again.

The only reason I even got the idea to lock up your penis in the first place was because I was frustrated that you were always exhausted and your sexual energies were increasingly diminished because you were working all the time, and just jacking off.

And... I know this is going to shock you... I want you to be free to fuck other women. You've earned it. You've worked hard all your life, you're incredibly handsome and successful, you always treat me well, and you've earned it. You should be able to enjoy fresh new pussy whenever you want. I know men need that to stay young, and I don't want you getting old on me.

When we get back, I want you to know that you can do that whenever you want. If you meet a girl somewhere, and she excites you, I want you to be able to flirt and charm and seduce and fuck her. As long as you promise to always come back home to me.

I love how powerful and confident and happy you are after you've had fresh pussy. I can tell how it affects you. It energizes you. It's pretty dramatic. And I like you like that.

But... I need to know that it's just going to be a sex thing. Just a physical thing. Just fun, and not more than that.

You really scared me with Emma. I know how close you got to her, and it scared me. I still don't totally understand that, but it scared me.

I don't want to lose you. I don't ever want to lose you. I need you to promise me.

Also... I want you to let me secretly watch sometimes, like you've watched me with other men. I really want to do that. I want to watch my stud hubby in action. I want to hear you make them screen.

And I still want to share a girl with you again. I think that would be so much fun!

I need to tell you that Marco and I have exchanged a few emails since we left. I need to show them to you.

I know I have a complicated thing with him, whatever it is. Obviously, he's very special to me.

To be honest, I've been toying with the idea of asking you to let him move in with us, but I now realize that's probably not a good idea.

I do, though, still want us to buy him a new car. He really needs one. He's always been there for me, and I just feel like that would be a really nice thing for us to do for him.

You know I love to tease you about Marco getting me pregnant, and having his baby. I'd be lying if I said I didn't fantasize about it a lot, because I do. There's a part of me that just wants to have all his babies.

But it's just teasing mostly. Obviously, I can't have a black man's baby and be married to you.

Like I told you last year during the whole DaddyBigBull/rehab disaster, you're the one I want to have a baby with. You need to be my baby daddy. And I want you to be. I need you to get me pregnant and give me your smart, beautiful baby. You have no idea how badly I want that. I feel like it will complete us.

With the way you've been fucking me this week, if I was off the pill right now, I probably already be pregnant!

When we get back home, I want to schedule an appointment with my doctor, and look at going off the pill. I also want to set up an appointment for you with your doctor regarding the whole sperm count thing again. I'm sure there are things we can do to make me more fertile, and you more potent.

And I want you to promise me that you're going to fill up with your baby juice every night until you get me pregnant.

Getting back to Marco... I know he's going to want pussy right away when we get back. You know how he is. He's been telling me in his emails how good he's going to fuck me when I get back.

And honestly, I do want to feel him between my legs again, I need that, but I'm not sure that's really a good idea right now.

So... I need you to please email him and tell him he's going to have to wait for it. Tell him that you and I need more alone time. Let him know that it's going to be at least a couple of weeks. Maybe longer.

I don't think he should fuck me until after you get me pregnant. I don't really want to be in a situation where I get pregnant but then don't really know who the father is. That would just be really weird.

I want you to email Marco because I need you to take control of that.

I need you... and I want you... to be my daddy. I don't want him or anyone else to fuck me unless they have your permission.

It's your pussy now, sweetie. You've earned it back.

Thank you, sweetie.

I love you so much!

My sexual satisfaction with my husband isn't directly comparable to what I experience with Marco. It's a different kind of sex. Both can be awesome, but they're awesome in a different way. And the orgasms are different.

When my hubby makes me cum with his mouth and tongue... which is the only way he can make me cum... my orgasms are sort of more frequent... like one, and then another, and then another, in rapid succession... but they are shallower and don't last as long. They're nice, but they don't rip my soul apart.

When Marco fucks me, and he's churning in and out of me, and then picks up the pace, and then really starts banging me hard and fast... the way he makes me cum is harder and deeper and longer lasting. It's much, much more intense. They just rip me open. And it's exhausting. In that moment, after he makes me cum, I just feel like I would do absolutely anything he wanted me to do, just so I can feel him give me another one.

I was very sincere about what I wrote to my husband. I meant every word of it. I hope he can live up to my hopes and expectations as far as him stepping up his game. I think he will. We're both very excited about things right now.

The Surprise

I can't believe this is happening!!!

I just found out why my husband has been so secretive about what we're doing tomorrow afternoon. He's made arrangements for us to renew our wedding vows in the courtyard of this beautiful restaurant we were at on Sunday.

Uhhhhh!! I'm so happy!!

Email to Marco

So... when I get back... what if I told you I wanted to strap you? And take your ass, instead of you taking mine? Can I?

Would you be my secret faggot? I promise I won't tell anyone. I bet you'd like it. Would you do that for me?

Email to my hubby

Sir, if you're going to be my daddy... and I really want you to be... I need you to please remember that your little girl needs lots and lots of black dick. Nice and big and thick, please! As much as you'll let me have. Every day would be perfect.

We're going to try switching roles every three months or so, but we're still trying to work out the rules of how that would happen.

Some rules we've already discussed...

... neither partner can use anything that the other partner did or didn't do in the prior period against the other partner in the subsequent period.

... the switch date and time has to be firm and unchangeable.

... we both have to respect and honor each other's safe words.

My taking on the more submissive role is going to be easy. The hardest part for me is trying to realistically see him in the more dominant role. I am committed, though, to doing everything I can to make this work.

Even if it means closing my eyes and submitting to the power of four-inch penis, ha ha.

My husband's already showed me a very different side of him while we've been in Spain, which has been extremely exciting for me. It's almost like he's been a totally different man here. And I like that man!

He's expressed interest in being the more dominant partner, and I want to give him that opportunity. I would absolutely love if he totally embraces it.

Chapter 13

Email to Marco

You better not be fucking any other bitches, or I'll lock up your dick too!

Thank you for being patient with me.

The good news is... no one else has been fucking it either.

The bad news is... no one else has been fucking it either.

What are your plans for the fourth? My hubby and I are going sailing with two other couples. I'm sure it will be boring.

Maybe we can hook up on Sunday??

Email to my hubby

Can I please have some big black cock this weekend? I'm missing it really, really badly. I'll do anything you want me to…

Email to my hubby

I received your email, and will do as you ask.

Regarding that other thing you wanted me to do, I texted Sauna Man as you instructed. He hasn't replied yet. I'm not sure how he's going to react, but I will do everything I can to make it happen.

Love you!

Texts with Sauna Man

We should get together again.

Been away from my phone. Just saw this. Hell yes!

I am sooooo horny!

Isn't your husband taking care you?

He wants to. And he does. But it just hurts me too much. His dick is too big. And he's always way too rough. I only let him fuck me like once a week.

Your husband doesn't know about me, right?

Of course not. He would kill me. And probably you.

He doesn't seem like a violent guy.

He's not, but he has his moments.

I'm leaving on Friday for the weekend. Sometime late next week work?

I really need to be fucked now! Are you going to make me speed dial someone else?

You got other guys on speed dial?

Yeah. But you're in my top ten, ha ha.

Damn. I got too much going on between now and getting out here on Friday. I'll make it up to you though.

Oh yeah?

I promise.

I wanna try something new with you. Do you know what strap-on sex is?

I've heard of it.

Would you do that with me? My husband won't let me fuck him that way.

I've never done that.

Haven't you ever had a girl put her finger in your ass while she's giving you a blowjob?

Yes.

And you liked it, right? Didn't it make you come right away?

A finger is different. Not sure I'd enjoy the strap on thing.

Are you kidding? You'll love it. I'll make it good for you.

Sounds painful.

It's not really. I'll use a small one. And go slow.

So, you've done it before?

Yeah. With this other guy. But he's kind of gone now.

What happened to him?

I met you, ha ha.

Got a call. I'll get back to you in a few.

Email from my hubby

I just got this email from him:

Along the lines of our previous discussion, I'd like you to write a sincere letter of apology to Emma. I want to see it before it goes out. Please get that done today.

Regarding the job I told you about, I secured an interview for you Tuesday next week. They will be sending you an email with details, and an application form. Please put that on your calendar.

I'll be by the house today just after 2pm. See you soon.

Email from my husband

I just got this from him:

I talked with Maria early this morning. I told her she could have the next 30 days off with full pay.

She seemed worried that I was firing her, but I assured her I was not. I encouraged her to take some time for herself and her children.

Instead, you're going to be responsible to make sure that everything gets done around the house, basically everything Maria does for us, the cleaning, laundry, dry cleaning drop off and delivery, grocery shopping, etc.

But I'd like you to do something different regarding the laundry. Rather than do it at the house, I want you to use a laundry mat where you do it yourself. I will give you the location tomorrow.

My email to Emma

This is what I wrote to her, at my husband's insistence, with his modifications:

This is far too late, I should have written this to you many months ago.

I want to apologize for my inappropriate behavior and scornful attitude towards you as regards my husband.

I realize now that you were only trying to be a friend to my husband during a very difficult time.

I was jealous and fearful about your relationship with him, but upon reflection, I now realize that my fears were unfounded, and mostly a reflection of what I was personally going through at the time.

I hurt my husband deeply by my actions, and then took out my frustrations on you and others around him.

Please know that I have no problem with you and my husband being friends.

Please accept my apology. I'm sorry.

22.

Texts with my husband

Did you get my email regarding the laundromat where you'll be washing/drying our clothes tomorrow?

Yes. I looked it up on GPS. That's like the ghetto part of town! Can't I do it somewhere closer to the house?

You didn't seem to have a problem going to the ghetto when you were seeing DaddyBigBull, as I recall.

That was different. I don't think it's very fair of you to keep bringing him up. That's past. That's over. I've apologized for that a million times.

And yet you brought him up again in your email to me earlier this week.

That was just a joke.

And not a very funny one.

Can I PLEASE go to a place closer to the house?

No. I think you'll fit right in at the place I selected for you. I drove by. It's nice and cheap and run down, with a liquor store, a pawn shop, and a massage parlor in the same strip center.

Sounds gross.

You'll fit in just fine. Just imagine you're back in the little shit town you grew up in. That strip center would be several steps up.

Now you're just being mean.

I also expect you to be appropriately dressed tomorrow when you're there.

Meaning?

What do young women wear when they do laundry? Shorts, tank top, flip-flops, no panties or bra, of course. And, as always, when you're in public, make sure you're wearing your spade tattoo.

If I go to a place like that, in that part of town, dressed like that, the guys there are all going to hit on me, like constantly. Is that what you want?

You like being the center of attention, as I recall. And men hitting on you.

If they're hot, maybe, but otherwise no. It's disgusting. I could get raped in a place like that.

Oh, I'm sure you can handle yourself just fine.

You're really serious about this, aren't you?

I am.

Can't you at least go with me? I'd feel much safer.

That's not really my kind of place. Besides, I'm going sailing with a few friends.

It's not my kind of place either!

It was before I met you. As I seem to recall, you lived in a rat hole apartment in exactly that kind of neighborhood.

I didn't live in the ghetto when you met me.

It was pretty close.

Can I ask why you're doing this?

I think you need a reminder of what life was like before you met me and before I moved you into the beach house.

Is that what this all about?

Oh, I'm just getting started. I haven't told you yet about the new gym you're going to join next week.

I like my sports and yoga gym, and the one at the country club. I have lots of friends there.

But they're very expensive, and I don't think you're going to be able to afford them after you start working. Not with what you're going to be making. Besides, you'll make new friends at the new gym.

Where is it?

I'm still researching. I need to pick the right one.

Uhhhhhh!! You're killing me here!!

BBQ Party

Diary, my husband and I are going to a BBQ party at Franco and Brandy's place late this afternoon. They have a beautiful home up in the hills that overlooks the city. They always have great parties.

Dress code for the women is bikini bottoms, crop tops, and barefoot.

For the men, it's weekend casual, whatever that means. My husband is going to wear khaki slacks, a polo shirt, and deck shoes.

Should be fun.

My Instructions

At the laundromat today, my husband's instructions:

1. I am not allowed to drive there. I must take a taxi to and from.

2. I am required to wear cut-off jean shorts, white tank top, flip-flops, no panties, no bra.

3. I'm required to wear my black spade tattoo on my ankle, and if asked about it, to say what it means (that sexually, I prefer black men).

4. I am not allowed to wear my wedding ring. If asked, I am required to say that I'm single.

5. If a man flirts with me, I am required to flirt back, and encourage his advances, no matter who he is, what he looks like, etc.

6. If a man asks for my phone number, I am required to give it to him, and get his.

Email to my hubby

I'm here. Things are okay. I feel safe.

The taxicab driver thought it was strange that I would come here to do laundry. I didn't even know what to say to him.

It's pretty disgusting here. And filthy. Could you have picked a more ghetto neighborhood? Except for the Chinese girls who work at the massage place next door (I assume they're Chinese??), I'm pretty sure I'm the only white girl within a mile of here. Oh joy.

Email to my husband

So... I've been a good girl and done exactly as you asked.

Only two men have flirted with me so far.

One of them noticed my spade tattoo right away, and knew right away what it meant. He kind of teased me about it, asked me if I had a boyfriend, I told him no, he asked me if I was looking for one, I told him "maybe", and he invited me to hang out with him tonight. I told him I was busy, but exchanged phone numbers with him, like you said I had to. He's actually still here.

The other black guy who flirted with me actually works in the liquor store a few doors down. I went there to get a Coke. The first thing he said to me was, "Damn, baby, ain't seen you here before. You one of Lonnie's girls?" I

smiled and just said, "I'm not that kind of girl." And he laughed. Lonnie is apparently a pimp around here. I told him I was just doing laundry. He told me his friend Lonnie is always looking for a new girl, and asked if I wanted to make some money. I politely declined, then he told me I had a "nice ass". Since you told me I had to flirt back, I asked him, "Yeah, you like it?" And he said I had the finest ass he had seen in a long time. Then another customer got behind me in line and I thought I should go, so I left.

Email from my husband

I just got this from him:
It sounds like you had a colorful experience today. I hope you learned a few things. I'm pleased that you did as I asked, but you failed to follow my instructions precisely to the letter. We'll discuss that tonight. I'll be home by 6pm. Please make sure the house is clean from top to bottom by the time I get home. Thank you, darling.

Frustrated

I'm so frustrated right now. I've done everything my husband has asked me to this past week, and he's still not letting me see Marco... or have any BBC. It's been almost four weeks now! My husband has been making love to me almost every night, which is nice. But he never makes me cum that way. The last four or five times, he's basically just getting himself off. After he ejaculates inside me, he rolls over, kisses me on the cheek, and falls asleep. He still goes down on me, but only before he puts his penis inside me, and not after.

Email to my hubby

I thought I did everything you asked. What are you thinking about that I didn't do? I've been trying very hard to obey you.

Email from my husband

I just got this from him:
Received your note about tonight.

It seems to me that you met a few fellas today that could use a good blowjob or two. If you're craving black cock that bad, maybe I'll pick one of them for you to service. How's that?

As far as Marco is concerned, I think you need more time away from him.

Incongruous

I love him, I really, really do. And I want to be with him. But sexually submitting to a man with a four-inch penis still seems incongruous to me. And wrong.

Email from my hubby

I just got this from him:
Regarding the three men you've recently met, I want you to flirt with them by text, be daring with them, make them want you, make sure they know how much you love to suck cock.

Regarding Marco, send him a quick response telling him you're busy, and that you'll get back to him tomorrow. Then don't. Wait until he contacts you again.

One other thing. Emma appreciated your apology. I talked to her over the weekend. She's going to email you today. Make sure your email back to her is respectful. I'd like you to invite her to lunch this week. I want you to patch things up with her. I need you two to get along. Please make that happen.

I love you.

Email to my hubby

Marco called and texted me today. He wants me to go see him. He wants pussy.

Can I go see him tonight? Or tomorrow? Or he could come to the house and you could watch if you want. Please??

Also... thought you might want to know... he and Dana have been talking/texting each other.

Texts with my husband

I'm not very happy with your behavior at lunch today with Emma. I talked with her as well.

Did the greasy bitch tell you how she ordered wine and went on and on about how good it was, and kept offering to me, and ignored me when I told her I couldn't drink?

She didn't mention that.

Yeah. I wonder why.

Still, I expect you to rise about that.

I hate her.

Emma is a very pleasant person. She isn't a threat to you.

Yeah, well, she's a threat to the cheese and donuts in my kitchen, so FUCK HER!

Alright. I'll handle that another way.

Good. Because I don't ever want to see her again. I'm sorry, but you wanted me to be honest with you about how I feel about things. That's how I feel about her.

Being honest with me about your feelings with me, and being polite and respectful to Emma are two different things.

Maybe I'm too blonde to understand the difference.

There's nothing blonde about how your brain works. You're one of the smartest women I've ever met.

You're just saying that so I won't be mad at you.

That's enough on that subject. I'll handle it another way. Regarding Marco, you do not have my permission to see him right now. That's going to need to wait, if it ever happens again at all.

You're not being fair. He's very special to me. You know that. Please let me see him tonight. He's getting really upset with me.

I think you two need more time apart. He's obviously became more than just recreation for you, which is a problem. You told me before that wasn't going to happen again, and then it happened again.

Well, like you said, Emma isn't a threat to me, and Marco's not a threat to you.

That's not how I see it.

You're just jealous of him.

I rather think it's more the other way around. But I'll tell you what, why don't I handle that another way too.

Meaning?

Don't push me on this 22.

I'm NOT pushing you!

You're not being obedient. You keep pushing.

You're doing this on purpose, aren't you?

Doing what on purpose?

Trying to hurt me. Trying to make me feel small.

I have go. We'll talk about this later. I'd like you to meet me for dinner. I'll text the location to you in a while.

I'm sorry. This is all very difficult for me.

I'll text you later.

This weekend

My husband told me last night that he's taking me to a lifestyle party in Malibu on Saturday, and that Emma will be going with us.

But rather than the fetish party we usually go to, where we know a lot of people, this will be a different one, hosted by someone else, where we don't know anyone.

Email from my husband

I just got this from him:
I picked out something beautiful for you to wear to the party tomorrow night. I think you're going to love it. Why don't you come by my office today at 1pm to model it for me?

See you soon.

Last Night

My husband's patience with me ran out last night.

We had a disagreement that turned into an argument, which morphed into a really nasty fight, although he was actually pretty calm the whole time and never raised his voice. I was the one alternating between shouting and crying.

I was extremely frustrated and felt like I had no control, and it all came out. Him telling me that Emma was going with us to the party tonight pushed me over the edge.

I said some things to him that I shouldn't have. About him. My life. Emma. His mother. Marco. My H addiction. My time in rehab. My fears. My frustrations. My desire for a child. Our marriage.

In a way, he basically just let me vent, just letting me talk.

And then he took control like I've never seen him do before.

He wrapped his arms around me, told me he loved me, that I was safe with him, held me for a minute, and then said, "I need you to listen now."

Then he proceeded to lecture me.

As he put it, he was tired of... "your disrespectful and insulting attitude towards my mother and Emma" ... "your sense of entitlement and lack of appreciation for the lifestyle that my success affords you" ... "your constant complaints that you're not getting enough sex" ... "the way you think the world revolves around you" ... "your lack of discretion regarding private sexual matters" ... "the way you involve other people in our life, and the way they get hurt".

He told me he still hasn't forgiven me for the Dana situation, saying, "She is like a daughter to me, and you threw her to the wolves. You took away her innocence. You are responsible for that."

Then he ordered me down to my knees, and continued to lecture me.

He told me to give him my hands, which I did, and took off my wedding rings and put them in his pocket.

He told me I was a spoiled child, a disrespectful wife, and too selfish and immature to be a mother.

By this time, I was crying.

He told me, "Go get me your purse."

And I did, running upstairs, then back down, and handed it to him.

He opened it and dumped out the contents on the floor, started going though things, to see what was in my purse, and put my gym and country club membership cards in his pocket.

Then he handed me the keys to my car and told me, "Go move your car out of the garage. Put it in the driveway. Then wait for me in the garage."

I did as he asked. And waited. And waited. I was probably in there twenty minutes before he came.

When he did, he was carrying two blankets and a pillow.

"You'll be sleeping in here tonight, on the floor, on the spot where your car was parked."

I didn't dare say anything.

"I'm not going to discipline you tonight. Instead, I'm going to do that tomorrow evening a few hours before we go to the party because I want those marks on your bottom for everyone to see."

He went on.

"I don't want to hear another word out of you tonight. In the morning, wake me up at 6am when breakfast is ready."

Then he hugged me, kissed my cheek, and said, "You'll be fine. I'll check on you in a few hours. If you need to use the bathroom you have my permission to use one of the bathrooms downstairs, as long as you come right back down here."

And then he left, turning off the light, leaving me in total darkness.

I didn't sleep a minute last night. Instead I kept getting up to check the time to make sure I wasn't late making his breakfast.

This morning he told me I would continue to sleep alone in the garage, and would not get the keys to my car back until my attitude improved.

He explained, "If you need to go anywhere, you can take the bus. I'll leave you enough money for that."

And he went on.

"We'll see how you do tonight. I expect complete, immediate, unquestioned, and utter obedience from you."

I asked him, "Is Emma going to spend the night here, after the party?"

"I don't know yet. Maybe. If I decide I want that to happen, I'll let you know."

Then he left to go play golf with his friends.

I Can't Do This

He's punishing me. Breaking me. Purposefully humiliating me, and forcing me to experience the grotesque.

After my nightmare this morning, when I was forced to listen (but not see) my husband make love to Emma, to say nothing of my humiliation at the lifestyle party last night, today, at the laundromat, I've been ordered to give some stranger a blowjob in his car in the parking lot. I'm supposed to resist and not let the guy touch my body otherwise. I'm supposed to ask the guy to take a picture of me sucking his cock using my phone.

My husband told me last night that if I wanted black cock, I was going to have to be satisfied with "real nigger dick" as he put it.

My husband isn't a racist or bigoted man, but every now and then his Southern upbringing... and the hateful voice and influence of his mother... come out.

So, who am I supposed to suck off, you ask? The second black guy who hits on me today, regardless of who he is or what he looks like. I'm supposed to flirt back and encourage him.

I'm supposed to offer to give him head in his car or wherever, and put a condom on his cock like a common prostitute, and suck his cock that way until he ejaculates in the condom.

I've been here almost two hours now. So far, only some drugged-out Mexican guy has hit on me. Thank God.

I only have about an hour more left to go before I get to leave this horrid place.

My Life Is Over

I'm in a lot of pain right now, physically, mentally, and every other kind. My butt is on fire right now. To say that I can't sit down is the least of it.

I'm here all alone at the house now with my cat. My husband went sailing and fishing with his friend Quinn.

He made it clear that he expects the house to be spotless when he gets back tonight, and the laundry all done. "Make sure you wash the dirty sheets," he reminded me.

Seriously, I ought to just burn them.

He put cash on the bathroom counter, a stack of one-dollar bills, for me to use for taxi cab fare and the laundromat.

My husband severely disciplined me early this morning with a leather strap until I was in tears and begged him to stop.

He had a water bottle that he used to spray my butt wet before he started hitting me. "I like the sound it makes, and it really brings out the color nicely," he said.

My ability before, to stoically hold it all in and just take his punishment without breaking down emotionally, has evaporated.

I started crying even before he started out of embarrassment and humiliation. And fear.

He calmly but firmly lectured me the whole time about my "spoiled, bratty behaviors", my "selfishness", my "disgusting sense of entitlement", and my

failure to totally and faithfully follow and honor all of his instructions last night at the party.

He was upset that I embarrassed him at the party, and warned me that there would be further consequences to pay for that.

He disciplined me this morning in front of Emma, who sat across the bedroom, her fat ass hanging over the edges of the bench, and looked on with a mixture of shock and bemusement.

Fucking swine bitch!!

Afterwards, my husband ordered me to crawl over to the pink-skinned cow, who then told me to turn around and proceeded to rub cold cream on my blistered ass, while my husband sat back and watched.

They had obviously planned it ahead of time because she already had the jar of cold cream on the table next to her.

I was still sobbing hysterically, having totally lost all control of my composure, and just followed his instructions.

I could tell she was enjoying every minute of it, as she condescendingly told me, "Owww… that looks like it hurts. This should make you feel better."

Then my husband ordered me to turn around to face the wall and kneel down in the corner, and left me there for over an hour while they went downstairs to have breakfast.

I could hear her laughing and cackling in the breakfast room at his jokes or whatever the fuck my son-of-a-hateful-Jew-bitch husband was saying.

When they came back upstairs, my husband tossed Emma's elephant-sized panties to me, and said, "Stand up. Put those on. You'll be wearing them today and tomorrow."

Uhhhhhh!!! Emma is like a size 16, at least, with an ass the size of a refrigerator, and a gaping, fisted bear cunt to match. I'm sure I probably looked like a skinny nine-year-old girl putting on her fat welfare aunt's panties.

As I stood there, trying to figure out how I was going to keep them from falling off me, I looked over and saw Emma in my dressing room looking at things in my jewelry drawers.

My husband walked over and kissed her, as she put her meat-bag hand on his shoulder and tip-toed to kiss him back, and she swooned like a teenage girl.

"You're such a good kisser," I heard her tell him.

That was the absolute fucking worst, watching him kiss her like that. Uhhhhhhh!!

"Take something, anything you like. It's yours," he said to her, looking at my jewelry drawers. She looked like a starving pig at the trough. "Really?"

He nodded. "Sure. Anything you like."

She didn't even bother to look over at me. She just ignored me.

I would have given up everything I own at that moment, perhaps even my life, to set her on fire.

I can't even bring myself to write about what happened last night yet. More later. Maybe. Unless I tie the bedsheets around my neck, jump off the balcony, and hang myself today.

Email to my husband

You wanted me to email you when I was on my way to the laundromat.

So… I'm on my way.

I'm dressed in tight jeans and a cut-off top, and wearing my spade tattoo, as you instructed.

I promise I will do exactly what you told me to do, with the second black man who hits on me, regardless of who he is or looks like, and text you a picture proving it.

I'm sure it will be horribly disgusting. Thank you for that.

Love you.

Email to my husband

I'm sorry that I don't have any pictures to send to you. I was only hit on by three men, two of them Mexican but only one of them was black.

I'm leaving to go home now.

Love you.

Texts with my husband

I've made some decisions about what I want to do where Marco is concerned.

Okay. What?

I'm not very comfortable with you seeing him anymore. He's trouble. You've allowed yourself to get too close. I want you to end things with him.

That's not fair.

I don't really think you're in any position to make that judgment. Nor do I care what your judgment is.

I can't just end things with him all of a sudden.

Either you do it, or I will. You won't like how I do it.

Are you serious about this?

Yes. I'm going to let you taper it off. You can see him two or three more times, and then that will be it.

I don't understand why you're hurting me like this.

The fact that you're putting it that way illustrates my point. You've allowed yourself to get too close to him.

And what about you with Emma?

Emma is not a threat to our marriage. Marco is.

So, I can't have sex with other men anymore? But you like that. I know you do.

I enjoy it sometimes, but you've allowed things to get out of control one too many times. You have a tendency to allow yourself to get too close, and give out too much information about us. And you tend to pick the wrong types of men. If you want to have sex with other men, I'm going to let you enjoy that on occasion, but there will be some rules associated with it.

Such as?

For starters, I will decide who the man will be. You have to use condoms. And you can't see anyone more than three times.

So, I can't even pick who I have sex with anymore?

You can make suggestions, and I'll consider it.

Are you going to keep seeing Emma?

Occasionally. I enjoy her company.

Even though you know it hurts me. I think she's a bigger threat to our marriage than Marco is.

So, you said. I disagree.

I'd be more comfortable if you saw three or five or even ten other women, then Emma. I hate her. And she hates me.

She doesn't hate you. She actually rather indifferent to you. She'll be around sometimes, when I want her to be around. And when I don't want her to be, she won't.

I don't want to talk about this anymore. I have to go.

We'll talk about it more when I get home, if you'd like.

You don't love me anymore, do you?

Oh, I love you. I've always loved you. I'm doing this BECAUSE I love you.

I liked you better the other way.

You just like being in control.

And you like to rub it in my face that you're rich, that you control all the money, and I have nothing.

I made the mistake of spoiling you before. Letting you have anything and everything you wanted. You don't really have the maturity to handle that.

So, I'm a child now?

The way you've been acting, some of the things you've done in the last year, yes, I would say so. An immature, spoiled child.

Why do you even want me then? You took away my weddings rings. Why did you do that?

To make a point with you.

What? That you're cruel? That you hate me now?

Always with the drama. Now I have to go. I'll see you at home later.

Okay. I'll be ready like you want.

Good girl. See you soon.

And Then Last Night

… and so after all that, this horrendous week from hell, where I'm just hating him, and afraid of what's happening between us… last night he puts on some music, pours me a bath, gently washes my back, washes me everywhere, talks with me, we reminisce about our life together, he puts my wedding rings back on my finger, tells me he loves me, shaves my legs and my pussy smooth, tells me I look beautiful, has me stand up, dries me off, takes me into the bedroom, kisses me everywhere, starting with my toes and works his way up, his penis is super-hard, I'm so dripping wet I'm soaking the sheets already, he makes sweet love to me, gently, taking his time, has me on verge of cumming with his penis moving and thrusting inside me, he ejaculates deep inside me, moves his head down between my legs, kisses me everywhere, goes down on me, licks me out and cleans up after himself, takes me to the edge of cumming like three times before backing off, and then gently then more firmly bites on my clit, clamps his mouth over my pussy, I can feel his tongue going crazy, and then I explode and cum all over his face until I'm like squirting everywhere.

I don't understand what's happening. This guy is driving me crazy.

Texts with my husband

Are you going to be in your office this afternoon?

Should be. Why?

I was going to have something nice delivered for you.

Sounds good. I be here.

Okay. Should be around 1pm or so, right after lunch.

Can I ask what it is?

It's a surprise. Flowers, and something else you'll like.

That sounds nice. Thank you.

You're welcome!

You doing alright?

Yes. I have that interview late this afternoon. I hope it goes well.

It's too bad that other job fell through for you.

I know. I'm sorry it's taking me longer to find something than I thought it would.

You have some time. How many more interviews do you have this week?

Three, besides the one this afternoon.

If you don't find a job soon, you might need to take something temporary to hold you over. Your car payment is coming up on the 25th.

I know.

Sex Anon Meeting

So... last evening at the meeting, the subject of "infidelity" was discussed, and the hurt and pain we cause our significant others when we can't control our sexual impulses.

That was interesting.

When it was my time to talk I talked about the subject of cuckold angst, and how my husband was both turned on and jealous that I fucked other men. That he both liked it and feared it.

Two different men at the meeting noticed my spade tattoo, and made comments about it during the break.

One of them tried to hit on me after the meeting but was stopped cold by one of the other women at the meeting who I was walking to the bus with.

She told him, "Hold on there, nigga, she ain't here to be your bitch, she here to get her life back straight like we all are, leave her alone and just get your ass on home."

Her name is Latisha. She's pretty tough; if she had a knife in her purse, it wouldn't surprise me. But she's always been very nice to me. We've bonded like only two women who have sucked black dick for drugs and money can.

Last night, she told me the story of how she met her pimp daddy, and I told her about DaddyBigBull.

Email to my hubby

Okay... so since I'm supposed to tell you everything now, instead of keeping all my dirty little secrets to myself... I thought about _____ today, like seven times.

But I didn't. I wanted to, and had like three offers, but I didn't. Because I'm trying to be a good girl for you. And because I love you.

PS: That guy who works at the liquor store next to the laundromat keeps texting me. And I've been flirting back like you told me to. So, he just now sent me a picture of his shriveled cock! Guess what he wants to see now?

Email from my hubby

I just got this from him:

Emma obviously knows about your sexual attraction to black men, and has expressed a curiosity about it, as in, she'd like to experience what that's like. She actually never has before.

I'd like you to please become her mentor in that regard. I can't think of anybody better to show her the ropes.

I think I would really enjoy watching the two of you take on a black man sometime soon. She's game for it. I'd like you to please set that up, and make that happen. Please coordinate with her and copy me on your communications.

Also, I told Emma about your Bad Dragon dildo collection, all the different ones you have. She asked if you had ever been on the receiving end of one, and I told her you hadn't. She seems to be rather keen on fucking you with one.

The next time we're all altogether, I'd like to see that happen.

Call me when you have a minute.

Email to my husband

They just called me regarding my job interview on Tuesday, and offered me the job! They said I could start a week from Monday, but they can only offer me a part-time position right now. And it's also not going to be a fixed schedule all the time. They said I would need to be flexible, but that if I did a good job, I might be able to transition to a full-time position in about six months.

The bad news is it doesn't pay as much as I had hoped, and it's also not exactly the type of job I would have wanted.

What do you want me to do?

Email to my husband

Have fun tonight. I guess.

It hurts me that you cancelled dinner with me... that we had planned all week... to go be with that Japanese girl you just met.

I won't be here when you get back. I need to get away for a while to think. Not sure for how long. A few days at least. Please don't call me or try to find me. Please respect that.

I love you. But I feel very hurt right now. And I need to be away from you.

I'm okay... back home now.

Text messages with my husband this afternoon...

——

Hi. I'm sorry I've been ignoring your calls and texts. I needed some time alone. I'm okay. Don't worry.

Where are you? Answer your phone!

I don't really want to talk right now. I'm sorry I failed you this weekend. I got scared.

Don't worry about that. Where are you? I've been calling and looking for you everywhere. Are you sure you're okay?

I'm okay.

Answer your phone!

Please don't be upset with me. I'm not in a very good place right now.

I'm not upset with you 22. I love you. I just want to know that you're safe.

I'm safe.

Are you alone?

Right now, yes.

Who else has been there with you?

It doesn't matter. You don't know him.

Where are you?

In a motel room. I've just been here.

Since Friday night?

Yes. Mostly.

Have you been using?

Please don't be upset with me.

I'm not upset. Have you been using?

Can we please not talk about this right now.

I love you. I just want to know that you're safe. I know you haven't been with Marco. I talked to him. And Tina and Ronnie. We're all very worried about you. Where are you?

I'm okay. I'm just here alone now. Can you please come pick me up?

Where are you?

I'll text you the address.

Where's your car?

It got stolen last night. I think he stole it.

Who stole it?

The guy who was here.

What guy?

I don't really know him. I just know his first name.

How do you know him?

Just from a bar I was at Friday night.

Where was the car stolen from?

The parking lot.

Of the bar?

No. The motel.

Who got the motel room?

I did.

Was that guy with you at the motel?

Yes.

Friday night?

Yes. And last night.

Did you report the car stolen?

No.

When did you find out it was gone?

About an hour ago.

When's the last time you saw him?

I don't really remember. Sometime last night. I was kind of out of it. When I woke up he was gone.

When did you wake up?

Just a while ago.

Send me the address where you are.

It's _____.

That's about an hour away. How did you end up there?

Can you please not with the thousand questions? Please just come pick me up.

I'll be right there. Are you sure you're okay?

Yes. Just tired.

Have you been using?

Can we please just talk about it later?

Just wait right there. I'm on my way.

Okay.

Should I call the police about the car?

Is there anything illegal in the room?

I don't think so.

You're not sure?

Not a hundred percent. There might be.

Don't do anything until I get there. Wait in the room. Don't call the police. And don't call anyone else.

Okay.

Do you need medical assistance?

I'm okay.

I'm leaving right now. Do you need anything?

I just need you. But I know I've already lost you.

You haven't lost me.

It feels like I have.

Stop panicking. I need to get driving. I'll be right there. Answer your phone. I'm going to call you so we can talk while I'm driving.

I don't really want a thousand questions right now. I'll just wait for you. I need to take a shower.

I'll be right there. I love you. It's going to take me about an hour to get there. Wait for me.

I'll be here. Thank you for picking me up.

See you in a bit.

Email to my husband

I'm sorry I screwed up again. I'm sorry I lied to you about going to meetings and about my sponsor.

I've used a few times, not that often, but a couple of times. And there are a few other things I've done that I haven't told you about that I need to.

I was scared, I panicked, I felt claustrophobic, I felt vulnerable, I was selfish, I got so dreadfully tired of fighting the urges, and I lost control.

I'm sorry I'm such a terrible wife. I know I don't deserve you. All you've ever done is love me and try to help me. I know that. And I love and appreciate you for that.

This has been very difficult for me, you being in the dominant position. And you getting re-involved with Emma makes me very nervous. I don't trust her.

But I trust you to make better decisions for me than I can for myself.

So... I promise that from now on, I'll do whatever you want me to do, and stop fighting and resisting you at every turn.

Please give me another chance.

I know I deserve to be disciplined. I promise I will submit to you, follow your rules, and accept your discipline whatever you decide it needs to be.

I love you.

Email from my husband

I just got this from him:
___

I received your note. Thank you for that. But quite frankly, I'm near the end of my rope with you. I'm not sure how much longer I can continue with this relationship. You have disappointed me one too many times, not to mention how you have degraded yourself.

I am not going to remain married to a woman who is a drug addict. I have tried to help you, multiple times. I paid to put you in one of the most expensive drug rehabilitation facilities in the country, for two months. Apparently, all for naught.

The idea that you fucked some guy you met in a bar on Friday night for drugs, and then spent the night with him again on Saturday night at a motel room, is unbelievable to me. And then he steals your car! The fact that its insured is beside the point.

Know this right now: I am not going to get you another new car. I will buy you a used car that will get you around, but you have driven your last Porsche.

It's clear to me that we are at a crossroads. We both have some important decisions to make. You say you want to make it up to me. Well, we'll see. Quite frankly, it's your actions that I care more about than yet more words and yet more promises.

I don't honestly care what you think of Emma. She is an honest and mature woman. She is reliable and stable. I like her low-drama personality, and enjoy her company. She may be a larger woman physically, but I find her to be very attractive. And it's refreshing that I don't have to worry about her suddenly running off and disappearing on me so she can go score drugs.

Emma is going to be part of my life. You can either accept it or not. At this point, I don't much care what you think. You have lost your right to have an opinion on the matter.

I've told you many times over the years that I don't mind if you want to occasionally have sex with other men. But your choice of men has always been highly questionable.

I've never understood why such a beautiful and intelligent woman would allow herself to essentially become a whore for strange men. The things you did with DaddyBigBull are just beyond anything I could ever imagine.

Your insatiable sexual attraction to black ghetto dick, as you yourself have phrased it, is beyond my comprehension. Your judgment is horrendous. I

love you, but quite honestly, I don't trust you to make competent decisions about anything.

You seem to continuously get yourself emotionally involved with other men without regard to how it may impact our marriage.

You forget that I've seen some of the videos that you made with DaddyBigBull. I heard what you said to him, what you said about me, our marriage, and the rest of it.

I've gone on long enough. I will inform you of my decisions later this week. Right now, though, my inclination is to start to think about a transition.

Write me your thoughts as you feel comfortable.

I will be late getting home tonight. I have some things to do after work. I should be home about 10-11pm.

I love you.

Email to my husband

It's not right for me to keep you from happiness. You deserve better.

I'm just a lying, selfish, junkie whore. I know it. And I also know that is all I will ever be.

Deep down inside, I knew this was never going to work. You met me in a strip club where I was dancing for drunks and thugs, and sucking cock in the back room to pay the rent. Who was I fooling?

I've been damaged goods since I was nine years old. I was the white trash slut who got passed around from black guy to black guy when I was in high school. Who am I kidding?

I used to dream of meeting and marrying a man like you, strong, educated, successful, refined, respected. Living the good life, in a beautiful home, with beautiful children to love. What was I thinking?

I love you. For as long as I am alive and breathing on this Earth, I will always love you. But I know it's time for me to go now. I've caused everyone enough pain.

I'm truly sorry for everything I've done to hurt you.

If you want to be with Emma, I understand. I won't stand in the way. It kills me to say it, but you're right, she is a better person than I am. She deserves you more than I do. If she makes you happy, then I'm happy for that.

I'll sign the divorce papers. I won't fight you. And I won't ask for anything.

Then afterwards, just please drive me out somewhere far away and throw me in a gutter. And make me gone.

Email to Marco

Things are kind of crazy here. And complicated. I guess they always are.

I'm going to be going away for a while, maybe a long while. And I really, really, really, really need to see you again before I go.

Can you come by tomorrow afternoon?

French Word?

I imagine there's probably a word in French for a girl who's finally come to the realization that she's just a man-eating whore, and that's all she ever will be. A girl who's forever doomed to paying for everything she wants and needs in life with her mouth and pussy and ass, because that's all she really has to offer. I think in English the word is cunt.

And life goes on...

I'm here, I'm safe, and all alone now. My husband just left a few hours ago. Tina drove up with my husband and I yesterday to bring me up here. She's been an amazing friend, as always.

My husband decided he wanted me in a different rehab place than last time. The atmosphere here is similar but different. It's not quite as cold/clinical as the place I was at last fall. People here seem more approachable.

After a good night sleep tonight, I go into detox tomorrow. I have to turn in my phone and iPad here in a bit, and won't get them back until after I complete detox.

I have no idea how this is all going to end up, and I'm scared. After what happened last weekend, my husband was beyond furious with me. I've never seen him raging mad like that before. He isn't very happy with me right now, but he's being very supportive, at least on the surface.

I'm sure my marriage is pretty much hanging by a thread right now. Part of me is regretting not going to see a lawyer about the divorce thing before coming here. I decided I needed to do and focus on this first, and not worry about the rest of it.

Marco came over to see me on Wednesday morning; that didn't really go so well. I had planned to tell him that I needed to end things with him, but he basically beat me to it. Maybe he anticipated what I was going to tell him, I don't know. He wasn't very happy that I had been putting him off since my husband and I got back from Spain. After much discussion and reliving memories... we didn't have sex, didn't make love... we agreed that the time had come for us to end this chapter of our lives. He picked me up, hugged me, held me, kissed me, and then he was gone. My heart is broken right now over him.

22

Chapter 14

The worst mistake I ever made was allowing myself to get drawn in and seduced by DaddyBigBull, and permitting things get to the point where I lost all sense of control, started doing drugs with him, and went down that dark and depraved road. I'll never make that mistake again.

The second mistake I made was giving in to my husband's whiny and persistent complaints and his pleading and begging and all the rest... and to my own sense of guilt... and releasing him from chastity too many times for too long a period of time. I should have kept his dick locked up 24/7, and been much, much stricter with him about release. I should have also stepped up the discipline when necessary. I'll never make that mistake again.

The third mistake I made was facilitating and encouraging my husband to get involved with Emma, because I felt sorry for the lonely bitch, not being there every time they got together, and allowing him to get emotionally close to her. I'll never make that mistake again.

The fourth mistake I made was allowing myself to get too deeply and emotionally involved with Marco. I should have kept our relationship on strictly physical terms. I should have diversified my Bulls, and not let myself get too close to any particular one. I'll never make that mistake again.

The fifth mistake I made was encouraging Marco to fuck Dana, and letting that happen. I should have kept my husband's niece out of it. I'll never make that mistake again.

Email to my hubby

Okay… so seriously, this so-called "recovery house" place is basically full of low-life's, criminals on probation, tattooed scum, and people who ought to be homeless.

This place makes the rehab facility look like a crystal palace. I've already seen two dead cockroaches.

Bunk beds and plastic drawers to put my clothes. Seriously?

And my roommate… I don't even want to go there. Jesus fuck Christ! She's skinny as a skeleton, has like a thousand tattoos, and is missing teeth! I'm pretty sure she sleeps with a knife.

The stupid bitch called me "Malibu Princess", which two of the other homeless women then picked up on… so now that's like my nickname. And they don't mean it in a good way.

This is like a fucking prison. Please get me out of here!! Please. I'll do anything. Anything.

Or just kill me now.

Call me. Please answer your phone.

Email to my hubby

Oh… and the stupid fucking bitch is a white supremacist. She even has a swastika tattoo around her navel, which she made a point to show me this morning.

ANSWER YOUR PHONE!!

Email to my hubby

So, I guess you're not answering your phone on purpose, for a reason. Or maybe you're on the boat and can't get a signal. I don't know.

I'm feeling pretty miserable today. I'll be okay, but it would be nice to hear your voice. I miss being home with you.

I'm sorry about Friday. I was just really frustrated, and overreacted.

Please call me when you get this. Please let me know we're okay.

My husband is just not a dominant man; not in the bedroom, anyway. And not with women.

He's highly competitive in the business world, and can be pretty ruthless when he wants to be, but it's all tied to his wealth. He uses his money and his contacts and the other things that money buys to control people and situations. But he is not instinctively dominant.

A man who is naturally dominant doesn't need money to be that way; he's that way biologically and psychologically regardless of his economic status.

Spider. That's the name she goes by. My new roommate. Skank City, Miss Meth America, where a full set of front teeth are optional.

Why Spider? Not entirely sure, but it could be on account of the gangster-style spiderweb tattoo on one of her elbows. I'm not sure which came first. Or that it matters.

Last night, after lights-out, I was treated to the sounds of Spider masturbating on the bunk bed above me, in the dark. I'm not sure which of eight claws she was using.

Never mind that I was there; that didn't stop her.

She sounded like a mutt puppy that had just been hit by a car, crying and whimpering for help.

Oh... but it didn't end there.

After my ears had been assaulted by the screeching, she picked up the pace and actually started to smack her pussy... at least that's what it sounded like.

Smack! Smack! Smack!

Then she starts moaning and talking out loud to herself, "Oh Poppy... that's it... Oh Poppy... fuck your bitch, fuck it, fuck it."

I'll stop there, because the rest of it was just obscene, and you might not yet have eaten lunch.

Yeah. That's what I got to hear before I fell asleep last night. Oh joy!

This morning after she got out of the shower (at least the bitch practices at least that level of hygiene), she's walking around the room topless, like she had something to be proud of. Which she most definitely does not.

I was still in bed. Almost afraid to get up.

Her tits look like the empty leathery sacs of breasts that used to be. If you can imagine a distended tit that's mostly all nipple, hanging down from loose folds of skin. They're fucking disgusting! Her nipples are like the chewed-up ends of two cigars that got passed around a redneck campfire.

Uhhhhh!!

She's only been here about two weeks, and already she's like the Queen Nazi. Something else I have to look forward to.

She said her boyfriend is in a skin head biker gang, which I refuse to believe, because that would mean he'd have to sometimes take her out in public, and let his friends see her, and I refuse to believe that there's any man out there who is that hard up.

Oh... and you'll never guess what her job is... Later Diary, I promise.

So... the new guy who checked in yesterday... the football player... has arms like The Rock, skin as dark as midnight, and a voice like Barry White... buttery and melodic, like smooth jazz.

My little white pussy is still creaming just from talking to him this morning at breakfast!

....

Ok... so Mr. Whites just left my room, dragging his magnificent horse cock back with him. Got the name when he was a Coke dealer, it stuck.

Tonight, was our last time together. He absolutely, positively, tore it the fuck up tonight. OMG! My little white pussy is going to gape forever! He snagged a condom from somebody, thank God.

I am so sore right now; walking tomorrow will be slow...

I leave here tomorrow to go to the recovery house I'll be staying at for the next 90 days. My husband is picking me up and taking me. I'm going to surprise him with a nice blowjob in the car.

I am so confused by this guy, my husband.

What does he want? Where is he coming from???

It's like one moment he's Mr. Dominant, using his money to try to control me, and issuing demands and edicts. And the next moment he's the same little-dick, quick-spurt faggot I married.

He picked me up yesterday from the rehab facility, late in the day. We went to have dinner at a nice place he had picked out.

He brought me a gift, wrapped up in a pretty box.

He abstained from wine… because of my stupid fucking problem! … which was very considerate of him; usually the wine list is the first thing he looks at.

We had a great conversation, talking about a hundred things, laughed, and had a great time.

He told me what was going on at his work, this new deal he's been working on, and his upcoming travel schedule.

We talked about my recovery, my plans to get a job, my plans for the future, my hopes for us being together again.

He was basically non-committal, and almost cold in a way. He said he supported me, and would continue to help me, but in the same breath said he wasn't sure what was going to happen.

We both avoided talking about the elephant in the room… Emma. I didn't ask him about her, or make any comments about her. I just tried to pretend she didn't exist.

He cruelly told me that all of my things… clothes, shoes, everything! … had been packed up, put in boxes, and moved to a storage unit. Except for my jewelry, which he put in a safe deposit box at the bank.

That ruined the mood for me, and I started crying, telling him I couldn't believe he really did that. Even the waiter noticed and asked if everything was okay.

My husband, in a flat, matter-of-fact voice, said: *"You've done a lot of damage to our marriage. I'm not sure what's going to happen. I want you to succeed. But you'll have to earn your way back into my life. "*
Great. Appreciate the pressure! Thank you!

Then he changed the subject to a trip he has planned with two of his friends; they're going to go deep-sea fishing in Cabo next month.

I asked him about his kids, and his father, and his mother. He said they were all fine. I delicately asked him what he had told them about us, about me. His response: "They don't need to know anything right now."

He mentioned Dana, that he had talked to her, and that she was happy but didn't like the college she was going to, and was having problems with her mother (who is my husband's sister).

And then we left.

The silence during the drive to the recovery house where he was going to drop me off was haunting; I felt like I was being driven to prison. My husband had this look on his face like he would rather be somewhere else.

Once we arrived, we sat in the car for a while and talked.

I could tell that his mood had shifted. He was now being very kind and sweet, and considerate. He hugged me and kissed my neck. And i kissed him on the lips.

At first, he seemed timid, and almost afraid to touch me.

The last time I had seen him... the Sunday before, he had barely held my hand while we went for a walk. And then it was just a quick hug and peck on the cheek when he left. But he's like that sometimes when he's in a bad mood.

But now, in the car, he was different, like he was wanting us to emotionally connect again. And then he started kissing me with more passion.

I told him I was sorry for everything I had done, and that I was going to make it up to him. That I loved him, and wanted to be with him; that I didn't want us to end.

His hand moved to my breast, and he held it, and gently squeezed it. Then his hand moved down and he put it between my legs (I was wearing a sun dress, and panties), and started rubbing my pussy, and bit into my neck.

I parted my legs for him.

Then he asked me, *"Were you a bad girl?"* And kind of grabbed my pussy when he said that.
Strange, I thought. Where is this guy coming from? 15 minutes ago, he was basically dismissing our relationship.

I didn't immediately answer him, somewhat confused, not sure if I should go there.

He asked me again, more insistently, *"Were you a bad girl?"*
"Yes," I answered him.
"What did you do?"
"I had sex with someone."
"With who?"
"His name is _____." (I told him Mr. White's real first name.)
"Where?"
"In my room."
"What did he do?"
"He fucked me."
"Did he use a condom?"
"Yes."

My husband was now kissing me with a passion he hadn't kissed me with in a long time… since before I entered rehab. And his left hand was a flurry between my legs, fingering me. I was already soaking wet.

"Did you enjoy it."
"Yes. He's really good."
"How many times were you with him?"
"Ummmm… a couple of times."
I let my hand drop down to my husband's lap, and could tell he was hard. I whispered to him, *"Let me take care of you. I want to taste you in my mouth."*
He moved his seat back, and lay back.

I didn't say anything else. Leaning over the center console… not easy in his car… I unfastened his belt and pants, and unzipped him.

He lifted his butt off the seat so I could pull his pants down, which I did.

His little dick was rock hard, and throbbing, and hot to the touch.

I leaned over to take it in my mouth, but then decided to tease him a little first.

I grabbed his balls with my right hand, firmly, and squeezed.

"You like that? You miss this?"
And then he started spurting all over. FUCK!!! WHAT THE FUCK!!

He couldn't even take me barely touching him like that!

He started apologizing profusely.

"I'm sorry. I'm sorry. I couldn't help it."
"It's okay, sweetie. I love you. It's okay."
I pretended like it was no big deal, to comfort him, to be nice, but inside, I was pissed. I couldn't believe it! He lasted like two minutes. He spurted before I even took his penis in my mouth.

"I'm really sorry."
"No, really. It's okay. I'm used to that with you."
"It's just been so long. I'm sorry."
"It's okay. I should probably go anyway. They're probably wondering where I am."
"Just give me a minute."
"Don't worry about it. Just open the trunk. I can carry it in. It's not that heavy."
When he didn't open the latch, I reached over and hit the button to open the trunk myself.

And then he got impatient. *"Just give me a minute."*
He had already opened the center console to get a napkin, and was wiping himself, but his pants were still down around his ankles.

"Sweetie, really, don't bother. Why don't you just zip up your pants, and go back to your fat chick. Maybe you'll last longer for her. "
And then I got out and left.

Email to Mr. Whites

Mmmmm... I'm glad you liked it. Normally I keep myself nice and smooth all over. The natural look is kind of new for me. I thought I'd try it for a while.

I can drop by to see you on Sunday if you want.

Thanks for your kind words about my transition here. I appreciate it. This is round two for me, and definitely my last!

I called your friend Andrew. He's going to get me an interview next week. Thank you for that.

Talk soon.

22.

Texts with my husband

Good morning. Are things calming down over there for you?

Yes. I'm adjusting. Thank you for understanding my crazy anxieties.

You'll be okay. Just ride it out. Be strong.

I will. I miss you.

I miss you too. Your car will be delivered today just before noon.

What is it?

It's a surprise. You'll see.

Ok. Thank you. I have two job interviews this afternoon.

I'm sure you'll do fine.

I feel so humbled here. So low sometimes. Life I've fallen off a cliff.

You needed humbling. Things got way out of control for you.

I know. I'm sorry.

I want you to do something for me.

Ok. What?

I married an extraordinary woman. Smart. Beautiful. Sexy. Interesting. Full of style and flair. Full of life. But you went down the wrong path. You got lost. And made some terrible decisions.

I know.

I love you. I support you. And I need you to get better. I want my wife back. The girl I married.

I'm trying, sweetie. I feel so ashamed right now. I disappointed everyone.

When you feel lost over there, and start feeling anxious, and are ready to give up, remember there are lots of people who love you. We all want you back happy and healthy.

I know. I'm going to do this. I promise.

Don't promise me. Promise yourself. And then just get it done.

I have. I wish you were here with me right now. I wish you could hold me.

We'll see each other soon. Let me know how the interviews go.

I will.

I have to get going. Busy day today. I love you 22.

I love you too, mister. Don't forget that.

Email to my hubby

So, I see you have a sense of humor regarding the car you got for me. It's even the exact same color. I guess I should be mad, but I'm not. I'm grateful. Thank you for getting me something to drive.

Regarding my interviews this afternoon, my first one went pretty well; I think I'll get an offer.

The second one, not so much. I don't really feel like I would fit in there very well.

I got confirmation today that I can have my job back at the construction company, if I want it. I was only there for three days, but they liked me.

I have another interview on Thursday regarding that yoga sports training opportunity I told you about. That one sounds really exciting to me. It would involve more travel, but it would also give me a lot more flexibility, and I'd

be doing something healthy that I really enjoy. That's my first choice, for now, if it works out.

Since you're going to be in SB this long weekend, would it be OK if I went by to visit Mr. Whites on Sunday? I would be a good girl and follow all of your instructions, and obey all of your rules, if I do.

If it's OK, I'd like to call you late tonight. I really need to hear your voice again.

Email to my hubby

Whether you were alone last night or with someone, Emma or whoever else, I hope you had a good night and slept well and woke up with a smile on your handsome face this morning.

I love you!

Spider Plans

So… Spider told me a while ago that she's going to have a late-night visitor in the room tonight, and asked if I had any condoms. Uhhhhhh…

Email to my hubby

Thank you for agreeing to let me go visit Mr. White on Sunday! I promise I'll be a good girl and only do what you said. Talk soon.

Email to Mr. Whites

So, it looks like I'll be by to see you on Sunday around 3pm, if that works. Any special requests?

JOB!!!

I had my interview with Andrew this morning. the guy Mr. White introduced me to.

Andrew owns a company that works closely with various sports teams and individual athletes around the country, both professional and college level. His company runs all kinds of sports and body conditioning and development programs, weight management and nutritional programs, injury rehabilitation, and other related services. It's a large company, with offices in all of the major markets.

They're looking for someone to help run one of their conditioning programs.

The interview went really well; it was with him first, and then afterwards, I met with two of his directors. I was there for almost three hours.

So… Andrew called me about an hour after the interviews and offered me the job!! He asked me what my salary expectation was, and I gave him a number that was way too high, because I figured I would probably need room to negotiate.

He didn't immediately respond, but instead asked me to tell him more about my time in high school and college on the volleyball and gymnastics teams, and spirit squads. And we talked for a bit about his time playing baseball, and how he started his company.

After talking on the phone about another 15 minutes, he said, *"I'll tell you what, Ms. _____, I know people, and I have a very good feeling about you. I think you're going to be a star here. Why don't we double your salary expectation, and have you start next week?"*
That's when I almost passed out from excitement, and had to stop myself from crying. And peeing in my pants.

As we ended the call, he mentioned that one of the assistant director positions was going to open up in March 2016, and that if I do well I would be perfectly positioned to apply for it.

I'm super excited!!!!!!!!!!!!!!!

Email to Mr. Whites

So... you're just awesome! Andrew offered me the job today after my interview with him (and some other people over there). I am so grateful to you for making the introduction and telling him about me.

You do realize that you get whatever you want, now... right? As often as you want it...

Chapter 15

I'm so happy and feel so good today. I feel clean and fresh and healthy and free. Life is good!

Email to my husband

I over-reacted this afternoon about Friday. I'm sorry. I shouldn't have said that.

Of course, I will be there. And I promise I will be on my best behavior with and towards Emma, and will do as I'm told.

Thank you.

Hubby cuck realizes that my BBC addiction is life-long and never going away. He knows he's never going to be able to stop me from fucking black men.

So, from his perspective, he wants me to be careful about the men I'm with, and wants me to be safe and always use condoms.

It used to turn him on that I fucked other men. He loved to watch me be a dirty little whore with black men. He really got off on that. And when he wasn't there to watch, it would excite him to hear about it afterwards.

Sometimes, I'd give him a nice handjob while I told him the details of what happened until he spurted all over himself.

But then something changed.

My involvement with DaddyBigBull, who was dangerous and violent and got me hooked on heroin… and my growing emotional attachment to Marco… made it not so fun for him anymore.

And he also started getting more religious.

He worries about the types of men I might get involved with. He grew up in the south, in a very conservative family, and has always looked down on people of color as less than. He thinks 90% of black men are thugs, criminals, lowlifes, losers, and drug users/dealers.

Email to Marco

I got your note. That was very nice of you.

I'm doing well. I'm out of rehab and in a recovery house right now. And I got a new job that I'm very excited about. I'm going to give it everything I have.

You'll have to tell me more about your communications with Dana. I'm very curious. I'm surprised she responded, actually, just based on what she had told me about you before… that you had seduced her, lied to her, ruined her life, or whatever. But that was probably more her vicious mother talking. The whole interracial thing was a huge problem for her.

Things with CHAD_ are extremely complicated. We're currently separated. I've moved out. But we're still talking. I'm not really sure what's going to happen there. But I love him and I need to try and fix things with him.

He's very confusing, though. Sometimes it seems like he wants us to get back together, and other times he's kind of dismissive of me. So, who knows. Right now, we're just "separated".

Of course, I miss you. And not just the sex. I still have that old dark green sweat shirt you gave me, that still smells of you. I've never washed it. I wear it to bed sometimes. It reminds me of the good times we had when

you'd come over on Saturday, and we'd spend the afternoon in bed together, and then let my husband "catch us" in bed when he got back from playing golf. And then you'd spend the night with me and we'd make him sleep in the guest room. I really miss that.

As far as us getting together... that's probably not a good idea right now. I don't want to further complicate things with my husband. He has his ways of finding things out. He's extremely jealous of you, and wouldn't like it. And I don't want you to be hurt. He can be quite vindictive sometimes. I also kind of promised him that I wouldn't. So... I need to see what's going to happen there first. I really need to fix things with him.

But thank you for your note. My sweet Marco boy. You already know I love you too.

Be safe

22.

Last Night

The son-of-a-bitch lied to me!

He didn't move *all* my clothes from the house into storage.
He kept my thin red leather belt, which I found on the dresser last night when he told me to go upstairs to the bedroom to wait for him and Emma. The same one I used to discipline him with.

And then he gave it to her.

Email from my husband

Last night was lesson one. Tonight, is lesson two. Please be here at 6pm. Your mouth and tongue will be busy tonight. Emma is anxiously looking forward to it. And so am I.

Night of Servitude.

I've never felt so humiliated in all my life.

I submitted to it, suffered through it, and did it for him, my husband, because he made it clear to me what his expectations were, because I promised him I would do what he wanted, that I would be obedient and be a good girl for him… but mostly I did it because I love him and I desperately want him back in my life.

Right now, I'm just trying to forget about this weekend. I'll write about it more later, maybe. But I just can't right now. I'm sorry.

Email to my husband

As you requested, I am writing to you this morning before work about my feelings regarding this weekend.

Thank you for permitting me to serve and service you and Emma.

I know I deserved to be disciplined for my negative attitude and misbehavior on Friday evening. Thank you for giving me what I need. To be honest, I was surprised that you had Emma do it, but I understand why you did.

I will be at the house for my disciplinary session tomorrow night after work, as you instructed.

It was my pleasure Saturday evening to wash and massage Emma's beautiful feet.

I enjoyed getting her ready for you with my mouth and tongue, and tasting her, and realize that I can expect to be doing that often in the future.

I enjoyed listening and watching the two of you make love from my position kneeling in the floor.

I know I've lost your favor, and realize that it's all my fault. I'm committed to doing my best to improve our relationship, and proving to you that I deserve to be part of your life.

I will continue to work on my jealousy issues.

I promise I will strive to improve my attitude and treat you both with respect.

I will follow the advice of my counselors.

I will focus on my new job and do the best I can.

I will avoid all negative temptations work hard to stay sober and healthy.

Thank you.

Email from my husband

To torture you, no. To teach you some things, yes.

If I didn't love you, 22, I would have let you rot and die in the gutter with DaddyBigBull. Surely you realize that, don't you?

And of course, I love you. I've always loved you. But love isn't enough to sustain a marriage. I do want you back in my life, but only if you can prove to me that you are past using drugs, and that you can control your unhealthy urges.

If we are ever back together again living in the same house, though, it's not going to be same as it was before. You need to understand that.

Email from my husband

I suspect that if you had a good reason for wanting to change the time you would have mentioned it in your email. But you didn't. So, I'll expect you at the house at 7pm tonight. Don't be late.

Regarding Emma disciplining you, I thought she did an excellent job this past weekend. I thought she really got your attention. I see no reason to make a change there.

Please don't make plans for Saturday evening. I have something very special planned for you that does not involve Emma. I think you're going to like it. I have something soft and beautiful picked out for you to wear.

I love you. I'll see you tonight.

Heroin is what turned the tables on me. And that's all my fault and responsibility.

But my husband... while I do believe he loves me, and is trying to help me... is also unfairly taking advantage of the situation (as is Emma), and is basically just being a little beta male fuck about it. The only thing dominant about him is the size of his bank account.

Part of me is starting to think that by doing what he's doing, whether he intends it or not, he's actually increasing my risk of relapsing. But I'm not going to let that happen. I am in control of my future and my destiny. I'm not working and fighting to stay off drugs for him; I'm doing it for me.

This too will pass, this pathetic attempt of his to be "dominant", and this whatever-fuck relationship he has with Emma. I'll do whatever he wants for now. I'll steel-up and suffer through it. I'll crawl through the fire. I'll debase and humiliate myself if that's what it takes. If that's what makes him happy. What doesn't kill me will make me stronger.

I'm not going to be down forever. And when I'm back, and strong and healthy, I will own him, and when I do, I'm going to cut his fucking balls off.

Email to my husband

I know you want me to be at the house at 7pm, but can I please change that to 8pm? And can I please ask you to discipline me, and not Emma?

Email to my husband

Are you doing all of this just to torture me? Do you secretly hate me? Are you ever going to want me again?

I haven't been able to write much this week. I've been extremely busy. Sorry.

My personal life is in turmoil. I know I criticize and am sometimes down on my husband for what he's doing, but I love him very much, and I trust his judgment. I cannot imagine my life without him, and there's no possible way I could stay off drugs and thugs over the long term without his love, support, and compassion. I'm willing and I'm going to do anything I have to do to win him back.

My new job is going extremely well. I'm very excited. Everyone I've met, they are like the best in their field, and very supportive. I'm learning a lot. One thing that excites me, after I complete my 90 days in recovery, I'm going to be doing a lot of traveling to the other facilities.

Living in the recovery house has not been much fun; Spider is just so weird, but we get along well. She's actually been a good friend to me, but I am kind of getting annoyed by the Malibu Princess thing. I now have an 11 PM curfew because I'm working. Everyone here is very supportive, and I'm very thankful for that.

My husband told me that DaddyBigBull refused a plea deal and is going to have his trial in November. That makes me kind of nervous. My husband didn't seem very happy about it either.

Tinder Morning

I met a man this morning at the Tinder house. There was a really long line, which he was already standing in, and he offered to get a drink for me.

Then he brought it to me and we sat and talked for a few minutes. He's ex-military, 32, single, white, talk dark and handsome, nicely built, and he smelled really nice! He said he works down the street; I told him I had just started a new job close by.

Hopefully, maybe... I'll see him again!

Email to my hubby

Good morning!

Can you please at least give me a hint about where we're going and what we're doing on Saturday? And the outfit you have picked out for me.

I love surprises, but this is more making me nervous.

Am I going to know anyone there?

Email to Mr. Whites

Ok… so I talked with Ronnie about the threesome thing, and she's totally game for it.

She liked the picture you sent me. I think you're going to like her. In the picture I'm sending, she's the 2nd girl from the left, wearing the blue top. You like?

So, when are you out? We need to party! Pussy needs hitting…

Yikes!

I saw Tinder Man again this morning at the Tinder house. He looked quite delicious in that Navy Seal hardbody kind of way. He was wearing tight 501 jeans, and I do think he might possibly have a nicer bubble butt than I do!

I was in a hurry, and didn't have much time to talk, but I gave him a smile that promised everything.

Dinner Party

So… my husband did have a really nice surprise for me last night! I'm still shaking.

He took me to a charity dinner event that his company was sponsoring. He got a hotel suite where the event was being held, and took me there to get dressed and ready before. Then we went down together, in the elevator, like we used to, as a couple.

I took everything I had to keep from crying, I was so happy.

I felt like Cinderella… he picked me up in a limo at the recovery house I've been staying at, and got me back before midnight.

I almost felt normal again last night.

It's going to be a crazy busy week.

I've been going through the training program at work, which ends on Friday. I'm really loving this job so far. There's some traveling required for the job, but they know I can't do that until after November, and are cool with it.

I've agreed to have lunch with Emma on Thursday, at her request. Still not sure what that's all about. I'm just trying to be patient with my husband and

let this play out. I know he'll eventually get tired of her. She is soooo not his type.

I haven't been properly fucked since Mr. Whites tore it up a few weeks ago. I went by to see him yesterday (which is visiting day), but it's impossible to actually do anything because of the rules; they don't let visitors past the front great room or the back outside grounds. He gets out next week, though, so I'm looking forward to that. We've already had the "booty call" conversation. I'm sure I'm just one of a hundred girls he can fuck whenever he wants. But that's okay. Casual is good.

I saw my friend Ronnie this past week, and we talk all the time. She's having a little trouble with Ty. She said he's getting way too attached, so she's working on dialing that down. I joked with her, "It's your fault! You got that nigga hooked on it."

She's terrified of being caught by her husband. His chemo treatments after his surgery are all done, and it looks like they caught it all. But his sexual dysfunction is apparently permanent, which is extremely frustrating for her (and I'm sure for him). Even with V pills, he can't get it hard anymore, which is very sad because according to Ronnie, he has a really nice dick.

My effort to hint and nudge him into letting her be a Hotwife (which is what she wants to be) didn't work. Ronnie carefully brought it up one time, in the context of my husband and I, and she got yelled at and smacked. Sam is kind of kind of emotionally volatile that way, which scares her.

Tina is doing well; has a new boyfriend; is the middle of changing jobs; thinks I need to just stab Emma to death in the parking lot and just be done with the bitch; is convinced that my husband is just having a midlife crisis with this Emma and Asian girl thing, and will eventually come crawling back to me; still thinks he's a closet faggot (she said, "Why else would he suck cock? And let those guys fuck him? I saw the videos. He likes it.") She doesn't understand why I even want him back. She thinks I should just get my half and leave him.

Spider's biker guy came by again last night before curfew, and I was once again treated to the sounds of hearing them fuck on the bunk bed above me. Oh joy! She makes so much noise! She sounds like a rabid squirrel getting fucked by a dog. It's just nasty.

I noticed last night that he has a swastika tattoo also, on his pectoral muscle. She has hers around her navel. If they knew I liked to fuck black guys I'm pretty sure they'd probably strangle me to death.

I'm extremely nervous about what's going on with DaddyBigBull. My husband has someone trying to find out what's going on behind the scenes. He's worried too, I can tell. It terrifies me that DaddyBigBull could ever get out of jail, because I think he knows who put him there. I hate him for what he did to me, getting me hooked on heroin. It scares me that I could have ended up with him.

Marco is… I just miss him. We've talked a few times, and it just makes me sad. I let myself fall in love with him, and now it just hurts.

Email to my husband

Just so you know, I've confirmed lunch with Emma for Thursday. I promise to be on my best behavior.

And I will be at the house on Friday night as you requested.

Saturday, I have something I wanted to do with Tina, if that's okay.

I hope you have an amazing day!

Update

I'm doing okay; just not feeling too good. The last few days have been very emotional for me.

My lunch Thursday with Emma didn't go very well. She was very much just rubbing it in, and making me feel horrible. My husband had warned me that morning that he expected me to be on my best behavior, and I didn't want to disappoint him. It took everything I had to remain civil and respectful towards her.

She drove to the outdoor cafe where we met in MY car! She asked me to rub her nasty feet under the table; which I bit my tongue and did. Then she put her foot under my skirt.

She told me my husband didn't respect me anymore, and didn't really want me back. She said that I should consider just moving on. She was like, "From what I hear, you'd probably be happier with all those niggers anyway, wouldn't you?"

Then she told me that my husband had shown her some of the videos of me doing things with DaddyBigBull, and said, "I can't believe you did those things. That was beyond disgusting. Chad was totally horrified. He told me he's never going to have sex with you again."

FUCK YOU!!!!!!!!!

And then Friday night when I went over to the house, as my husband requested, and the things that happened... it all just reminded me how far I have fallen, and how far I have to go if I ever hope to win my husband back.

We were all in bed together. They were both naked; at my husband's instruction, I was fully clothed. He told me he wanted to watch me use a dildo on Emma. Which I thought to myself, "Okay, that's better than going down on her rancid, sardine-smelling cunt like he made me do last time."

But Mr. FuckHead had apparently been shopping, and it wasn't just any dildo. It was this big flesh-colored one attached to this face mask thing that you have to wear on your head.

As he was putting it on me, strapping it around the back of my head, Emma was giggling like a fat girl about to get cake.

Fucking her that way with the dildo, wearing it on my face... her in bed, on her back, with her chunky legs up in the air, with me laying on my stomach with my face bobbing between her legs... was bad enough.

I know I'm in a place right now where I shouldn't complain. I know that if I ever hope to win my husband back, I'm going to have to go through a period of time when I just have to obey him and do whatever he wants, and let him work out whatever demons are currently driving him.

But when Emma turned over and wanted the dildo in her ass, I just about lost it. I don't think I've ever come that close to actually vomiting while engaged in some kind of sexual activity. For the first time in a long time, I wished I was just flying high out of my mind on heroin so I could just forget.

I think sometimes my husband gets off on just crushing my spirit. It's like he sees this as revenge time to get back at me for all the things I made him do over the years. And God knows he has a lot of things to punish me for.

I'm just feeling very depressed right now.

Spider's has been sensing my mood, although I haven't told her any of the details of what's going on in my life. She knows I'm married, and that my husband and I are currently separated, but that's about it.

She asked me a few days ago how long it's been since I've been fucked, and I told her, "I barely even remember what it's like."

She told me this morning that her guy is coming over to see her again tonight, which means I get to hear them pig-fuck again, with her disgusting squeals. Oh joy!

Last week, when her guy was here visiting, some other guy was with him; another white supremacist, tattooed biker type. Just to be polite, I conversed with everyone.

Yesterday, Spider was like, "Ronald is pretty sweet on you. He thinks you're hot."

Uhhhhhhhh!!! Just kill me now.

Text message from my husband's phone

Chad wanted me to take a picture, and asked me to get his phone. After I took the picture, I couldn't help but notice that he had some text messages from you.

I hope you don't mind if I read them.

FYI, he's kind of busy eating pussy right now. And after that, we got some fucking to do.

Did you want to see the picture I just took of him with all my juices all over his face?

Emma

Email to my husband

I know I deserve to be punished. I know you're testing me. And that's okay. I love you anyway. Because I always have, and because I know you don't really love her. My counselor thinks she's just a temporary distraction for you. Which I think too. Eventually you'll tire of her. She'll fade away. And you and I will be together again. I pray for that every day.

I hope you have a great evening. I miss you.

Email to my husband

Spider's biker boyfriend took some pictures of my tits and my pussy and texted them to his friend Ronald, who wants to fuck me.

Did you want to see the pictures he took? Or are you still busy with your new girlfriend Emma?

Texts with Ronald

I knew you were hot but I had no idea. Wow! Those pics are awesome.

You like that?

Yeah. We should hook up.

But I'm a married woman.

I thought you were separated?

I am, but I'm still married.

We could just hang out then.

And what?

Whatever you want.

Anything I want?

Yeah. No problem. Whatever.

Anything?

What do you have in mind?

What if I had an enemy that I need to get rid of? Would you help me?

We could talk about that.

Let's do. Are you free tomorrow night?

I am now.

I could meet you somewhere.

Sounds like a plan.

Texts with my husband

Emma invited me to have lunch with her again on Thursday. Can you please join us and be there? I'll do whatever you want... I'm just asking. Please.

I know. She mentioned it to me before she asked you. I don't see that I need to be involved with that. You two have fun.

I'd just feel a lot more comfortable if you were there.

I have a very busy day Thursday. I likely won't take lunch as it is.

This weekend, can we get together alone, just you and I, without her?

Where's this coming from?

I just miss being with you, just us.

I'll talk to Emma about it, and get her thoughts.

Why do you have to ask her??

I don't have to ask her, but I want her input. She's important to me.

I'm scared about what's going on between you and her. Am I just wasting my time here? Do we have a future together?

That's entirely up to you, 22_. We'll see how you do. We'll see how committed you are to staying clean and healthy and making better choices and decisions. We've talked about this a thousand times.

I'm trying really, really hard. You don't know how difficult this is for me.

I don't think you know how difficult this entire fiasco has been for me. And everyone else. You mostly just think about yourself. That's part of your problem.

I'm sorry. I didn't mean to negate your feelings. But Emma is totally stressing me out! She scares me.

Don't worry about Emma. Worry about yourself, your job, and getting back on track.

I feel sometimes like you're pushing me to fail. Like you're just testing me.

I am testing you.

Why??

Because I need to see how you handle it. How you handle adversity and stress. Whether you are strong enough to resist the temptation to use drugs again. Or whether you are just looking for the easy way out.

You don't have to be so mean about it. You should be gentle with me. I really need that right now.

I'm very proud of you, 22_. You've made it this far. You found what appears to be a very good job. You appear to be committed to changing your life. But it's still early. When you left rehab last year, I thought you had beat the addiction. I went to a lot of effort to solve your other problem. But then about six months later you were back to using again, and trying to hide it from me. When you disappeared for three days and ended up in some motel room with some random guy you met in a bar, that was it for me. I don't trust you right now. That's going to take a long time to fix.

I know. I'm sorry.

I have to get going. We can talk tonight if you want. Call me after 8pm.

Okay. I will. I love you.

We'll talk later.

I love you!

Have a good afternoon

22

Email to Emma

So yeah, lunch on Thursday sounds good. Same place and time works. I look forward to it.

I'm sorry I've been such a bitch sometimes. I want nothing more than for us to get along better. I know you're a kind person who only wants the best for my husband. I have no problem with your friendship with him.

Email from Emma

I appreciate the apology yesterday. I'm glad you've reached the point in your recovery where you can at least acknowledge your responsibility for the devastation you've caused.

You have hurt CHAD deeply. He's shared his feelings with me about a lot of things. You have embarrassed and ashamed and humiliated him time after time with all that you've done.

It hurts him that you can't seem to stay away from the drugs and the niggers. He's really disgusted by it.

Did you know that he had his entire house searched by two men with drug dogs to find all the things you hid everywhere? They found what you hid inside the buddha statute in the garden. And the syringe packets you taped underneath the bathroom cabinet in the pool house.

I wish he had never shown me those videos of you with that horrible man you got involved with. I don't even know what to think about the nasty things I saw you do in those videos. CHAD told me you were drugged and didn't really know what was happening, but I'm not so sure about that. It seemed to me like maybe you liked it. In one of the videos you even started barking like a bitch dog when that disgusting man asked you what you wanted, and then you bent over and spread yourself to show him. I could be wrong, but you seemed perfectly sober to me.

The true tragedy is that CHAD loves you. I don't honestly understand it, but he tells me that all the time. On the other hand, he's also seriously conflicted between what he wants and what is realistic. It's like you have him brainwashed or something.

I was with him the night he made the decision to move all of your things out of his house, and forbid your return. He didn't want to do it, but after we discussed it, with him crying on my shoulder, and my comforting him, he came to the realization that you really left him no choice.

I hope you can find it in your heart to leave him be. Go be with your niggers if that's what you really want. You've put CHAD through enough pain and sorrow, don't you think?

Our Lord is a compassionate and loving God, and I sincerely hope He forgives you for what you've done to that poor man.

I should have perhaps saved all of this for our lunch on Thursday, but I'm so angry with you right now, I felt like I needed to get this off my chest. Please forgive me for my honestly.

Email from my husband

Emma is entitled to her opinions just as everyone else is. I agree with some of what she has to say, but not everything.

She doesn't think you'll be able to stay off drugs. I, on the other hand, have a great deal of confidence in your ability to accomplish whatever you set your mind to. I've seen that character in you many times before. You are an extremely smart, clever, and determined person. I know you can do it, if you want to.

I strongly suggest you maintain your focus on staying sober, working the program, listening to your counselors, and putting your life back together.

Focus on your new job and doing well there. Be the best you can be. Impress everyone with your intelligence and your talent. And stop worrying about what other people think of you.

I'd like you to keep your lunch date with Emma, please. I expect you to be be on your best behavior with her. Don't hate on her. Instead, prove her wrong. Show me what you're capable of.

Email to Emma

Thank you for your honest thoughts. I need to hear it. I appreciate what you're doing for my husband. He needs a really good friend right now. He's told me many times how much he enjoys your company. I know you just want the best for him.

See you tomorrow!

Email to my husband

I received the attached email from your new girlfriend today.

I haven't responded.

I need to know if you agree with what she's saying, please.

Text to Ronald

I'm running a little late, about 45 minutes, but I'll be there. See you soon!

I'm not interested in Ronald sexually. I'm interested in what he might be able to do to help me solve my Emma problem.

It's always good to have friends in both high and low places.

Mr. Whites gets out of rehab on Saturday!!! YAY!

Chapter 16

Texts with Emma

Hi 22_. It's Emma. This is my new number. The new iPhone is great!

Okay.

I really appreciated the time we spent yesterday at lunch. I feel like we're breaking down some barriers between us. There's no reason why we can't get along better. CHAD is very happy about that.

I'm sure he is.

CHAD just called me. He's having dinner with Yoko tonight, but I thought you and I might spend some time together.

That's going to be difficult. I have plans with my friend Ronnie.

Really? What are you doing?

Not sure yet. We're meeting up at her house.

I understand. Perhaps you can reschedule that. I have a surprise for you. A present. Actually, it's from CHAD, but he asked me to give it to you.

Why doesn't he give it to me?

I know. He probably should. But you know how busy he is all the time. He's all work, work, work!

I could meet up with you tomorrow afternoon.

Not to be a pain, but it really needs to be tonight. Please make plans to be at house at 7pm. But go in through the side entrance. I'll leave the gate unlocked for you. I'll be in the pool house.

Okay. But I need to leave by 8pm.

I'm not sure that's going to be possible. You should probably plan on at least three hours. I know you have the 11pm curfew where you're staying, so no problem there. You'll be back on time, I promise.

Can I ask what the gift is?

Well, if I told you it wouldn't be a surprise, would it?

You said it's from my husband?

Yes.

He bought it especially for you. We kind of picked it out together, actually.

Oh really?

Yes.

Oh, before I forget, he would like you to test again tonight when we meet. You've been doing great so far, so I'm sure it isn't even necessary, but you know how he is. He's just being careful!

Okay.

He actually wants me to hold the cup while you pee, to make sure you don't try to cheat.

Oh, he does, does he?

I told him it's silly, but you know how he is sometimes. He's still not quite trusting you.

Fine. No problem. I have nothing to hide.

Great! Then 7pm it is. I'll see you in a few hours.

Bye Emma.

See you soon 22_. I look forward to it!

Email from Emma

I swear, you're going to turn me into a fat lesbian with that mouth of yours! OMG! My legs are still trembling! You are so good at that! The way you use your fingers, it almost feels like you have three tongues. I still can't believe you got your whole hand inside me! That felt awesome!

No one's ever smacked my pussy that way before. You made squirt all over and soaked the mattress!!

Honestly, if you don't mind me saying it, you're even better with your mouth than CHAD. I mean he's really good, but you obviously taught him how to do it. Promise me you won't tell him, even though it was his idea for me to get you to start doing that.

I hope you're enjoying your new gift. CHAD thought it would help keep you away from all the ghetto niggers that you seem to like so much. The silly sharpie writing on your belly was my idea.

I hope it's not too uncomfortable. I think it's kind of silly, because obviously you can still give blowjobs, and it also leaves your asshole exposed, and CHAD told me how much you love anal. But he wants you to wear it, and wants me to keep the key.

I know you're disappointed that he doesn't go down on you anymore, but he's pretty adamant about that. Partly that's my fault for sharing my concerns with him about you being with so many black men. He realizes now how immoral and unhealthy that was and is.

It's too late today, but I'd really love it if you went to my church with me next Sunday. There is a beauty and purity to prayer that I'd love to share with you. CHAD_ would really love if we did that together. Obviously, we both need to ask the Lord's forgiveness for our sins of the flesh, right? We're so naughty!

Thank you again for last night! You're right, I didn't miss Chad's little dick at all, lol.

Emma

PS: I have this really curious desire to kiss you, and experience what that would be like. I've never, with a girl before. But I would want you to initiate that. I think I'd be too embarrassed.

Email to my husband

I tried calling you, but keep getting your voicemail. I guess you're busy doing whatever.

I've been in a certain mood all day. Not terrible, but not great. Just blahhh.

I wish I was home in your arms right now. But I'm starting to realize that may not ever happen again.

You're seeing Emma, and allowing her to live in the pool house. You're dating that Yoko girl, and whoever else, I don't know.

I'm in my room right now, just reading. My roommate isn't here yet. She sent me a text telling me that her guy is going to come over tonight.

I am so sorry for everything I've done to hurt you. I know I don't deserve you.

It really hurt when Emma told me that you no longer want to have sex with me because of what I've done before.

And it especially hurts that you showed her all those videos that DaddyBigBull sent you. You know I was high on drugs when all of that happened, and barely have any memory of what was happening. Those videos were extremely personal. I feel totally humiliated that you shared those with her.

Email to my husband

Emma told me you've been spending more time with Yoko lately. It's funny that I had to hear that from her, and not from you. Should I be worried?

I'm sure you probably feel huge to her. You need to be careful not to hurt her with your little penis.

I'm wearing your "gift" right now. Thank you. Although I wish it had been you who put it on me rather than your girlfriend Emma. I'm trying really hard to do what you want to please you.

Update re Mr. Whites

I'm hooking up with Mr. Whites tonight after work. Finally, ... I get to have some fun

Email to my husband

Good morning! I hope you have a great day. I miss you.

Can I take you on a date Friday?

Email to Mr. Whites

I can still taste your cock in my mouth. You sure do love your blowjobs, don't you? Ha ha.

Thank you for last night. And thank you for not being gentle with me. You owe me a new pair of panties, ha ha.

Chapter 17

Confused

Is my love for my husband really just attachment?

Is my desire to win him back unrealistic?

Is my fear of losing him really just my fear of being alone?

Does he still love me, or is he just playing with my emotions?

Is he really trying to help me, or is he just pushing me away?

My friend Tina thinks my husband is already gone, and that he's just going through the motions, trying to make me the one who finally ends things. She thinks he's pushing me to fail in my treatment plan. She thinks he's

angling to protect his financial position if we get divorced. She thinks I need to immediately hire a lawyer to protect myself.

My friend Ronnie still thinks there's hope. She thinks there's a lot of good in my husband, and that he still loves me. She thinks he's acting out of a combination of hurt and compassion. She thinks his interest in Emma and Yoko and whoever else will eventually fade away, and that he'll come back to me. She thinks I just need to be patient and keep working on my treatment plan.

Me? I have no fucking idea. One day I agree with Ronnie, the next day I agree with Tina, and the third day I'm in between.

Texts with my husband

I appreciate the offer regarding Friday, but I have something planned that would be difficult cancel. Maybe we can instead have breakfast at the house on Sunday.

Okay. Are you doing something with Emma?

No.

With Yoko?

Yes.

What?

A friend of hers owns our gallery, and they're have a show going on for a new artist.

It seems like you've been seeing her more often lately.

Not really. Once or twice a week or so. But that's not something you really need to concern yourself with.

To be honest, I'm jealous.

Jealousy is really the least of your concerns right now. Focus on your treatment plan, your job, and don't worry about anyone else.

Emma wants me to go to church with her on Sunday. A Catholic church.

Good. You should. I think more spirituality in your life would be good for you.

So, while we're at the church, should I talk about how she's committing adultery by coveting and trying to steal another woman's husband? Or how she has been engaging in lesbian sex?

22_, please. Sarcastic and negative thinking like that isn't helpful.

Well it's true. The idea that Emma is supposedly religious is ridiculous. It's all just a stupid front she's putting up. You don't really believe it, do you?

People have different reasons for wanting to attend church. That's a personal choice of theirs. One which I think you should respect.

Do I really have to go? Don't I have a choice?

I'd like you to go. I think the experience would be good for you. I want you and Emma to get along better, and spending more time together helps accomplish that.

Okay. I'll do it. I don't want to do it. But I'll do it for you. I'm not doing it for her.

That's fine. I'd like you to please do what she asks, and respect her.

Okay. I feel like I'm losing you some times.

You're not losing me, you're just not in control of everything anymore. I think that's what's really bothering you.

True. But we hardly spend any time together anymore. Alone time, just with each other.

We're separated 22. I'm here, and you're there. For a lot of different reasons that I hardly need to repeat. I agreed not to divorce you, against the advice of virtually everyone I talked to about it. We're still married, but obviously things are not the same. And I'm not sure they ever will be. But I agreed to give it time, as you requested, and so will see how things go.

Please don't be mean to me. I don't need that right now. What I'm going through is really, really difficult.

I know it is. But I'm not going to coddle you through this. And I'm not going to put my life on hold just because you decided to become a heroin addict. You're going to need to find your own internal source of strength, and get through this on your own. If you do that, successfully, over the long term, that will tell me a lot about your commitment not only to your own life and health and safety, but to any relationship with you may wish to have with me.

Okay. I understand. Does 9 AM work, on Sunday?

Yes.

Can I please get a sticker for my car so the guards will let me past the front gate, so I don't have to stop and give my name and then wait for them to find my name on the guest list to let me in? It's embarrassing. They know who I am.

I'll think about it.

Okay. I'd appreciate that.

Email to Ronald

Sorry I'm late getting back to you. It's been a crazy week. Tomorrow at your place works. I'm looking forward to it.

But... you still haven't promised you won't try to fuck me. You need to promise! I need to be faithful to my husband, even though he doesn't deserve it.

So...??

Night with Ronald

Just got home, a little past curfew, after spending the evening with Ronald.

My ass is on fire right now. I'm going to have marks for days. But it burns sooooo good!

He kept his promise to me, and didn't try to fuck me, which I'm very happy about. I'm not sure I'm ready for that with him, or even want it.

He did, though, touch me all over while he was disciplining me... and that was okay.

Texts with Ronald

I can see we're going to have to maybe have a few new rules the next time we hook up.

Like what?

You promised you wouldn't try to fuck me, which you were good about, and which I appreciate, but you still tried to touch me all over while you were disciplining me.

Was that a problem?

You're not supposed to put your fingers inside me.

Didn't you like that?

That's not really the point. You're not supposed to do that. You're just supposed to spank me for being a bad girl.

Seemed like you were enjoying it to me.

I'm supposed to be a good girl. You need to help me be a good girl.

Alright. Is that going to be a new rule? No touching you?

I didn't say it's a new rule, I'm just saying you shouldn't be touching my privates that way.

So, it's not a new rule?

We shouldn't have to have a rule for everything. You should just not do that.

So, if I do that again, are you going to be upset?

That depends.

On what?

On whether if feels good or not.

Email to Ronnie

Okay... so I confirmed with Mr. Whites regarding Friday night. He wants to take us dancing, and then later to his place. He said we'd probably meet up with some of his friends.

He knows we're married, and wants us to wear our wedding rings. You're going to love him. He's like a total stud in bed! I told him you like it nasty... ha ha.

Tinder Man

I'm so excited! I ran into Tinder Man again this morning. He was handsome and charming as ever.

His eyes went immediately to my wedding ring, but he didn't say anything.

Yeah!!

I got approved for my own credit card today, in my own name, without using my husband's credit. It only has a $800 credit limit, but it's a start. Thank you Capitol One!

Email to my husband

I couldn't help but notice that you've been conspicuously silent today ever since I sent you the email about Marvis texting me last night. Is that because you miss it, and you're thinking about it? It could just be our little secret...

Email to my husband

I wasn't sure if I should tell you... but I got a random text from Marvis last night, asking about you. He said he misses your mouth, and your tight little ass. He made a joke about how the hetero guys are sometimes the best cocksuckers, and wondered if you were available.

The last time I talked with him, I think it was back in April/May, before we went to Spain, and he wanted you to go over, I told him you were taking a break from sucking cock... which disappointed him.

I haven't responded to his text yet. Should I tell him you're still on break, or??

Texts with Emma

Hello 22_. I missed having our Thursday lunch yesterday. I apologize I wasn't available.

That's okay.

I was thinking maybe we could meet up for a drink on Monday or Tuesday.

I'm not allowed to drink, and I'd prefer not to go to a bar.

Oh, don't be silly. One glass of wine isn't going to hurt.

I'm trying to stay away from all types of drugs and stimulants, unless I have a prescription for it. And alcohol is a drug.

Alcohol isn't a drug, it's not a pill or something. You don't shoot it up with a needle. It's just naturally in wine. I'm sure you'll be fine.

Talk to my husband about it. He knows.

So, everyone else is supposed to not drink just because you don't want to?

No, it's not that. I just prefer to avoid the temptation. You can drink all you want, I don't care. Just not around me. Please.

Are you really that weak still, that you can't even go to a bar without wanting to get drunk?

It's not that I'm weak, and not that I want to get drunk. I just prefer to avoid the temptation.

Have you been staying away from the niggers?

I really wish you wouldn't use that word. It's offensive.

Why is it offensive to you? You're not one.

It's insensitive.

Well I'm not going to change how I think or how I talk just because someone gets offended or whatever. You didn't answer my question, though. Have you been staying away from them?

Why do you care who I see or what I do?

Because CHAD is a very busy man, and he asked me to check up on what you're doing, to make sure you're not doing anything to embarrass him.

My friendships with black men have never embarrassed him before.

Yes, it has. You just don't know him. He tells me things, how he feels.

I'm pretty sure I know my husband better than you do.

Oh? Is that why you're living where you are now? Because you care about him so much?

I don't want to argue with you, Emma. Please. My husband has asked me to respect you, be nice to you, to get to know you better, to do as you ask, and that's what I'm trying to do.

You may think you know him, but you don't. He's embarrassed by the things you do. The men. The drugs. The recklessness. He's tired of covering for you. He just wants to move on with his life. If you truly loved him, you'd let him go.

I do love him, which is why I'm NOT letting him go. You can have your fun with him for now, Emma. That's fine. Go for it. But he's my husband.

I know he is, but he's very special to me. I love him, and he loves me.

Oh, I seriously doubt that.

I know he does. He's told me so.

Is that why he takes you everywhere, to all his business dinners, and charity functions, and meet ups with his friends? Out to dinner, and all that? Is that why he's always showing you off in public, because he loves you? Because he really wants to be with you?

He's not comfortable doing that yet because he's still married to you. He's trying to be a gentleman.

And you think that's the only reason, huh?

Yes.

Emma, please. Wake the fuck up. Look in a mirror. He doesn't take you anywhere, and will never allow himself to be seen in public with you, because you are short and fat and look like Yoda. And I got to go. Bye Emma!

Email to Emma

Since you seem to be so interested in knowing what I'm doing...

... that nigger fucked me so good last night, he made me cum like a bitch in heat! And then he fucked my friend Ronnie.

This morning when I got up to take a shower, I could still feel his semen dripping down my leg.

Any more details you'd like to know?

Did you get your fill of four-inch white penis last night?

Did he take you anywhere, or did he keep you hidden as usual behind closed doors?

Email from my husband

Emma forwarded me your recent text and email communications. I understand you two also got into a shouting match on the phone this morning.

Needless to say, I'm very disappointed in you. And in her. I can see that you both still have significant trust issues with each other.

Reading through the texts and emails, I find fault with both of your actions. You are both being selfish, inconsiderate towards each other, and acting like children. This needs to stop.

I'd like you to please come by the house tomorrow afternoon. The three of us need to sit down and have a serious talk about all of this.

If you are at all serious about trying to repair our relationship, I'll expect you here at 3pm.

Email to my husband

I've read and reread the text and email communications I've recently had with Email. And with you. And yes, you're right, she and I did get into a shouting match on the phone this morning.

Needless to say, I'm very disappointed in you. And in her. I can see that you think it's fun to continue to torture me, which is exacerbating my trust issues where you're concerned.

Reading through the texts and emails, I find fault with your twisted-fuck efforts to get revenge on me. That is what you're doing, isn't it?

I'm in recovery; I have this demon I'm trying to defeat. It's the most difficult thing I've ever tried to do. I'm sick. I'm weak. I'm extremely vulnerable. Recovery is physically painful, emotionally exhausting, and seemingly never-ending. And it's humiliating.

But rather than being here for me... really being here! ... you've turned your back on me, and seem bent on doing everything you can to cause me to relapse. You've paid for everything, which I am grateful for, but let's not kid ourselves, it's pocket change for you. It's like me, on my salary now, buying lunch.

You mostly ignore me. You barely talk to me. You moved Emma into the pool house. And you haven't touched me in three months. You have no idea how much that hurts.

I've tried. I've really tried to do what you want. But I can't escape the conclusion that you're being selfish and spiteful and mean and hateful towards the woman you supposedly love. Supposedly. Well, this ends today.

You're right; we need to have a serious talk about all of this. But before that, you can kiss my ass, and get your fucking tongue all up in it, and show me that you're still worth my time.

If you are at all serious about trying to repair our relationship, I'll expect you here... you know where I'm staying... at 3pm tomorrow afternoon. Alone.

You've got a choice to make. You can choose the fat bitch, or you can choose your money. Because you ain't getting both.

Monday morning, we will either wake up together, in each other's arms, and start our life anew... or you can spend the morning talking to my lawyers. Because I am fucking done.

Men

I'm going to take a break from men for a while. Not sure why; it's just a feeling I have, like an experiment. To clear my head, maybe. To take away all the distractions. To focus on me. To see if I can do it.

We'll see how long it lasts.

Two errands to run tomorrow:

- Appointment with the Lawyers
- Battery store

The End of Days

My husband didn't come today. Or call me, or text, or email. And I was too prideful to contact him. So, nothing happened.

Back when I was seeing DaddyBigBull, I'd go over to see him sometimes, and he knew right away what I wanted, what I needed. I would undress for him like I always did... he always wanted me completely naked and barefoot... he wasn't one for fancy sexy dress outfits likes Marco was... and I'd climb into his warm bed. Sometimes he'd already be in bed when I got there, or would join me right away, and other times I'd be alone for a while, and he'd come into the bedroom later.

I would leave my right or sometimes my left foot out and dangle it over the edge of the bed. DaddyBigBull knew what that meant. It meant that I was ready to chase the dragon, that I wanted him to shoot me up so I could go up the ramp, through the tunnel, down the chute, and across that long narrow dangerous bridge into that special dark crazy world that only heroin addicts know.

DaddyBigBull got me hooked on heroin, against my will, but it was me who kept going back to him for it.

He'd take my foot in his hands and kiss it. Sometimes he'd suck on my toes. He could be very gentle that way. My feet would always look so tiny and white in his big dark hands. I don't know why, but that would always excite me. Before he met me, he had never had a girl give him a foot job before, and I loved doing that for him. I busted his footjob cherry, ha. But unlike my husband... I used to make him lick off his own semen from my feet and toes... DaddyBigBull would go get a warm towel and wash my feet for me afterwards. I always loved that!

DaddyBigBull was many things... aggressive to the point of being violent, dangerous, unpredictable, coercive and manipulative... but one thing I could count on was that when it came to drugs and sex, he never disappointed. He always reliably had a stash of pharmaceuticals, and he was always horned up and ready to fuck. He wasn't just my black pimp daddy, he was my drug daddy. And I loved being his dirty little whore. His pretty white girl. His bitch.

He'd usually shoot me up between my toes, sometimes on top of my foot, or behind my knee. A few times he shot me up on my thigh, and in the groin area between my legs, but I was always terrified that my husband... when he went down on me... would see or notice something, so I didn't let DaddyBigBull do that too often. Not there.

Once I felt the rush of poison in my veins, I'd close my eyes and disappear. And then DaddyBigBull would fuck me. And fuck me. And fuck me all night. He'd fuck me front and back and sideways. He'd fuck me on the bed, standing up against the wall, and on the floor. He'd grab me by the hair and fuck my mouth like it was a pussy. He'd smack my face with his dick. He's rape my ass without asking, because like most black men, they never ask.

And sometimes it wasn't just him. Sometimes I didn't even know their names. Sometimes I never saw their faces. Sometimes they never saw mine.

I never really cared, because one of the things that heroin would do is make me extremely, intensely, insatiably, crazy-bitch horny. There were nights when I lost track of how many men I had sex with. I'd just close my eyes, opened my legs, or bend over and put my ass up, and just let them do whatever.

Some nights, it wasn't just men. The first time DaddyBigBull made me do that, I resisted and got whipped, and cried afterwards and wanted to kill myself. A month later, whenever he snapped his fingers and whistled, I automatically get down on all fours and assumed the bitch position. The one thing I never knew at the time was that he videotaped it a few times, which he then later sent to my husband. That didn't go over too well.

Ever since I was a very young girl, and discovered that special, magical feeling that the corner of my mother's vibrating washing machine provided, I've always been perpetually horny. I had my first orgasms that way, in the garage (we didn't have a utility room), even before I knew what they were, when my pubic hair was just starting to grow out. I'm not ashamed to admit that I still occasionally masturbate that way, on the vibrating corner of the washing machine. I know I'm not the only one because girls talk about that!

After my love affair with Kenmore, about a year later, it was daddy's rough thick fingers moving between my legs, in my room, late at night, in the dark, when my mother was at work. Not that it mattered so much that she was at work because later on, when I tried to tell her what he was doing, to get her to stop him, she accused me of lying about it, slapped me across the face, and told me to never ever mention it again. My daddy basically took that as a signal that he could go ahead and escalate things during those filthy humid nights and start making me perform oral sex on him.

Several years later, I found myself at a party, getting stoned for the first time with strangers. I had just made the freshman cheerleading squad, and was in my uniform. Somehow, I don't remember exactly how, I ended up in one of the upstairs bedrooms with a much older black man who took out his penis, pushed my head down, and held it until he had satisfied himself in my mouth. I was scared, but also intensely, strangely curious and excited about the whole experience. By that time, I knew what to do when a man put his cock in my mouth, so it's not like I didn't know what I was doing.

He wanted to fuck me that night, and managed to get my underwear off, but I somehow managed to keep him from doing that telling him I was a virgin, that my daddy was a police officer, and by promising him that I'd suck his cock whenever you wanted, a promise he took advantage of several times over the next several months. I had lied to him about my father being a police officer, and got smacked for that when he found out. I had to lie to my friends and teachers about how I got my first black eye.

Then one time we were at his apartment, where I'd meet him after school. He was being very aggressive with me, and asked me to show him my "white pussy". It was clear to me that he wasn't going to take no for an

I remember feeling this strange momentary sense of relief that he wasn't inside my twat. I remember thinking, when it was finally over, and I was in the bathroom cleaning myself up, that I would at least still be a virgin, and feeling somehow relieved by that. It sounds so stupid and weird to think about that now, but that's what I thought about.

He raped me that night... forcefully, violently. I never told anyone... partly because I was scared and didn't want anyone to know, partly because I didn't think anybody would believe me, partly because I knew my daddy would probably beat me to death for being with a nigger (as he called them), partly because I was convinced it was mostly my fault anyway because I had led him on, and partly because I knew he was a man and that men can't always help themselves around pretty girls who flirt. (My daddy used to say that.) I had teased him. I had showed him my titties. I had let him touch me. I had sucked his cock. I had let him cum in my mouth. I had encouraged him. And it was all my fault. At least, that's what I believed.

That night wasn't the last time I saw him. Most girls in that situation would have run far, far away from a man like that. I didn't run. What I did, about a week later, was go back to him. I have no idea why. But I saw him again, and again, and again. Until one afternoon, at his apartment again, this time in his bed, he took my cherry... my real cherry... not because he forced me, but because I wanted him to, because I laid back on the bed, put my legs up, and wanted to feel something different than him just fucking me in the ass again.

And so that's how it started. By the time I graduated from high school I had probably been with 50 different men, almost all of them black, many of them friends with each other. I would go to parties sometimes, and there would be like five or six different guys there that I had been with.

I was raised by a violently racist father. My mother hated them too. I grew up in a very conservative area of the south where interracial relationships were not accepted. And so, once it got around at school that I had been with a black guy, none of the white boys at school would date me. They would barely even talk to me. The corollary was that once word got out that a white girl liked black dick, every single black guy in town would hit on her.

By the time I was a senior in high school, I was the pretty white cheerleader that the black athletes passed around between them. During football season, it was the football players. During basketball season, it was the basketball players. During baseball season, it was the baseball players. During the summer, it was all of them. The only athletes I didn't have sex with were the guys who played soccer, and that was because they were all white.

I was the party girl; the crazy one. I was the girl who would do anything. I was the fun girl who was always up for anything daring and dangerous. I was the girl who fucked on the first date. I was the girl who would give them head in the locker room. I was the girl who got gang-banged at parties. I was the girl who liked the big black penis, and everyone knew it. I was the girl who loved to fuck as much as any guy.

I learned a lot from boys. I learned about my body. I learned how to fear sex, and I learned how to love it. I learned about that strange, curious, mixture of pain and pleasure. I learned not only to love sex, I grew to crave it. It would sometimes scare me how much I liked it. I wanted to be fucked every day. I learned how to make myself cum by rubbing myself with my fingers while getting fucked in the ass. I learned how to please a man, and I learned how to please myself. I learned how to use sex to get what I wanted from a guy. New dress? Handjob after school. New shoes? A blowjob in the parking lot. Weekend shopping trip to Atlanta? A quickie in the camping trailer.

I learned that sex is how you keep a man happy, and make him like you. I was also taught that when a man wants something, you give him what he wants, you let him do what he wants, and you don't question him.

I mention this only because through therapy I've learned and discovered that I am the sum total of my experiences. My early sexual experiences hardwired certain desires and behaviors into my brain and my psyche. And not just the good, safe, and healthy ones.

I've been in therapy for a really long time. I haven't always been consistent with it, but at various times, I've seen therapists ever since college; and for a lot of reasons. I've been diagnosed with a bipolar condition, and with borderline personality disorder (BPD). I try to control it as best I can with various medications, although there isn't really anything that helps BPD, except talk therapy. And I've been known to sometimes go off my medication because I hate some of the side effects.

I wasn't honest with my husband when I first met about any of this. I kept things from him because I knew instinctively that if he knew, he might not want anything to do with me, and certainly wouldn't marry me. I didn't tell him that I had been with black men before, because he was one of those same rich white boys in high school who ignored and looked down upon and hated on me. I didn't tell him that I had been a party girl because he had never been a party boy. I didn't tell him about my medical or psychological issues for obvious reasons. And sure enough, my suspicions were borne out

about a year into our marriage when I finally did tell him everything... gradually, not all at one... and he almost left me.

I'm writing this partially because my therapist, who is a psychologist, encourages me to write as a form of self-therapy in between the times when I see her. She's all about the journal writing... which is partly what this diary is for me. And if you think this is crazy, you should read the things I write in my journals that I don't post, ha ha.

I guess I'm just feeling kind of lost today. Sad. Disappointed. Crushed. Afraid of the future.

I've lost my husband. I know that. And I'm probably never going to get him back. And it's all my fault. I don't blame him. I wouldn't want me either.

I'm going to be okay. I'm much stronger than I was a few months ago. I have a strong support team, and great friends. And a job I love. I have a future!

Part of me wants to go into battle mode, get what I can get from my husband financially to protect my future, and utterly and completely destroy Emma.

Another part of me just wants to forgive him, take nothing from him, and move on.

And then there's that other part of me, that reckless, dangerous part of my personality that would probably drive across town to go see DaddyBigBull right now if he wasn't in jail... get naked for him, climb into his bed, and dangle my foot off the edge so I can go to that dark special place again, and forget.

Scared

I'm so scared right now, I'm shaking. I feel like I've been kicked in the stomach.

I have no idea what's going to happen today. All I know is after my argument with Emma on the phone yesterday, and then getting that email from my husband, I couldn't take it anymore.

Last night, it took everything I had not to go back crawling to the dragon. My sponsor came over, we talked and cried together, and she kept me strong.

I've received so many kind and generous notes from my readers; thank you!! It means a lot to me.

I want my husband back. That's what I really, really want. I want my life back with him.

But if our relationship is damaged beyond repair, and I've lost him forever, and he really wants to be with Emma, I'm going to be okay. I can handle whatever happens because I know I tried.

It's Time

Though I have still mixed feelings about it, I'm meeting with the lawyers tomorrow. I don't want to get caught unawares. I have to take control of my destiny right now, and protect myself.

It's time to get this party started.

Lawyers

I just got back from meeting with my lawyers.

I got up early this morning, went for a run, went through my yoga routine, and showered before heading to the meeting.

I'm feeling very good. This isn't going to be easy, but I can do it.

My lawyers reassured me that the separation documents my husband made me sign last month are not enforceable due to the circumstances surrounding my being forced to sign them while I was in rehab and my husband had total control of everything. They said the documents aren't worth the paper they're written on.

They were also pleased to hear that I did not sign a prenuptial agreement when I married my husband like he had wanted me to (at his mother's insistence).

They said I am basically entitled to receive at least half of the increase in his net worth since we've been married, as well as spousal support. They are

going to hire what they called a forensic accountant to analyze all the financial information.

They're going to file the divorce case in court tomorrow, and then get my husband served. I asked them to please serve him at his office.

They said they are going to file an emergency request with the court to force my husband to immediately start giving me half of his income, and require him to pay my lawyers.

They asked me if I wanted to move back into the house and force him to leave, but I declined. I'm going to finish out my 90-day program here at the recovery house before looking for another place to live. One of my lawyers joked, and told me, "If you like the beach, go find another beach house to rent for now, and we'll make him pay for it."

They asked me if I wanted the court to order that my car be returned to me, but I declined that also. I can't imagine I'd ever be able to get the Emma stink out of my car; she can keep it. I asked my lawyers if I could force my husband to get me another one, a new one, and he said, "Consider it done."

I haven't heard a single word from my husband since we exchanged emails on Saturday. I called him last night, just to at least make sure he was okay, but it went to voice mail. I left him a message, which he hasn't returned.

I also sent him flowers today, for delivery at his office... an arrangement of lilies, with a single pink/white orchid in the center.

Life Mystery

If we're not supposed to stab and carve out the hearts of our enemies, then why are knives so cheap?

That got his attention!

After ignoring me since Saturday, my husband has been blowing up my phone for the last hour; phone calls, leaving voice mails, text messages, and emails.

I guess he must have been served... ha ha

I think I'll let him simmer in that for a while before returning his calls.

One Man?

A handsome, successful man who respects women, and will worship the pussy every night with his mouth and tongue... draw her hot baths and massage her feet... and a man with a big, thick cock who will rip it up and fuck her brains out every night... a confident professional in the board room, and a muscled-up thug in the bedroom... a man who gives a woman what she needs, and at the same time just takes what he wants...

is it ever going to be possible to find all of these qualities in just one man?

Email to my husband

Oh, I'm sorry sweetie... I just noticed you've been trying to contact me. Did my lawyers accidentally leave their phone numbers off the paperwork?

Email to my husband

I'm not in much of a mood to communicate with you right now, but I didn't want to totally ignore your efforts to communicate with me today.

Obviously, much has happened to get us to this point. I don't think it would be particularly helpful to rehash everything here.

I love you. I have always loved you. But apparently that's not enough.

I greatly appreciate everything you've done for me. But I really think it's time for both of us to move on.

You've made your choice. I wish you the very best with Emma. I think she's going to make a beautiful bride for you.

I bet you can't wait to tell your mother that you finally got rid of me. I'm sure she'll be pleased. I hope she doesn't get too upset with you, though, when she finds out that I didn't sign the prenuptial agreement you wanted me to, and that you lied to her that I had.

If it's OK with you I'd like to text a picture of Emma to Dana, so she can see who her new aunt is going to be.

By the way, good news! Tina found the backup drive that I thought I lost which has all of our personal photos and videos. If you'd like, I can make copies of the ones with you in them and mail them to your office. Please let me know. I'll do it however way you want me to.

Email to Emma

Oh my God! I feel so hot and thin and sexy this morning. I have the day off, and just got back from a run.

Mmmmm... I got fucked soooo good last night. He had a big ole' black dick. Tore my little white pussy up! I am sooo sore right now! His name was Leon or Lamar or... it was one of those L names, or something. My blonde brain, I swear, I can never remember things like that.

What about you? Are you still sleeping with my husband? Did you get some of that semi-hard, four-inch white penis? I bet that was super awesome! Did my husband at least get it out of his pants before he spurted? I hope you didn't have to finish yourself with your hand, like I always had to. That's always so sad, isn't it?

So... Fall Jubilee is coming up at the country club. I'm sure my husband is taking you, right? Show you off to all his rich friends? Have you picked out a dress yet? Or maybe a tent? I hear the canvas ones are on sale at Walmart. Don't forget to cut off the tags!

I really miss our Thursday lunches, Emma. You were always so kind and sweet to me, ordering wine, and making comments about how good it tasted. Thank you for that! It was amusing to hear you talk about different wineries and vintages, as if you'd know, ha ha.

You'll have to tell me how you've been. I'm so incredibly interested and curious.

Do you hear that clock ticking? Is it getting louder?

Email to my hubby

So... my lawyers asked me to put together a list of potential witnesses... names, addresses, phone numbers... and I couldn't remember Marvis's address. I thought you might, since you used to go there when he made you suck his big black cock. Do you have it?

Email from my husband

Please 22, can we just talk. I'll meet you anywhere you want. Please.

I don't want to do this. We need to stop hurting each other.

Please talk to me. Let's meet somewhere. I'm begging you.

Please answer your phone.

Email from my husband

Please 22, let's not go down this road. I've never hit you, and you know it.

I have a bigger problem that I'm dealing with, and I need to speak with you. We need to stay together on this.

Can you meet me at _____, near my office? Or I can go to you. Your call. Please let me know.

And can you please tell your lawyers to hold off on what they're doing? Lawyers are like vultures. They don't care about human relationships, they only care about the money.

Let's talk about this, please.

Texts with my husband

Oh yeah, so what's your "bigger problem"?

We need to talk about it in person. Not on here.

Why?

Can we just meet? Please.

I think you're trying to trick me.

I am not trying to trick you. I have a very sensitive issue going on that I need to deal with, and we need to be together on it.

What does it have to do with me?

It affects you. It affects both of us.

What is it?

We need to speak in person.

I'm not really comfortable with that right now. My lawyers told me you might try to trick me into saying things or whatever. And I know how you are with your little words.

Why are you blowing everything up here? You don't have to do this.

Fuck you Chad. You put me here. I could be home right now, but you moved all my things out of the house. And took my keys. Fuck you.

22, please. Let's talk. This is important.

You can talk to my lawyers.

What do I have to do here? Please 22.

I'll think about it and let you know.

We need to talk today.

We're talking right now.

I mean in person.

Where's Emma?

I don't know. At work I suppose.

Is she still staying in the pool house?

I have a delicate situation with her.

Is she still living there?

She still has her apartment.

You're not answering me. And I'm getting bored with this conversation.

What do you want from me??

You want a list?

If that's what it is.

I'll have my lawyers sent you a list.

Can we please keep this between just us?

Why? Are you nervous?

We don't need to self-destruct here.

I have to go.

Please, let's meet up.

Not today. Maybe tomorrow.

This is critically important 22_.

So, you say. I'm bored again.

I need to talk with you in person.

I have to go. Bye Chad.

Wait! When can we meet?

22. You there? Please answer me.

Go away, Chad. You bore me.

Email to my husband

I'm sorry, but I don't trust you right now. I don't want to get hit again.

If we meet to talk, it would have to be in a public place. And I have to ask my lawyer if it's alright.

Where and when were you thinking?

Email to my husband

I'll agree to meet up with you, in a public place to discuss whatever you want, but I can't do it until tomorrow after work, and I'm taking Tina with me. And you better be alone. I'll text you the location tomorrow.

Email to my husband

I've been really angry with you lately, upset, frustrated, and annoyed. But today, you broke my heart.

You can deal with your "situation" however way you want to. Keep me out of it. Emma can have your bastard child for all I care. Or a dozen of them. Whatever. You've lied to me for the last time. I don't trust you anymore.

I don't believe for a second that it was "accidental". I think she had this planned all along, and you're too fucking stupid to recognize it even now. She doesn't love you, she just wants 20k a month in child support. What a dumb fuck you are.

Good news is... at least your little dick works. Kind of. I guess that's something. You got the fat chick pregnant. Nice accomplishment Chad. I bet your mother will be proud of you.

I'm going to focus on and complete my program, and get healthy. That's number one for me. And nothing you do is going to derail my plans.

It's time for me to move on. I'm not calling off the divorce.

You're right about one thing: Us splitting up doesn't have to get ugly. It can be done in a calm and reasonable fashion. I'd much prefer it that way. I have no desire to burn the house down. But ultimately, it's up to you.

Sometime soon my lawyers will be sending you a proposal to resolve things. I suggest you take it very, very seriously. All I ask is that you treat me fairly. I hope you have it in you to do that. Otherwise, I have other options.

Congratulations, daddy.

Days of Contemplation

No... I'm not using again. I know that's what everyone thinks whenever I go quiet for a while. That's one of the curses of having been a drug addict before; people will forever just think of you as a drug addict and always expect you to go back to using.

This has been a very trying time for me. This week, in particular, I've had to make some decisions that I never thought I'd have to make. And face something I never thought could happen.

I'm surrounded by friends and supporters, but I feel alone. I think I know what I want, but I'm also confused. I make a decision, and then I want to change it. My sponsor is a gift from God. She's been a constant supportive presence this week. I'm grateful to her. She knows what I'm going through.

My continued sobriety is by no means a foregone conclusion. I've been doing well, working the program, and I feel good, happy, healthy, and in control. I'm still staying at the recovery house, looking to get my own apartment next month. My job is perfect for me. I love it. I'm making great money doing what I love to do. I owe Mr. Whites big time for recommending me for this opportunity. My boss, Andrew, is awesome. And I'm making lots of new friends.

But I have no illusions that I'm walking, every day, on the knife's edge. At any moment, of any given day, I'm one bad decision away from the needle. I'm two decisions away from ending up in some ghetto apartment as some drug dealer's whore. And perhaps three decisions away from a drug overdose and death.

I know who to call to get drugs. The numbers aren't saved on my phone anymore, but they don't have to be. I memorized them long ago.

I know where to go to get drugs. I know the street and the house that DaddyBigBull used to take me to. I know the guy's name who answers the door. The last time I was there... about three months ago... Streets... that's what they call him... again refused to take money for it. Instead he invited me in, looked quickly to the sides to make sure I was alone, and then took me into the back room and made me pay for it with pussy.

I remember every detail of the last time I went to go see him, desperate for a fix, nervous, willing to anything to get it. I remember how the room smelled of beer and dirty clothes, the filthy mattress on the floor, the distant

sounds of police sirens in the background, some baby crying in the apartment next door, the rough way he touched me, taking the condom from my purse and putting it on his cock to make sure he was wearing one, how it seemed like it took him forever to cum. I remember laying there, looking up at the ceiling fan, as he was banging into me, grunting, saliva dripping off his lip onto my neck, thinking, "this is your life now, on heroin".

I remember how I felt afterwards, sore between my legs, walking barefoot back to my car, carrying my purse and heels, the dogs barking in the dark behind someone's fence, still high out of my mind, with a g pack of heroin and new syringes in my purse. And more condoms, because I had to go back and fuck Street three more times for it. It was either that or, "I'll come find you, baby".

I was hiding it all from my husband, of course, lying to him about everything, living in fear that he would find out; which he eventually did.

Fast forward to the present.

I've now gone through rehab for the second time in a year with my husband's support. I feel grateful that he's paid for everything, but also guilty. And stupid.

What kills me about this whole fiasco with Emma is the fact that I'm the one who introduced him to her at the fetish party. I'm the one who encouraged him to spend time with her as part of my game. But back then, I knew he wasn't attracted to overweight women, and got a kick out of making him go down on her, knowing he was going to find it disgusting. I was in control of it. Now, I control nothing. And now she's pregnant.

He knows she is for sure because after she told him, they did a second test where she had him hold the stick between her legs while she sat on the toilet and peed on it. That's a disgusting sight to think about. And then she went to the doctor to confirm.

She's two months pregnant now. He's known for several weeks and had no intention of ever telling me about it. Or anyone. He said he's been trying to "finesse it". Worried about upsetting her. Trying to keep her close, figuring he'd have more influence with her that way.

He said he tried to gently raise the possibility of her terminating her pregnancy, but she was adamant about wanting to keep the baby. She's been pushing him to leave me. He also admitted to me that Emma was

trying to get me to start using again. And that he knew she was trying to do that.

My husband is now begging me to take him back and cancel the divorce. I met with him again this morning. Just us. We went for a quiet walk on the beach, talking, and then sat for a long time listening to and staring at the crashing waves, not talking.

I'm skeptical. I know how manipulative my husband can be. I've seen what he does with other people. I can't help but feel that the only reason he wants me back is to protect his financial position.

I'm very angry with him. Not a hateful anger, just a sad, resigned, frustrated anger. But I also still love him. He's been there for me so many times. We've been through a lot together. Part of me feels like I owe him.

But I'm also tired of being totally dependent on him financially and emotionally. I'm tired of him constantly trying to control me with his money. I want my freedom and independence.

If down the road, after a time apart, we're meant to be together again, then it will happen. For the right reasons. Not because it's forced. Not because one of us feels vulnerable. But because it's something that we both want.

Email to my husband

Thank you for the flowers. They were just delivered. And they're beautiful.

I also got your voice mail early this morning. To be honest, I'm not really up for seeing and having dinner with you tonight. Or this week. I need time alone for a while to think. And talking with you right now just confuses me.

I'm not going to ask my lawyers to put the divorce on hold, as you requested. Instead, I plan to move forward on that for now. But if you have some kind of specific proposal you'd like to make, I'll consider it.

My move out date at the recovery house, by the way, is going to be November 27. So, I need to find a place to live here pretty quick.

I hope you have a nice day.

22.

Email to Emma

So... I've heard the good news, and understand that congratulations are in order regarding the sad little bastard you're carrying. Nice trick! I hope that goes well for you. With half of your DNA in it, what could possibly go wrong?

Just remember, though... after you give birth to your calf next year, you only get your meager piece of monthly child support from Chad after I've taken half of everything he owns.

He's yours. You can have him. Good luck with that.

Email to my husband

Just curious... have you told your colleagues at work and your friends at the country club that you knocked up some trailer park fat chick? Or your mother? Does your son and your daughter know that they're going to have to share their inheritance with your putrid bastard?

Dana sent me a text this morning asking me how things were going. I haven't responded yet. Do you mind if I share a pic I have of Emma with her, so she can know who her new aunt is going to be?

Email from my husband

I know you're hurt 22_, and I feel terrible about it. I'm feel hurt too, albeit for different reasons. I can't work or eat or sleep over this. I desperately need you by my side.

Can we at least please call a truce here, and stop with all the hurtful thoughts and comments? I'd really like your help with this situation. Please. We both need to be on the same page here. This is a problem that affects us both. I've been trying to handle this on my own, without having to involve you, but obviously I've failed.

You're right about Emma, and her intentions. I've been a fool for not seeing it. I know you warned me. I should have listened.

For God sakes, please don't involve Dana with this. Or my family or friends. No one but you and I know about this, and I'd like to please keep it that way. Not even my lawyer knows.

If the situation were reversed, and Marco had gotten you pregnant, I wouldn't be happy about the situation, but I would have been there for you to love and support you no matter what, even if it involved us having to raise that child as our own. I would have done that for you, no question.

Please don't abandon me here. I need you. And I love you. Let's work together on this, please.

Email to my husband

I've thought about this long and hard. All night. You're not the only one losing a lot of sleep over this whole fiasco.

I'm trying to be strong, and you're trying to make me weak. You've playing the victim card, trying to make me feel guilty. Rather than help me up, I feel like you're trying to keep me down. You're trying to make everything about you, forgetting the absolute hell I've been through these last few months.

You forced me to go to rehab, for the second time, and paid for everything... I know it was astronomically expensive... which I am grateful for.

But then...

... you essentially abandoned me and left me to deal with this alone,

... you kicked me out of my own home,

... you removed all of my things out of the house and put them in storage,

... you started seeing Emma and eventually moved her into the pool house,

... you showed Emma the videos that DaddyBigBull sent you,

... you took away my car and gave it to her,

... you bought me a piece of junk car as a sick joke,

... you took my name off all the bank accounts and put me on a monthly "allowance" that is less than what you spend on a bottle of wine sometimes,

... you took away all my credit cards except for one with a very small limit,

... you forced me to sign a totally one-sided "separation agreement" while I was vulnerable and still in rehab,

... you made me do all kinds of disgusting things with Emma to prove my loyalty to you and test my resolve,

... you got the fucking bitch pregnant because you're just fucking stupid, and then you tried to hide it from me and everyone else because you know what people would think of you if they knew,

... and then... this is the most hurtful and outrageous thing you did... you knew Emma was deliberately stressing me out, forcing me to do these disgusting and vile things, and trying to get me relapse and start using drugs again, so you would leave me for good, and she could be with you... AND YOU DID NOTHING ABOUT IT. YOU FUCKING LET HER DO IT! It's going to take me a very long time to forgive you for that, if ever.

I love you... I've never stopped loving you... I'll probably always love you... but I'm not going to be manipulated by your corporate boardroom tactics and your feigned hurt. I know what you do to other people. I've seen you do it. I know how ruthless you can be. I know what a good actor you are. I know how facile you are with words.

I may be blonde, lack your professional credentials, and world experience, but I can hold my own against anyone and handle whatever you want to throw at me.

I have a meeting with my lawyers today. I'm going to instruct them to get a proposal to your lawyer tomorrow. It's going to lay everything out, in detail.

I suggest you make arrangements to go sign the documents by Friday noon. I don't want to hear that you disagree with something, or that you've made a counter proposal, or that you want to further negotiate this or that provision. I want to hear that you've signed the documents without so much as changing a comma.

Once the documents are signed and approved by the court, and you do everything you're supposed to do under the agreement, I'll help you with your Emma problem. I'll do whatever you want me to do. I won't tell anyone in your family or any of your friends about you getting her pregnant. And I'll continue to keep your secrets about what you did to DaddyBigBull.

And after that's done, and Emma is living in fucking Greenland with a barren cunt, you can apply for the boyfriend position with me, and maybe I'll consider it.

That's the deal. This isn't a negotiation.

Proposal

My lawyers just emailed me the proposal draft. Just a few more changes, and we're good to go.

And then it was done.

My husband signed the divorce papers that my lawyers prepared; I went in to sign them late this afternoon. Everything will be finalized next week.

I have agreed to have lunch with Chad on Sunday.

I'm sad but happy at the same time. This had to happen. It was time.

New Day

New life, new challenges, new opportunities, new chapter, new day.

Excitement tempered by caution.

Let it begin…

Chapter 18

Late Lunch with Chad

This meeting today is going to be more than a little awkward. I'm very nervous about it.

We both signed the documents on Friday, so that part is done. I'm grateful to him for not fighting me on that. Everything is going to be finalized in the next week.

I'm also grateful that we're not ending our relationship as enemies. I don't hate Chad, but if I'm completely honest with myself, I also don't love him in the same way I used to. I still love and care for him, but in a different way... in a way that's hard to describe. I feel tightly bonded to him emotionally, but in many ways, maybe it's just a familiarity and a dependence thing.

I'm very much looking forward to being free from his control. Obviously, I always had a lot of sexual freedom in my marriage, but hanging over my head every day was the fact that he always controlled the money, and would use that to control me at various times.

We still have a lot we need to talk about. He has a number of issues and concerns that I've agreed to help him with... how he's going to handle the news at work, what he's going to tell his family, the nature of my ongoing contact/relationship with his two older children (a son and a daughter) who I am very close to, and, of course, the Emma problem. I've also agreed to keep his secrets regarding his sexual activities with me, with other men, him getting Emma pregnant, the things he did to put DaddyBigBull where he is now, and some financial things that I know about regarding his business and partners.

Under our agreement...

We both signed a mutual non-disclosure and confidentiality agreement which prevents either one of us from talking about the intimate details and activities of our marriage, including all sexual matters between us. I'm prevented from disclosing to anyone that he fathered a child with another woman during our marriage. He is prevented from disclosing to anyone anything about my drug addiction or sexual involvement with other men.

I get to keep all of my personal property, jewelry, art, clothes, shoes, and the rest. Most of it is still in storage for now, until I get a new place.

He's required to pay for my clothing expenses, up to $5,000 per month, for a period of 72 months.

He's required to pay for my personal care and grooming expenses (hair, nails, salon, spa, massage, etc.) for the next 72 months.

He's required to pay for my health, dental, and vision insurance, and all out-of-pocket expenses (including all expenses associated with any future drug rehabilitation events) for a period of 72 months.

He's required to pay for one health club and one country club memberships of my choice for a period of 72 months.

He's required to pay for all care and veterinarian expenses for my pets for a period of 72 months.

He's required to pay all expenses for me and a friend to go on vacation, three times per year, for up to 10 days each time, to the destination of my choice, for the next 72 months.

He's required to buy me a new car of my choosing, with a $100k limit, and pay for all of the ongoing insurance, maintenance, and repair expenses associated with it, including car cleaning and detailing expenses. And I get a new car every 24 months, until the final one at 72 months.

He's required under the marital settlement agreement to buy me a new house to live in, of my choosing, with a $5 million limit on price. He also has to pay for all of the ongoing expenses to keep and properly maintain the house (property taxes, government assessments, membership and association fees, insurance, repairs and maintenance, housekeeping, landscaping, and gardening) for as long as I own the house. He's also required to pay all costs to fully furnish and decorate (and remodel if necessary) the inside of the home, including art work, up to 10% of the value of the house.

He's required to pay for the delivery of fresh flowers for my home (entry room, great room, kitchen, master bedroom and bathroom) every week for the next 72 months.

The rest of the settlement money is going to be put into two trusts; an Income Trust which will pay me a fixed amount of money every month for the rest of my life, regardless of whether I ever get married again, and a Settlement Trust, from which I will receive a lump sum in January 2016, another lump sum in 24 months, another lump sum in 48 months, and a final lump sum in 72 months. This payment scheme from trusts that my husband is required to immediately and fully fund was at the strong suggestion of my lawyers who wanted to make sure I was protected, even from myself.

Chad gets to keep the beach house property and everything in it, along with his personal property, jewelry, art, clothes, electronics, and such. He also gets to keep his ownership interests in his business, his retirement and other financial accounts, his family trust income, and all other assets that he had since before we got married. And he keeps the sail boat.

He is also required to pay all of my legal and other related expenses.

And so the next chapter of my life begins...

Email to Ronald

So... that thing we talked about, that bitch having an affair with my husband, let's meet up to talk about that again. Wednesday or Thursday after work?

Text to Marc

I know a white girl who's giving away the pussy this week. She needs to be banged really good. And likes it hard and rough and nasty.

You want her number?

Email to Chad

I hope you're feeling better. It hurt me to see you so upset yesterday. You're not normally that emotional, I know.

We've been on a long journey together, sweetie. A lot has happened along the way. We had a lot of great times together. And stressful ones. Obviously, both of us have made our share of mistakes.

But as much as I wanted everything to somehow work out between us, the reality is that not all stories have a happy ending. Sometimes relationships just end and become something else.

I still care about you very much. You're very special to me. It's hard for me to imagine my life without you. But I needed to do this. As much as I need to continue to work the program regarding my drug addiction, so I can break free of that demon hold on me, I also need my freedom from your control. I need my independence. I need room to breathe.

I know you have this hope that we will someday be together again, and who knows, maybe that can happen. But I can't promise you anything.

I do want to remain in contact with you, obviously. I don't want to lose my close friendship with you. And, as we talked about yesterday, I'd like to keep and maintain my relationship with your two wonderful children who I love very much, and I appreciate your being agreeable to that.

Anyway, I had a few moments and wanted to share this with you. I hope you have a great day.

22.

Marco is in my rear-view mirror, and he's staying there. But we're still friends.

Otherwise, I'm wiping the slate clean. Mostly. Except for an old booty call or two. Because a girl has her needs, ha ha.

I'm moving forward... new life, new opportunities, new challenges, new people, new adventures.

Up early this morning. Yoga class. Busy day today at work. Getting ready for a three-day business trip to Dallas next week with Andrew.

Marc reminded me once again last night why he's number two on my Booty Call Speed Dial. Oh yes!

He's the guy I know from the club back when I was dancing; he was one of my regulars. He's never known that I was married. Didn't know then, doesn't know now.

I went to meet him at his place. He had my tiny little panties off in two minutes, and then tore up the Golden Snatch. God, I love a guy who can get hard and stay hard all night and not instantly go soft after he cums the first time.

I love this deliciously sweet-sore feeling between my legs right now.

I'm still all natural down there, just slightly trimmed, the way Chad wanted me to keep it while he was off getting the fat chick pregnant. I know now that he only wanted me that way because he knew most black guys like the white pussy smooth.

I want to go smooth again... my longtime preference... but I kind of have a wicked little plan about that.

Email to Emma

Things didn't end well between us, I know. And I'm sorry for that.

You were right all along. As much as it pains me to admit it, Chad does love you, and wants to be with you. He told me so himself. He's very happy with you. I never imagined that could ever happen, but it did. And it has.

Quite honestly, I don't blame him. He deserves someone who will love him and care for him as you have shown you can and want to.

I was a terrible wife and a horrible person to him. I know that now.

I'm sure he probably told you that our divorce settlement is done and final.

Part of my recovery program requires that I acknowledge and take responsibility for my actions, particularly those that have hurt other people.

With your permission, I'd like to please do that with you. I'm deeply sorry for all the hurtful things I did and said to you, or about you to others. Please accept my apology.

I wish you the best in life. I hope you and Chad have a happy and healthy baby. He or she is going to be so cute! I know you're going to be a better wife to him and mother of his children that I ever was or could be.

After all that's happened, I don't know that you and I could ever be friends. But I would like that if possible.

Email to my husband

My lawyers told me they got confirmation of the wire transfer regarding the monies to fund the marital settlement trusts. Thank you for that.

I copied you on the email I sent Emma this morning, just so you'll have it.

I hope you have a great day!

Email to Marc

Thank you for last night. That really hit the spot! So, can I have some of that whenever I want?

Texts with Mr. Whites

Your sweet ass. My place. Tonight. Bring your friend Ronnie.

Really?

8pm. Don't be late.

Just you, or?
Just us three.

That works. I'll call her.

Make it happen baby.

I loved watching you with her last time. I'd love to get her ready for you.

Oh yeah.

Yes. But she's kind of shy that way. The girl thing, I mean. But if you made me do it...

Is that what you want?

Yes. Before and after. I'd love it.

I can do that baby. Be here by 8pm.

I'll call her. I'm sure she can get away.

Don't be late. I need my bitches to be on time.

Yes sir!

Email to Mr. Whites

Thank you for noticing I wasn't wearing my wedding rings last night. Was the pussy different? Ha ha.

So... after last night... Ronnie and I decided that:

1. We want to be your bitches forever.

2. You're not using your bitches enough.

3. We like it when you share us with your friends.

And Ronnie is jealous that you took my ass last night, and not hers. She wants you to give her a whore's ass next time.

PS: Thank you for "making me" get her pussy ready for you. She tastes delicious... especially after you fucked her. Oh yes!

PSS: Ronnie got in trouble with her husband last night when she got home, but she said it was worth it.

PSSS: I don't have a husband you need to worry about anymore.

Email to Chad

Sweetie... I'm so used to saying that to you... I don't mind you emailing or texting me. Anytime, as often as you like. It's not that. And I know how difficult this is for you. It is for me too. But I don't think it's a good idea for us to have dinner, or Tinder, or meet up right now. I don't mean to sound harsh, but I need to be away from you right now. It's confusing for me emotionally to see you. We are where we are for a thousand different reasons. It was time for me to move on. I'm a drug addict. You told me very explicitly that you didn't want to be married to a drug addict, and I respect that. So now you're not. Now you're free to live your wealthy charmed life with whoever you want. I've learned from my program that I will always be a drug addict. I may be in recovery, and not using, but my addiction is my addiction. It's never going to go away.

I still love you and care for you, but I need some distance, please. I may change my mind tomorrow... you know how I can be that way... but right now, I can't really see you. Please understand.

I sent the email you wanted me to send to Emma. I hope that was helpful to you. I'm sure she believed it because we both know how fucking stupid she is. You really picked a winner, Chad. Fat and stupid. But at least she's pretty. I guess.

I'll do whatever else you want me to do to help you solve your Emma problem, as I promised. I don't really need or want to know what your plans are. Just do whatever you're going to do and leave me out of it, please.

And yes, I miss you too.

22.

Email from Chad

Thank you for sending that email to Emma. It seems to have changed her entire attitude towards you. And, partially, with me. She told me yesterday that she doesn't see any reason why you and she can't part as friends.

Wanting her to feel included, I talked with her yesterday about your desire to still spend time and see _____ and _____. I told her how close you are to them, and how much they like doing things with you. I asked her what she thought about that. I'm certain she would have been against the idea before you sent that letter of apology, but now she is warmed up to the idea, which is progress.

I'm taking her out on the boat Saturday. Jack has arranged for a catered dinner, similar to what he's done for you and I before. I plan to speak with Emma then about what you and I have discussed. I think your plan is good. I think it will work. I never wanted to believe it before, but I can see now that you were right all along about her intentions and what she wanted. I seriously misjudged her. Obviously, it's all my fault for letting things get to this point.

I hope your plan works. I hate to think about my having to resort to something more drastic if it doesn't. But I promise you that Emma is not going to have my child. That is never going to happen.

I know how hard this has been for you, 22_. I appreciate your agreeing to help me with this. I'm so very sorry for what I've done to cause you pain. I never did deserve you, and I certainly don't deserve someone as wonderful and beautiful as you now. I hope someday you can forgive me for ruining what we had together.

I'll let you know how things go on Saturday. Wish me luck. I love you 22.

Chad

Yes!!!!!!

I'm sitting at a small table at the Tinder house right now, before going in to work, and he just walked in and got in line. Tinder Man!!!!! I haven't seen him in almost a month…. Yes!!!

Email to Chad

Received your note about Saturday. Good luck. I hope that works out for you.

22.

Email to Tinder Man

It was nice to see you again today. You look so handsome in your suit!

I'd be disappointed if you didn't think of me all day today.

Email to Marc

I got your message. You know, I can't just drop everything I'm doing and drive all the way over there just because you want pussy, ha ha. Just kidding. But can we hook up tomorrow night instead?

Email to Chad

I wanted to reach out to wish you well regarding what you have planned for tomorrow with Emma. I hope it works out the way he you want. I think it will, if you do it right, and follow through on the things we discussed. Fortunately for you, she's selfish and greedy and stupid enough to fall for it.

I know this isn't easy for you, but I also know that you're strong enough to get through this. I hope you do, because honestly, the idea of Emma having your baby is just fucking gross. If she ever does, you will never get rid of her, she'll take you for upwards of $20,000 per month in child support (according to my lawyers), and she'll be in your life for the next 20 years.

I sincerely hope it works. Be well.

22.

Email to Chad

I had another dream about you last night.

I was living in Miami... my friend Wendy from college and I were living together... and you somehow snuck in the house in the middle of the night while I was asleep. You got into bed with me and slipped down and put your face between my legs, and started going down on me, which woke me up. Except that I didn't have a pussy... I had a dick... but that didn't stop you, and you were sucking me off like you had been missing it, like slobbering all over it. I was confused and it felt strange because I couldn't understand why I had a dick.

As you sucked it, it started growing and growing and getting harder and harder, until it didn't fit in your mouth anymore. Your legs were wrapped around my leg, squeezing it between yours, and I could feel moisture, like it was wet or something. And I thought you had spurted.

But then you moved up and turned over on your back and opened your legs and I noticed that your balls were missing. And you didn't have a penis anymore. You had a pussy. But it wasn't just any pussy, it was Emma's pussy, all natural and hairy like her pussy is, and you wanted me to fuck you, and I started yelling at you to get out of my house, but you wouldn't leave, and you were reaching for my dick trying to put it inside you, lifting your butt up off the bed, and I started screaming out loud until Wendy walked in and you ran off.

#

Luck to Chad

I've done my part. I came up with a plan that I think can work, I helped him set it in motion, and now it's up to him to execute it.

I wish Chad luck today with Emma. The dumb hippo-fucker is going to need it. I hope it all works out for him.

Charity Man

I kind of sort of hooked up with Charity Man last night. I hadn't been to the gym/sauna at the country club in a while, and decided to take Ronnie with me. While we were waiting for our massages, I noticed that Charity Man was there working out. I hadn't seen him in a really long time.

We talked. He flirted. We talked. I teased. He noticed I wasn't wearing my wedding ring, and asked about it. I just joked, "That never stopped you from wanting to fuck me before."

For those of you new to my diary, Charity Man is a guy who sits on a charity board with my ex-husband Chad. He and his wife also attend various charity functions that Chad and I would also attend. I've hooked up with him a few times over the last two years. Chad knew that I had sex with a man at the charity dinner… but I refused to tell him who the guy was; I kind of loved leaving Chad wondering.

Anyway… Charity Man and I agreed to meet up later that night. He got a hotel room, and I met him there. He had my panties off in two minutes, and we fucked. As we lay in bed afterwards, me gently rubbing his balls, he told me he was scheduled to play golf at a tournament on Saturday, and that he and his partner had been paired up with Chad. And a guy from San Diego.

#
Email to Emma

Chad granted me the courtesy of telling me the news, so at least I didn't have to find out from a stranger. I guess you finally got what you wanted.

I hope you're not expecting me to congratulate you. As far along as I am in my recovery program, I'm not quite there yet. I'm trying really hard not to hate you, but I can't help but feel like you've cruelly taken something from me. You'll deny it, I know, but you have. The hardest part is that deep down inside, I know I'm largely to blame for what's happened. And to think that I'm the one who introduced you to him.

It's Chad's life, though, and he can do whatever he wants. You'll be his third wife, so there's that. It's too bad you missed out on enjoying his company when he was younger. With the new baby coming along, you're probably not going to enjoy all the fun traveling and other activities he likes to do. Those were always my favorite times with him. But hey, you can always watch our

old travel videos; I know Chad still has them. Or if you do ever travel somewhere, I can babysit your little bastard, ha ha.

I sincerely hope you love him the way he deserves to be loved, and treat him well. Chad's a wonderful, kind, and loving man. He deserves the best.

Be well, Emma.

PussyBoy

I'm in the mood to bust some balls today... and I know there are balls out there that need busting.

I need to make me a new PussyBoy.

Email to Chad

Don't let it go to your head... but to be perfectly honest, my sex life has been kind of boring without you.

I've been with five different men since we separated, and it's been fun, but not as fun as it could have been.

I was with Charity Man the other night. Not a planned thing; I ran into him at the country club while I was there getting a massage with Ronnie. And we hooked up later.

Now that we're divorced, I feel like I should probably tell you who he is, but I don't want you to freak out about it.

Pretty much the whole time I was with him, though, I thought of you. I guess maybe because he knows who you are. In fact, he asked about you. I don't know if you remember but he's the guy I lied to; I told him you have a really big dick, and that you kind of hurt me with it. I got a kick out of telling him that, and watching his reaction. He's not much bigger than you are, and he thinks you're like this totally hung stud, ha ha.

I've been missing you. The sound of your voice.

I miss feeling your mouth between my legs in the morning, and waking me up that way. I miss fucking you with my strap-on. I miss the sweet PussyBoy sounds you used to make.

But you're engaged to be married to someone else now, so I probably shouldn't be writing this...

Thanksgiving

Tina and I basically had no place to celebrate Thanksgiving yesterday. We're in New York City until Sunday, shopping, sightseeing, and visiting with two of my girlfriends who live here. So, we ended up having dinner together at the W, which was really nice, elegant. This is such a beautiful hotel.

Afterwards we went for a walk... New York is great for walking... and went to a few bars. It was a little strange being in a bar and not drinking alcohol, and even stranger seemingly being the only one who wasn't drinking. But I love the atmosphere of a fun, lively bar. I'm pretty far along in my program, and didn't feel the least bit tempted, so that was good. And Tina was with me to make sure I was a good girl.

My Dom from ten years ago lives in Manhattan, and I was tempted to look him up, but decided not to. I did notice from Facebook that he's still the perpetual bachelor. No doubt he has a few hot little bitches on call to satisfy his voracious sex drive. I remember what that was like with him. :)

We're here until Sunday, then head back home. I've decided to move in with her for a while to give me more time to look for a place to buy. I love my Tina girl, she's such a good friend.

I told her about my... um... experience with the taxi cab driver. She laughed, and joked that my sex addict therapist (who I've been seeing for three months) is obviously incompetent, ha ha.

I need more dark meat tonight... getting banged in the backseat of a taxicab was exciting, but I need more than just a quickie tonight... and I fully intend to satisfy my craving.

Tina and I decided we're going to share a guy tonight. Now we just have to go out and meet him. Fortunately, there's an endless supply of good black dick in NYC, ha ha.

Email to Chad

I didn't want to contact you yesterday and interrupt whatever you had going on with your family. But I thought of you. I hope everything was pleasant and enjoyable.

On this day, especially, I am extremely grateful and thankful for everything you have done for me. For being there. For helping me. For being such a good, kind, and loving husband. I wish I could have been a better wife to you. I'm broken and flawed and you deserve much better. It kills me to say it, but I hope Emma can be the one for you, and bring you happiness.

I wish you love.

Flowers

I hadn't told my ex-husband Chad where Tina and I were staying... he knew we were in New York, but not which hotel... but somehow, he figured it out, and had flowers delivered to the room early this morning. Two vases of flowers, one for each of us.

On mine, the card read... "From a man who will always love you."

On Tina's, the card read... "Thank you for being a good friend to her."

Good boy!

Email to Chad

We're the limo, on our way to the airport.

It was a fun but short trip.

Quincy asked about you, wondering how you were. We talked about that trip the four of us took to Miami two years ago when we sailed to the Keys and you did your Jimmy Buffett impression, and had us all rolling on the floor.

Tina got ridiculously crazy last night. A bit of control, actually. But we had fun.

Thank you again for the flowers. That was very thoughtful of you. Good boy!

I have so many mixed feelings right now. I know you've been wanting to meet up for Tinder or something, but I'm not quite ready for that yet. My feelings are still too raw right now.

I need to focus on my program, get my move situated, get a car, and continue to perform at work. Andrew told me he'd consider me for promotion in February/March, so I'm kind of focused on that. I'm sure you can understand.

Ronald texted me that you guys are going to meet this week. Please be careful with him. Those biker guys, I'm not sure how much you can really trust them.

Chapter 19

Email from Chad

When I said I would do anything for you, I meant it, 22_. I wish I could somehow reverse events and get us back to a better time and place together.

Can we please meet sometime to talk?

Email to Chad

I'm curious what you think "a better time and place together" was?

I have my own ideas about that, but I'm not sure you'd agree with me.

As much as I want to, I don't think it's appropriate for you and I to meet up while another woman is carrying your child.

Solve your Emma problem. Then we can maybe talk.

Texts with Chad

Are you around? I just arrived back at my office and saw the package from you on my desk. And just opened it.

Oh, good. I'm glad you got it.

I didn't think you were serious about that.

Of course, I was serious. I'd love it if you washed them for me. By hand in the sink like you used to.

I'm not sure what to think about this.

You said you'd do anything for me, right?

Yes.

Well, my panties are filthy. And they need to be washed.

You're serious?

Of course. Besides, it'll give you a chance to do something nice for me.

If that's what you want, I'll do it. But I'd really like us to meet and talk 22_.

I know you would. But I'm not quite ready for that yet. I'm still kind of mad at you.

I suppose we both have a lot to be mad about. That's why we should talk. I can meet you tonight, where ever you want. I can leave the office whenever.

I'm serious about what I told you the other day. Solve your Emma problem, and then maybe we can meet. Are you any closer to that? You're running out of time. After three months it gets more difficult. She thinks you're going to marry her for God's sake!

She's agreed to terminate her pregnancy. We're going on Tuesday. She wants me to go with her.

Good. You should, to make sure she goes through with it. Maybe she'll code blue on the table.

I just want to get through this with as little complication as possible.

How are you going to handle her afterwards?

Give it about a week, and then just break up with her.

I think you should do something to make her break up with you. Something that will make her want to stay away for good.

Like what?

You could try heroin.

That's not funny 22. Don't even joke about that. I'm not going to inject her with drugs for God's sake. That's insane.

I don't mean her. I mean you. Not actually do it, but make her think you're using. Poke yourself with a fork or something to give you some marks. Let her find something in the bathroom. Get mad, pretend like you're shocked that she found out, accuse her of violating your privacy, and then confess. Cry. Make it real.

How about I just keep it simple and break up with her, tell her it's not going to work.

That's kind of boring. You should do something fun that she'll never forget. So, she'll never want to talk with you again.

I've had enough drama in my life this year, 22_. I just want out of this mess quietly with as little drama as possible.

My way would be more fun.

Your way is more likely to blow up in my face. Besides, I don't have your acting skills.

Going Shopping!

Ronnie and I are going Christmas shopping today, and have decided to have some naughty fun by wearing our Queen of Spades tattoos discreetly on our ankles, outside left leg. Looking forward to maybe getting ourselves in some trouble…

Email to Chad

I got your note that my panties are ready. Thank you for doing that for me!

Normally I'd want you to personally deliver them, of course, but due to present circumstances, please have them delivered by courier to my office in a nice, pretty, gift-wrapped box on Monday.

If you get done what you're supposed to get done this week with your fiancé, I'll agree to meet and have lunch with you on Friday. But I'm going to want to see the receipt to prove that the deed has been done.

With respect to how and when you break things off with Emma, I'll tell you on Friday how I want you to do that. Until then, keep things normal with her.

Talk soon.

Texts with Chad

I understand 22. I'll have them delivered to you first thing on Monday. I'll do it the way you like.

Good boy! Thank you.

Are you confident about Tuesday?

Yes. I think it will go as planned. She and I talked about it again yesterday.

I hope it does. The idea of Emma having your child is disgusting.

I know how you feel. I was thinking rather than us meeting for lunch on Friday, can we meet after work instead? I'd like to have more time to talk. We can get dinner.

I've agreed to meet with you, Chad, as you've been requesting, but I'm concerned about you getting your hopes up. This is not about us getting back together. Too much has happened. Us meeting is just to talk. So, I think a lunch would be more appropriate.

I miss you so much 22. I've made so many mistakes. I never thought I would lose you. I'm miserable without you.

We both made mistakes, sweetie. I'm certainly not without fault for what's happened.

I never meant to hurt you. I wish you could find it in your heart to forgive me.

I have forgiven you, but it still hurts. It doesn't just go away.

I know.

Things are different now. I'm hoping we can both move forward as friends. I don't ever want to lose that with you.

I don't want to just be friends with you, 22. You know that.

Well, we'll see. The future is full of possibilities. Did you want to keep our lunch on Friday?

Yes, absolutely.

Why don't you pick nice quiet place for us, so we can talk.

I will.

Good. I hope you're in the appropriate state of mind when we meet.

I'm not sure what you mean.

Oh, I think you do. And I hope you don't disappoint me.

Texts with Ronnie

I told Mr. Whites we'd be there at 8pm.

That works. Did you want to drive together?

Normally, yeah, but he wants me to spend the night with him, and since you can't, I'm going to need my car.

I'm jealous. I want to spend the night too!

You wish. But you have to be a good wife and go back to your husband afterwards. Besides, Mr. White's a freaking animal in the morning, and you're way too delicate, ha ha.

Email to Mr. Whites

If you were serious about Round 2 tonight... and I'm pretty sure you were... I can be there at 8pm if that works. And, if you like, I can bring my friend Ronnie with me. Let me know.

Email to Chad

I'm happy to hear that Emma is doing better. Pregnancy terminations don't always go as planned. I'm sorry that hers was difficult.

You need to keep things even with her, and not rock the boat until December 23rd. That's the day you're going to let her go. We'll talk about the details about how I want you to do it on Friday.

You did the right thing, and have nothing to feel guilty about. Don't let Emma drag you down into her own emotional morass. Be strong. Be a man about it.

Regarding our Friday lunch, I have certain expectations that you need to know about:

I expect you to be precisely on time, and on your best behavior. That means: polite, kind, and respectful.

If you whine or complain about anything, the lunch is over.

if you fail to follow my instructions in advance of our meeting, the lunch is over.

If you meet my expectations Friday, and don't disappoint me, I'll consider having lunch with you again next week.

Email from Chad (earlier today)

Emma's procedure is done, but with complications.

They did what they called a D&C, but then they had a 'situation' with her, and decided to admit her into the hospital. Nothing serious, it would appear,

mostly just for observation regarding the excess bleeding complication. She's also a mess emotionally, still. They even called in a mental health counselor for her to talk with.

Anyway, I'm here at the hospital with her now. Not sure for how long.

Email to Chad

I am, of course, devastated by the news. Emma is a bleeder. Who knew!

Email to Chad

You're going to get a delivery from me today at your office; a package, with a note inside. I expect you to follow my instructions.

Regarding Emma, I know she had given notice at her apartment a few weeks ago, and was planning to move into your house at the end of the month. I want you to accelerate that, and get her moved in this weekend. Pay who you need to, and do what you have to get that done.

Email to Marc

You made a comment to me one time, a long time ago, back when I first met you at the club, and I danced for you in the VIP room. You said that if you ever got inside my panties you were going to fuck the white off my pussy. You also said you were going to tear up and ruin it for white boys.

And so, I think we've had sex like maybe 20 or 30 times since then, and even though you always fuck me really good, I still have a white pussy, and it's not nearly as torn up and ruined as you promised it would be.

I can't help but feel that you have failed.

I can't help but feel that my nigga isn't doing his job.

You also told me one time that I had the prettiest pussy you've ever seen.

But I don't want to have a pretty pussy. I want to have a dirty little whore pussy. When I open my legs, and men see it, I want them to know just by looking at it that all the niggas in town have been hitting it. I want white

boys to be scared of it. I want them to be scared of putting their little dicks inside me.

Maybe next week when we hook up, you can finally do what you said you were going to do, and give me the kind of pussy I want.

Or maybe I need to find myself another nigga who will, ha ha.

Email to Chad

My dear sweet Chad,

I have to admit that I was skeptical about meeting you today. To be honest, I was worried about your expectations. But I thought our conversation went well. I'm trying to be totally honest with you about how I feel about everything.

I was pleased to see that you followed all of my instructions and were on your best behavior during our lunch. I missed seeing your handsome face! And thank you again for the beautiful flowers.

As I mentioned, I had not planned on any kind of physical interaction between us. I don't think that's appropriate right now. You are, after all, a man who's engaged to marry another woman. But you were such a good boy today, I felt like you deserved a little reward.

I hope you enjoyed the foot job under the table as much as I did, even though it was through your pants and not skin-to-skin. I could tell how hard your little penis was, though! Hopefully you weren't too embarrassed walking out of the cafe after cumming in your pants. I don't think anyone noticed.

I loved the foot massage you gave me under the table. I'll have to see about putting you on my schedule for more of those!

Finally, I appreciate your agreeing to follow my lead regarding Emma, and the process of ending things with her. I promised you several weeks ago that I would help you with that, and I intend to follow thorough. It's going to be a break up she's never going to forget.

Talk soon,

22.

Email to Chad

Okay… it honestly pains me to say this… but I want you to make this week the most beautiful and loving and caring and thoughtful week you've ever had with Emma. I'm sure her experience last week was very traumatic for her. You need to be there for her every day.

I want you to make sure she orgasms 3-4 times a day. That means every morning… your face between her legs. That means every day after work… your face between her legs. That means every night before bed… your face between her legs. Pour her a bath. Massage her feet. Pamper her.

And you need to get her flowers every day.

Last night with Marc

He got my email yesterday. Called me at 11pm, wanting pussy. I drove over to see him. He fucked me on the floor like an animal when I got there. Then he dragged me to his bed in the other room and fucked me again. We fell asleep. He woke me up at 4am, wanting pussy again. This time he had me ride him until he busted his nut inside me. We fell asleep. I woke him up with a blowjob around 8am. He flipped me over and took my ass using just spit for lube. Afterwards, we got up and took a shower together. I washed his cock and balls for him. He wanted another blowjob before I left.

I just got home… feeling tingly and beautiful all over…

Email to Emma

I'm forwarding this party invitation to you because it was accidentally sent to me. I guess just because I'm still on the list from last year. I'm sure Chad probably already mentioned the party to you, but I'm forwarding it just in case he didn't get it.

It's a dinner party type event for charity. Lots of people; lots of fun. Very fancy. A dress up affair. A lot of Chad's business friends and colleagues will be there. I'm sure he'll want to take you and introduce you around.

Have fun!

I know we haven't communicated in a while; lots of water under the bridge, obviously, but I hope things are going well for you and Chad. I'm doing well in my program; on my 9th step!

I know Chad will probably never tell you... he's not really emotional that way... but I know he's super excited to be a daddy again. I hope you and baby are doing well.

22.

Email to Marc

I woke up this morning feeling parts of my body that I didn't even know existed. I am sooooo sore all over.

I had a dream last night that I was captured by these two black guys who decided I was just a piece of fuck meat for them to use and abuse. They took turns fucking me like... I have no idea how many times. I feel asleep between them on the bed, and then in the morning they fucked me again.

So... yeah... thank you for my dream last night. You guys were awesome!!! And thank you for fucking the white off my pussy. It's all just black now, inside and out, and torn up the way it should be.

And your friend Creed, damn... you didn't' tell me I was going to be getting linebacker dick last night. He's huge! OMG! You were right about him, though. That nigga can fuck... like times three! Damn! I'm sorry I doubted you. The next time you want to give out my number to one of your friends, you don't need my permission first, ha ha.

I have a date with this white boy I've been dating on Wednesday. But I'm thinking I might have to cancel on him now, because I'm pretty sure my pussy is still going to taste like black dick. But then another part of me kind of wants him to find out.

I hope you have an awesome week!

22.

Email to Marvis

Thanks for responding. I don't know the exact date yet, but it will be sometime next week. I'll let you know. Thank you for doing this for me!

Email to Chad

You told me you were sincere about wanting to end things with Emma, and I promised to help you do that. You've done good so far, and now it's time for the final step.

This break up needs to be final and irrevocable, not one that drags on and on and on. And not one that leaves any room for some kind of later reconciliation.

I have something planned that I need you to cooperate with. I need to meet with you later this week to discuss the details and the logistics.

I need you to please email me Emma's work schedule, and yours next week. Be sure to let me know about any plans you have with her in the evenings, if any.

Does Thursday lunch work?

Email to Chad

Thank you for sending me your schedule, and Emma's.

I think Tuesday afternoon around 2pm is going to work best, so I need you to plan for that. I'll give you the details tomorrow at lunch.

Please meet me there at 11:45am. Get a table for us in the back room.

Please make sure you're in the appropriate mood, and on your best behavior. I don't expect that you will disappoint me.

If you're a good boy, maybe I'll give you another footjob under the table. Maybe I'll even touch it with my bare feet this time. Maybe.

Talk soon.

Email to Marc

So... I have a date with my white boy tonight... and I'm pretty sure my pussy still tastes like black dick, thanks to you and Creed.

Part of me is worried he's going to be able to tell, and another part of me wants him to know what a dirty little whore I am, ha ha.

I hope you have a great day!

22.

Email to Mr. Whites

The office party tomorrow starts at 6pm; we should get there at 6:30pm. Thank you for being my date! I have this great dress I'm going to wear for you. I think you're going to like it.

After the party, I'm yours all night... and the next morning, if you want.

I hope you have a great day!

22.

Holy shit!

Chad just called me. The charges against DaddyBigBull were dismissed today by the judge because of something the police messed up in the investigation. I think I'm just going to die.

Email to Chad

This news about DaddyBigBull is extremely upsetting to me. I'm frightened. We need to be very careful. He's capable of anything. I don't know for sure, but you need to assume he knows you were behind what happened.

I need time to process this.

I'm going to go ahead and change my cell number this morning.

At lunch today, we need to talk about what we're going to do. We need to be smart about this.

Meanwhile, we're going to have to put things off regarding Emma. You're going to have to stay with her at least through the holidays. This isn't the right time to rock the boat there. It really bothers me that you showed her some of those videos of me with DaddyBigBull. That was incredibly thoughtful of you.

See you soon.

22

Gone for a few days

Little bit of turmoil going on right now, with DaddyBigBull getting out of jail, but nothing Chad and I can't handle.

We've decided to go up to Santa Barbara for the weekend to talk about things in a more private setting. He told Emma he's going up to see friends.

I'll be away for a few days and probably write you Diary for a while. Or maybe I'll update while I'm up there.

I wasn't quite sure how things were going to go, but after Chad begged and pleaded with me to go up there with him for the weekend "just to talk, away from everything and everyone", I agreed.

It was nice... but... we both have different agendas, different wants/desires, and are pretty far apart regarding how we see our lives in a year or two or five. So, I'm not sure about much of anything.

We had a nice, quiet time, more as best friends than anything else. I insisted that we get two different rooms and not sleep together. He didn't like that, but went along with it. I was also determined that there be no sexual activity between us... I don't really need the confusion of that right now. And so, there wasn't.

Chad promised me he'd "handle" DaddyBigBull; but how, I have no idea. His last plan pretty much fell apart, although I don't really blame him for that. At least he tried. I know he was sincere in his efforts to get DaddyBigBull out of my life.

What I don't know, that I really wish I knew, is what DaddyBigBull knows. I have no clue. I don't know if he blames my husband or not; or if he is totally clueless about how and why he got arrested. I'm afraid of him and wish he would just disappear.

As far as Emma is concerned, I'm kind of starting to lose interest with whatever happens to her. Before I found out that DaddyBigBull got out of prison, I was focused on "getting" Emma. Now, I feel like DaddyBigBull is the more serious risk as far as my future is concerned.

I told Chad yesterday... basically... "do whatever you want, break up with her, stay with her, marry her, whatever, I don't really care, it's your life."

Why is life always so complicated?

Email to Chad

I tried calling you, but you're not picking up!!

I just now noticed all your messages, and that you've been trying to get ahold of me. I'm sorry. I've had my phone off since around 6pm last night. We had our Christmas party at work, and then I spent the night with a friend. I'm sorry. I didn't mean to worry you.

I kind of told my friend about the situation... not the details... just that one of my ex-boyfriends got out of prison, and that I'm frightened because he's upset with me.

I'm going to stay here at least a few more nights. My friend has offered to let me stay here as long as I want. Don't worry. He'll keep me safe.

DaddyBigBull has no way of knowing where I work, so I'm not too worried about that. And he doesn't know who Tina is. I'm more worried about you. DaddyBigBull obviously knows your name, and where you work and live.

Thank you for the offer regarding the security men. I think that's a good idea. Have them call me on my new number, and I'll meet with them.

I can't really meet you for lunch today. We have this project at work, and have meetings through lunch. But I can get off early around 3pm and meet you then. Just let me know where.

Talk soon.

Email to Chad

While I appreciate your concern last night, and know your intentions are good, I don't appreciate being stalked. Please don't turn into one of those men. It's beneath you. Honestly, it's kind of pathetic.

The guy I met up with last night is just a fuck date. That's all.

Please don't follow me again. It's weird and it scares me.

I don't need you to protect me. I'm strong enough to protect myself. Believe me, I know how important it is for me to stay off drugs. I'm motivated and focused. I know that my life depends on it.

Go back to your fat bitch. She's probably hungry again. Stay with her, break up with her, or whatever. I don't really care.

Email to Chad

I'm sorry I keep pushing you away. I do that when I'm scared. That, or I run away. I don't want to be hurt again. I can't survive that right now. I'm sorry.

Low Key Afternoon

I spent last evening (Christmas eve) with Tina and Ronnie and a few other friends who came over. It was a girl's night thing.

Chad called me early this morning to wish me Merry Christmas; wanted to see me today, but I declined. He admitted to me that he hasn't broken up with Emma yet, that he didn't want to do that to her the day before Christmas; so, she's still there. He said he's going to tell her on Saturday.

I just got home a bit ago. Spent a few hours visiting with Tinder Man this afternoon. That was very, very nice! It was very low key, we talked, watched a movie, we made out for a while, he gave me a shoulder massage, and a foot massage. Then I asked him to take off his shirt, and I gave him a back massage. He wanted more, but I politely demurred. Like a gentleman, he kept his penis in his pants. Good boy!

As he walked me to my car, he asked me what I was doing for New Year's Night; I told him I didn't really have any plans. He said, *"Yes you do. With me."* He explained that a friend of his in-Laguna Beach has a catered party bash every year with a bon fire and fireworks, and he invited me to go as his date. So... yeah... I'm really starting to like this man, ha ha.

Drama at Chad's house

Chad finally told her. I just got several text messages from him. He and Emma have been arguing/fighting all morning. He said she was in a rage, threw a Tinder cup at him, and locked herself in the bedroom.

Email to Chad

I'm sorry I wasn't able to respond to your flurry of text messages last night. I was out with a friend, and he always makes me turn my phone off when I'm with him.

I'm sorry about the drama you're going through with Emma. I always thought that extricating yourself from that situation was going to be a little messy.

You can't just get a fat girl pregnant, leave your wife for her, have her move in with you, manipulate her into getting an abortion when she's already three months pregnant, and then dump her right after Christmas... and not expect some drama.

At least she only threw a Tinder cup at you! You're lucky she hasn't burned your house down.

That's strange to me that she just went to work this morning. Don't you think?

My recommendation: While she's at work today, you need to have all of her clothes and other stuff removed from the house and put in all storage. Pay for a month in advance. Then you need to notify the guards not to let her past the gate (tip them well to make sure they don't fuck that up), and immediately change the garage door codes and the locks to the house. Since she gave up her apartment to move in with you, and has no place to go, you need to get her a motel room and at least pay for the first week. I'm thinking a nice gritty Motel 6 off the freeway should work. Then have the key cards to the storage unit and the motel room delivered to her at work.

If you need any further advice about anything, please let me know, ha ha.

Email to Emma

I heard about the drama yesterday, and your nasty little tantrums. I'm so sorry you're going through that. I'm not sure, but maybe he's upset because you killed his baby. Can you spell "Motel 6"?

Email to Emma

Chad just told me that he took the car away from you today, and left you stranded at work. You know... the car that was never yours. I swear, I have no idea why he's being so mean to you. He was going to marry you, wasn't he? You don't think that was just a pre-abortion thing, do you?

Have you ever heard of Uber? I'm pretty sure they'll pick you up at Motel 6 to take you to work tomorrow.

Warmest personal regards,

22.

Texts with Chad

Emma is blowing up my phone still. She said you've sent her a couple of emails, and she's really pissed off.

So, turn off your phone. Or block her.

That will only make things worse. I don't want her calling my office.

So, what do you want from me?

Can you please just leave that alone.

I suppose I could, but I don't want to.

Please 22. There's no need to antagonize her any more than is necessary. She knows a lot of things about us.

Whatever. I don't care. I'm not afraid of her. And there is no "us" anymore, Chad.

Please. You don't need to do this. You've won. You don't need to rub her face in it.

But that's the best part of revenge. That's how this bitch rolls.

She can do a lot of damage with what she knows. Please. Let it go.

I'm kind of busy right now, Chad. We can talk more tomorrow if you want.

Please promise me you'll stop antagonizing her.

Is she still alive?

What does that mean?

I have to go. Good night, Chad.

Email to Emma

I was at Chad's house early this morning... we had Tinder... and he showed me the intake and discharge report and the receipt for your abortion. He said he found them in an envelope in one of the dresser drawers underneath some of your sweaters. Chad was just going to throw them away, but I'm sure you probably need these important documents for your memories.

I wanted to mail them to you, but I wasn't sure what your permanent address was going to be. Mailing them to you at the motel where you're staying seemed kind of crass. And then I remembered that church you took me to a few times, the one where you said you knew the priest. I think you said his name was Father Paul, if I remember right. Is it okay if I mail them to you there? I'm sure he'll get them to you.

Please me know.

Warmest personal regards,

22.

Email to Chad

I think you deserve a reward for what you've been through this week.

I'd like to drop by tonight to give you something.

Please let me know if 8pm works.

Email to Chad

I'm very proud of you. I know this wasn't an easy week, but you did what had to be done.

I can't help but think that if your little dick had been locked up as consistently as it should have before, you never would have gotten yourself into such a mess. I blame myself for that. I'm sorry I wasn't the kind of wife that I should have been to you. Obviously, I'm sorry for a thousand other things too.

Last night with you was very special for me. I really missed sharing that with you.

I don't know what the future holds for me, or you, or possibly "us", but I've learned a lot from what we've both been through this past year. I'm sure we both have.

I hope your 2016 is amazing! You deserve it.

Happy New Year!

PS: I have a date tonight, but I'd love to have brunch with you on Saturday, if you're up for it.

My Pussyboy:

I went over, and we talked. We were both kind of nervous. He knew better than to try to touch me without permission, and didn't try. Eventually he kissed me. He was very emotional.

I kind of mothered him in a way. Held him, and gently teased him if he had missed "mommy". I removed my top and let him suckle on my breasts and eventually nudged his face down between my legs. I let him take in my scent for a while before I allowed him to do anything else. Then I spread my legs and invited him to pleasure me with his mouth and tongue until he gave me an orgasm.

We eventually made our way in the guest room, where he made love to me (with a condom). Afterward he ejaculated (it didn't take him very long), I removed the condom, tied it around his nuts, and had him turn over for me. And then I gently and lovingly prepared him for my strap-on. I penetrated him slowly and carefully at first. It had been a long time, and was uncomfortable for him at first. It almost felt like I was taking his cherry all over again. Then after a while I picked up the pace and started fucking him harder and deeper... the way I missed fucking him. I used one of the smaller and perfectly smooth dildos; it's only about six inches long, and not very thick. I had earlier decided that I would wait until another time to use one of my Bad Dragon dildos on him, and make him take the knot for me.

Afterwards we took a shower together and then we fell asleep until morning.

It was quite a beautiful evening, actually.

Email to Chad

That was nice last night. I hope you enjoyed that as much as I did. I missed doing that with you.

Chapter 20

Email to Chad

I got home really late last night from a date with this guy I've been seeing. And my pussy was filthy.

I miss the way you used to go down on me and clean me up after I was with another man. I really miss experiencing that with you. You were always so good at that.

If I had called you up late last night on my way home wanting to come over, would you have turned me down?

Email to Creed

Okay... so I was writing something in my diary this morning, and I couldn't help but read back a little to the night I first met you, when Marc introduced me to you.

I hope you don't mind that I've given you a special nickname in my diary.

Since that night, my diary reveals that we've hooked up seven times, not including the four times you've driven to my work during the noon hour and I've given you head in the car outside in the parking lot.

Why have you been ignoring me!

Creed isn't the most attractive man in the world... he's a former linebacker for UCLA, and is a really huge guy, like 6-6 and 260... but in bed he's the bomb. That boy can fuck! And he cums like a firehose.

Email to Marc

I got your note about the birthday party for your cousin next week. I'd love to dance for you guys! I haven't actually danced in a while, though, so I might have to practice a little before.

But I don't want to be the only girl there! I'd like to bring Ronnie. I'm sure she'd love to go. She's never danced, but she's always a lot of fun.

Email to Creed

I bought another box of condoms for you today, just your size. But some other nigga borrowed one a little while ago. Hope that's not a problem, ha ha.

Hope you're having a good night.

Email to Marc

So, as far as tonight is concerned, I was thinking about maybe doing something different.

There's a movie I'd really like to see. Let's go do that instead. And then afterwards, your choice.

Call me in a while.

22.

Email to Chad

I'm sorry about tonight; that I can't make it. You need to please give me more notice than that. I'm sorry that I already had other plans.

But I was thinking, if you're up for it, maybe we could go for a run together tomorrow morning near your house. And maybe a swim after?

I'd like that.

Let me know…

Email to Chad

You've been such a sweet and wonderful guy lately, kind and strong and supportive, and I appreciate that. I know you've been wanting to get back together, which I've been resisting, because I'm just in a very different place now.

I don't want to make any promises to you that I can't keep, and so I've been taking things slow and just kind of experiencing things day by day.

From your perspective, I'm sure you probably just see me as wavering and inconsistent.

I want to have fun with you, and share life with you, but I don't want to be hurt again. And I don't want to hurt you again. We've both been through enough.

I had a vision last night of a possible future you and I might have together, that I wanted to share with you and discuss.

I'd like to drop by tonight. I can be there early, about 630, and make dinner for us, if you'd like.

I need you to please have an open mind tonight about my proposal.

Please let me know if tonight works.

22

Email to Chad

I thought our conversation went well last night; I hope you feel the same, but I'm not actually sure. I felt like you were giving me a lot of mixed signals.

I know it wasn't everything you wanted to hear, but I felt I needed to be totally honest with you about everything.

I don't want you to communicate with me for ten days, until next Sunday. During that time, I want you to really think seriously about what we discussed. If you agree with my proposal, and you're ready, or if it's something you don't think you want or can do, you can let me know then. But not before.

I hope you have a great week!

Nervous

I'm starting to get a little nervous about the party tomorrow night. It's been a long time since I've danced for men at a party like that. I know what they're all going to want and expect. Ronnie, on the other hand, is chomping at the bit because she's never been with more than two men at a time.

#

Texts with Ronnie

I just got off the phone with Marc regarding the party Friday. I hope you're ready girl, ha ha.

I'm totally ready!

Good! Party starts at 8pm; Marc wants us there at 830. He just texted me the hotel suite. It's going to be at the Island. I got us a room for after.

So, the plan is??

Dance, mess around with the birthday boy, take care of him.

And the other guys?

Of course! If they're hot.

How many guys?

He said about 12, if everyone shows up.

What are you going to wear?

Short red cocktail dress, black lace bra, g-string, black heels.

You?

Not sure yet.

Drive together?

Yes. Can you pick me up?

Sure. Does Tina know?

Yes. I invited her, but you know how she is about black guys.

She's still never?

No. Can you believe it. In all this time.

How did it go with Chad yesterday?

Not sure yet. I was pretty honest and direct with him about what I had in mind. Not sure he's going to be interested. He cried again... UHHHHHH!!!

Well, that's your PussyBoy, lol. You broke him.

I know. When he cries I just want to smack him!

You got your claws in him deep. I'm sure he'll go for it.

Maybe. I hope so. It would be fun. We'll see.

And Tinder Man?

He travels so much, it sucks. He's gone off again to who knows where.

When's he back?

Don't know. He emailed me yesterday to say he was okay, but that's about it. I'm going to send him a naughty email reply maybe tomorrow.

Send him pictures from the party Friday.

I wish. Don't want to scare him away.

Have you decided on a house yet?

I have it narrowed down to four. I'm going to think about it and go see them all again this weekend. You're still coming with me, right?

Yes. I like the one with that travertine entry and the fountain. And it's on the cove.

It's a little over my budget, though. I'd have to get Chad to help me cover it.

He'll do it.

Probably. We'll see.

Confession

I've never been involved in a gang-bang before... when I wasn't the only girl there, and when I was totally, 100% sober.

I'm getting extremely anxious and nervous about tonight. Right now, for me, the struggle is not how many men are going to be at the party, or what's going to happen sexually to Ronnie and I... it's walking into that room without taking something first, alcohol or drugs, to get me in the right frame of mind, to calm me down, to numb me to where I'm kind of floating and have absolutely no inhibitions.

I want to do this. I'm excited, and looking forward to it. But still kind of anxious.

Countdown...

I'm Happy. Drug Free. Feeling Powerful. And Super-Horny Excited.

I'm going to dance sexy nasty for the niggas, tease them, show them my creamy white tits, get their big black dicks hard, let them touch the pussy, work them into a mad frenzy... and get myself thoroughly FUCKED tonight!!!

I deserve it. It's been too long...

The Island Fuckery

Still at the hotel. In bed. Exhausted. Recovering.

Ronnie's in the shower right now. Her pussy was destroyed last night. They all fucked her. Every one of them. I've never seen her that way. She was totally off the hook. Slutty white bitch in heat.

I've never done a party like this sober before. Wasn't sure if I could. I was so nervous! But actually, it was even more intense and... amazing that way. All of my senses... sight, hearing, smell, taste, touch... were on fire. And unlike the other times, this time, I remember every single detail.

I'm sore, no matter which way I move. My jaw and tongue feel like they're just going to fall off. I've never sucked that much cock in my life. And my ass. OMG! At some point last night I heard Marc tell someone that I liked it

in the asshole. Four of them had me that way... until I couldn't take it anymore.

I'm feeling free and happy and beautiful this morning. I really needed that. I really, really needed that.

More later...

Back Home

... soaking in the tub. Yes!!

Email to Marc

Thank you for the other night. It was awesome! We couldn't have done it without you being there to make sure we were safe.

I love the way you share me with your friends, and don't get jealous or possessive. I love being your dirty girl.

PS: Ronnie wants to know when the next party is. I told her I'm sure our Pimp Daddy would let us know, ha ha.

Ronnie

The party Friday night was Ronnie's first gang-bang. She'd never been with more than two men at once before.

I've been involved in a few... more than just a few, actually... but I've never been totally sober during it. I've always been either high on H or E, or very, very drunk. I never thought I could do it if I wasn't high and kind of zoned out. But actually, being totally sober made it even more intense and amazing. And unlike many of the other times, this time I can remember every detail of what happened.

Ronnie spent a good part of the afternoon yesterday at home in bed with a bag of frozen peas between her legs, ha ha. They totally destroyed her pussy.

I had sex with five of the guys at the party, including Marc, but all eleven of them fucked Ronnie; for about three hours non-stop. It was like one after the other kept mounting her.

I was actually more the fluffer girl at the party.

At one point the guys dragged one of the mattresses to the balcony, picked up and carried Ronnie outside, and fucked her out there.

She had the time of her life, though.

Her husband Sam gets back into town tomorrow. I call him the Clueless Cuckold… because he still has no idea that Ronnie fucks other men.

Ronnie would love to be a hotwife for him, and play openly, but she's scared to come out and ask him. She's tried to kind of broach the subject a few times, using me as an example (Sam knew that my then-husband Chad was a cuckold, and that I occasionally had sex other men), but it's never worked. He immediately shut her down and insulted my virtue. Bastard!

Lisp?

So… is it possible to develop a lisp from sucking too much cock? Because I swear, for the last several days, since Friday night, people keep asking me if I got my tongue pierced or something!

Business Trip

I'll be in Washington DC next week for three days. Looking to get nasty with a local boy or two who meets my criteria. Handsome. Athletic. Strong. Dominant. Black. Nicely hung. Can fuck all night, with a three-nut minimum. Cuz I don't fuck no slackers!

Decision Time

So… tomorrow is the day; Chad's day to decide.

The last time we spoke, we discussed the parameters of what might be.

I explained that I wasn't really interested in getting back together with him in the traditional sense, as a married couple, but that I did care for him, and wanted to occasionally see and spend time with him, and share experiences.

I told him that I loved my new freedom, that I might possibly relocate at some point later this year to Miami, and that I was wanted to fully explore my relationship options with other men.

I told him that despite my attraction to dominant black men, that I also enjoyed having a submissive PussyBoy in my life, and that he was free to apply for the position.

I told him I didn't really want to live with him, or any other man; that I wanted to have my own place.

When he asked if there was a possibility that down the road we might be a couple again, married and living together as we were before (which is what he clearly wants), I told him anything was possible, but that I couldn't make him any promises.

He asked me what I meant by "applying for the PussyBoy position".

I explained that it meant exactly that, applying for it. I also told him I fully expected that at some point I might meet another man interested in the position.

I then told him of my interest in what I call FemDom Dating; which I envision as a variation of traditional dating, but one where the woman both intellectually and sexually asserts herself from the very beginning, and makes it clear to him what her expectations are.

In FemDom Dating, the man would find out very early that the woman's pleasure and orgasm is primary, and that sexual activity isn't always going to involve his penis. He'd be expected to master his oral skills, for example, before she would ever touch his penis. And strap-on penetration of the male would likely be introduced long before regular intercourse with the female.

In addition, in a FemDom Dating relationship, enforced male chastity would likely be introduced very early in order to help him focus his efforts on her.

I told Chad that he obviously had an advantage over other possible applicants because I knew him, I knew what he was capable of, and he had plenty of experience as a PussyBoy.

He asked me to clarify what my expectations would be.

I told him they were really very simple: "I want to have fun. I want to be cherished and adored. And I expect your loyalty and obedience."

The conversation then turned to sucking cock and anal penetration.

He told me that he didn't enjoy doing that with other men, that it was extremely humiliating for him, made him feel like less of a man, and wondered if that could be excluded.

I told him I was surprised he would ask me that question.

I said, "I think you already know what I expect in that regard. I know what a good little cocksucker you are, and what a sweet tight ass you have. I love watching that. It totally turns me on. To me, that's like the ultimate form of submission for a PussyBoy. If you still have a problem with that, it makes me think that perhaps you're not really interested in or right for the position."

At that point he got very quiet, looked down at the floor, and started fidgeting with the keys in his pocket.

After watching him equivocate like that for a few moments I told him, "Well sweetie, it sounds like you have something to think about. I don't want you going into this halfway. You're either in or not. I know plenty of other men who would give up their balls for the position. I want you to really think about it, and decide if this is really what you want."

I then asked him not to communicate with me for 10 days, and let me know (tomorrow Sunday) what his decision was.

So, we'll see what he decides.

He just called me...

Chad just called me; we spoke for a few minutes.

He asked me to dinner tonight. Except he didn't phrase it that way. What he said was, "If you don't have any other plans, I'd like to take you to dinner tonight." My response, "I do have other plans, but I'll cancel them."

So, we're meeting up tonight at 7pm. He's picking me up.

I don't yet know for sure, but something in the tone of his voice, a certain quiet deference, tells me that PussyBoy is coming back home to mommy...

Email to Creed

Sorry for the last-minute notice, but something came up that I need to deal with.

Can we hook up tomorrow night instead? Or Tuesday?

PussyBoy is Back

He made his decision and informed me last night at dinner.

Email to Chad

Good morning, my sweet!

I set up an appointment for you Saturday morning at the salon, the same one I've taken you to before. It's at 10am.

If you're going to be my PussyBoy, I want you nice and smooth below the waist, including your feet.

Then afterwards, we're going shopping, and having lunch together. Tina is going to meet us at the mall.

Obviously, I'm going to need you to cancel your golf game.

Talk soon.

Email to Chad

One of the things I really miss with you...

... the beautiful way you'd always wake me up in the morning, with your handsome face between my legs, the way you'd feast on the pussy, make me cum, and then gently turn me over and eat out my ass.

You're so good at that!

I wish we lived closer. You could be doing that for me right now...

Creed just left...

That's what I love about Creed. There's no pretension. No conversation. No frustration. No consternation. No complication.

Just massive cock inflation, hip gyration, glistening perspiration, hammer-time stimulation, pussy dislocation, anal violation, mild strangulation, incredible sensation, sweet exhilaration, and orgasmic transportation.

He just comes by, we go into the bedroom, and we get to fucking. He gets hard, stays hard, tears up the pussy, and is always good for three nuts. That's why he's my favorite Bull now.

Email to Chad

So, I ran into somebody you know today at lunch. I was at K Grill with some people from work, when he walked over, introduced himself, and asked me how I was doing. And then he pretty much hit on me, and asked me if I liked to sail.

So, is your lawyer always like that? Isn't that unethical or something?

Email to Chad

You were such a good PussyBoy yesterday, I'm very proud of you! You met every one of my expectations. Even Tina was impressed. I think we're going to have a lot of fun together.

As I mentioned, I have something very special planned for you next weekend. Something old, something new, something borrowed, and something blue...

I have a date tonight, and I was thinking of dropping by your house afterwards. And if it's okay, I'd like to spend the night. Maybe we can go for an early run together. What do you think?

Text messages with Chad

I received your email. That would be great about tonight. Do you know about what time?

Not sure. Probably late, around midnight. Is that okay? I can text you when I'm on the way.

Sure. I'd love to see you.

I'm going to want you to clean me up.

I know.

Are you ready to start doing that for me again?

Yes.

No matter who I've been with?

Yes.

Good sissy boy!

Email to Chad

I can't help but feel that you deserve to be punished for all that went on between you and Emma.

You betrayed my trust, took advantage of me while I was vulnerable, and let your pathetic little dick get yourself in a mess. Your actions hurt me deeply, made me lose trust in you, and caused a lot of damage to our relationship.

Tina thinks I should just cut off your balls. Like, literally cut them off. Have them removed. Gone. She doesn't think you'll even miss them much.

Ronnie thinks that's way too harsh. She argues in favor of some kind of behavior modification counseling or therapy.

Personally, I think you need to get the belt. I was always struck by how effective physical discipline was with you. You having such a very low pain threshold is part of it, but I think it's mostly due to the way you were spanked and whipped as a child by your mother and your aunt.

At any rate, we need to have a conversation about this.

Email to Chad

I'm a little disappointed that you still haven't got back to me regarding the house, and whether you're going to help me get it.

I promised my agent I would get back to her by 4 PM today. The sellers are sitting on another offer which expires at 5pm.

I'd really like to get this house. It's the perfect size, great views, with beach access, and is within walking distance to yours. I also think it's a great investment.

If you could please let me know by noon today, I'd appreciate it. Thank you.

Chapter 21

I communicate with Dana every now and then. She's doing good.

Marco barely even talks to me anymore. He's never forgiven me for my relapse last summer and the way I treated him.

Letting Marco loose on Dana like that was probably a mistake. I kind of messed things up there. I should have realized that wasn't going to turn out well. Chad was very hurt by that.

Email to Chad

You need to check out Dana's Facebook page. She posted some photos last week from a birthday party she went to for one of her friends. There's a bunch of people in the pictures, but look closely at the second photo. Look at the tall black guy standing next to her, and notice where his hand is, on the front of her leg. It's very subtle. There's no way she'd let him touch her there, in that way, if they're weren't intimate. He's totally fucking her, I'm sure of it!!!

Email to Chad

I KNEW Dana was going to go "back to black" after experiencing sex with Marco. I knew it!!! I'm so proud of her...

Email to Dana

How have you been? I saw your post on Facebook today about your friend's birthday party last weekend, and couldn't help but notice you standing next to Mr. Gorgeous! Who is he? Are you dating him?

Frustrated

I'm feel so frustrated right now. Sad. Afraid. Trapped. Lost. Didn't get the house I wanted. Still driving my old crappy car cuz I can't make a decision.

I can't sleep. Have a million things to do at work. Business trip to Chicago next week with my boss Andrew and two other employees. There's this scheming bitch at work who hates me and is trying to get me fired. She's a fucking cunt! Had to go meet with HR last week. Message: need to improve my impulse control, be more considerate of others.

Whatever. I don't even need this stupid job.

Heroin is calling out to me, it's out there, in the wind, singing about the good life, telling me I'm beautiful. And wanted.

No! No! No! No! No! No! No!

Ronnie got caught...

Drama at Ronnie's house late last night.

She got home late; had told her husband Sam she having dinner with a woman she works with. But she wasn't. She was with some guy, one of the guys from the party that she's been hooking up with.

Sam was waiting up for her, in a rage. Apparently, he had gone through her gym bag a few weeks ago and found some condoms.

They got into this huge argument. She admitted she had been seeing other men. And basically... Sam beat the shit out of her.

She's on her way over now...

Sam, the Dickless Wonder

Finding out that his wife has been cheating on him may be humiliating for a man, but it does NOT give him the right to beat her. This isn't fucking Pakistan!

Super Bowl Party Bust

Ronnie and I were invited to a party at Mr. White's house, but obviously won't be attending due to recent events. We're okay, though. We're just going to hang out here with each other. Party time can wait…

Ronnie and Sam

She decided to get him served with a restraining order today, and have him removed from the house.

I just got off the phone with her.

Apparently when the sheriff's department showed up at his house to serve him with the papers, he got in an argument with them, and ended up getting arrested.

Oh boy! Here we go…

Tinder Crazy

OK, so I guess I must be the last woman on earth to have discovered Tinder.

OMG!!!

There's like 10,000 Black Bulls to choose from within about a 50-mile radius! And they're all looking for white pussy…

Email to Chad

Looks like I'll be there about 9:30 PM.

I hope you're ready for me, PussyBoy. It's Bad Dragon Dildo Night…

Ronnie & Sam

Unfortunately, things are getting even more complicated between them.

Sam has been charged with felony battery on a police officer because he was drunk and apparently got into a fight with the sheriff deputy who was trying to serve him with the restraining order that Ronnie filed. So now he could like go to prison or something!

And it looks like his employer is probably going to fire him. He works as a manager for some defense contractor who suspended his security clearance and put him on unpaid leave.

Ronnie is feeling really bad about this whole thing, feeling sorry for him, and is thinking about dropping the restraining order against him.

Uhhhhh!!

Email to Chad

I had such a great time with you last night. I loved the flowers, and really especially appreciate how thoughtful you were, and the way you so openly shared your feelings with me. I know that's hard for you sometimes.

I don't know what the future holds for us... if you'll eventually meet and marry someone else, or if I will... but one thing I do know, I want you to be part of my life. I'm not ever going to let you go again. You're going to be my PussyBoy forever!!

I'm thinking that every Monday night should be Bad Dragon night for you. But next time, you're taking the knot for me, boy.

And sometime soon, you're going to need to remind me what a good little cocksucker you are...

22

Tinder Bull

I'm going to meet up with my first Tinder Bull tonight. We chatted for a while, exchanged pics, and talked on the phone.

He's actually from out of town, but here on business for a few days. We'll see how it goes. I'm going to wear something special for him...

Email to my Tinder Bull No. 1

Thank you for popping my Tinder Cherry last night. Does your cock always taste that good? I miss it already...

Email to Marc

Thank you for agreeing to be the go-between on Saturday.

Ronnie's husband Sam is allowed to go by the house to get his clothes and personal things. There will be a police officer there just to make sure there isn't any trouble. Your job is just to make sure that Sam only takes the boxes with his name on them in the garage.

You're a sweetheart for doing this for her. I appreciate it.

My First Tinder Bull

Psychologists say that when a woman first meets a man, she decides within twelve seconds if she's going to have sex with him.

Last night, after meeting Nate, it only took me about five.

We met in the bar of the hotel room he was staying at near the airport. He was every bit as gorgeous as I thought and was hoping he'd be.

About 20 minutes later, he had me upstairs in his room down on my knees with his cock in my mouth, joking with me, "Is that what you came up here for, baby?"

He wasn't shy about the fucking part either. Oh yes! Pussy got torn up last night.

I was with him for about two hours. In the elevator afterwards, my legs still kind of shaking, I was like, "Did that just happen?"

He kept my panties as a souvenir.

I think I'm going to like this Tinder thing!

Tinder Bulls

Just when I thought I was out, they pull me back in!

Three more giant cocked African Bulls contacted me on Tinder this afternoon wanting pussy this weekend!

I don't see how I could possibly refuse them, ha ha.

Email to Chad

I've been thinking about things, and I realize that I need to apologize to you for something. I promised my therapist that I would reach out to you about this, and I'm keeping my promise.

A long time ago, when I was spending a lot of time with Marco, back when I was making you suck his cock, and we were all in the bedroom together, and he flipped you over and fucked you that night, the first time, I realize now that he basically raped you. It wasn't consensual, you weren't expecting it, and you resisted, you were looking to me for protection, but he held you down, made you take it, and I encouraged him.

And to be perfectly honest, I did more than just encourage him, I had told him ahead of time that I wanted to watch him fuck you. Obviously, he did it because I asked him to. Marco asked me the day before what he should do if you resisted, and I basically told him to fuck you anyway.

I wanted you to experience what it was like to be forcefully fucked, to be turned out, and feel what it was like to be a man's bitch. I wanted you to experience that not just physically, but psychologically. I want to Marco to break you down and take your masculinity. You were already sucking his cock at the time, and I thought it was only natural to take you to the next step.

Anyway, I realize now that it was wrong of me to do that. I got lost in the fantasy and wasn't thinking about the consequences.

I remember how aggressive Marco that night, how painful it was for you, and how you were screaming out, trying to make him stop.

I remember how emotionally traumatized you were afterwards, the way you curled up into a ball on the bed and sobbed and cried while I held and comforted you.

I also remember how you barely even talked to me for almost a week.

Looking back on the situation now, I realize that I should've handled it differently. I should've talked to you about it first. And most importantly, I should have made sure you consented and were okay with it. And when you resisted, and tried to get Marco to stop, I should not have told Marco to just keep fucking you.

It was very wrong of me to do that, and I'm sorry.

I know a lot has happened in our lives and between us since then, but I wanted you to know how sorry I am for what I did. And for what Marco did.

I hope you can forgive me. I never meant to hurt you.

22.

Email from Chad

I absolutely and unconditionally accept your apology, and forgive you.

I know that I have at various times sent you mixed signals about a lot of things. I don't blame you in the least for my failures to clearly communicate. The fault lies with me, not you.

All I have ever wanted to be, is your husband. All I have ever wanted to do, is love you. I realize that my own failures are what caused you to decide that you didn't want to be married to me. I was disloyal and failed you in so many ways.

I can't imagine my life without you. I never want to even contemplate that. Whether you choose to spend an hour a week with me, or a day, or a night, or seven days, I am grateful for whatever amount of time you deem appropriate, and whatever time you are comfortable with.

I want to reiterate to you my offer that Ronnie is welcome to stay at the house, or in the pool house if she prefers, for as long as she wants. I am desperately sorry for what has happened between her and Sam.

I love you.

Email to Sam

I'm very sorry about what's happened. Obviously, Ronnie has kept me informed.

Because of the restraining order she took out against you, Ronnie isn't allowed to contact you directly, so she's asked me to reach out to see if you'd be willing to meet with me to talk about how you guys might possibly resolve things. You don't have to, it's just an offer.

I know I haven't always been your favorite person, but I'm sincerely motivated to help Ronnie with this situation. I know she really loves you and is very sorry about what's happened. She's in pain right now, as I'm sure you are also. Please know that she never meant to hurt you, and doesn't want you to be prosecuted or go to jail.

You did a horrific thing, the way you violently beat her, but I also know that we all have our breaking points, and are all capable of extreme and uncharacteristic behavior in certain circumstances. I don't judge you Sam. My only motivation is to help.

Please contact me if you'd be agreeable to meet and talk.

Email to Marc

Let me know how the property pick up goes today. I really appreciate you doing this for Ronnie.

Remember, Sam is only allowed to take the boxes in the garage with his name on them. He's not allowed to go in the house. The police will be there to "escort" him, so there won't be any trouble. They will have a copy of the court order.

I want you to look and act like you just got done fucking his wife; like your kind of annoyed for being interrupted; like she's upstairs in the bedroom

waiting for more. That's why I'd like you to be barefoot, and shirtless, wearing just a pair of shorts or something, so he can see the outline of that big cock of yours. But be casual about it. Don't say anything. You won't need to.

Talk soon.

Email from Sam

22,

I'll agree to meet with you. Of course. Please tell Rach I'm very sorry for what I did. I was drunk and lost control of my emotions. That will never, EVER happen again. Tell her I promise. I'm willing to do counseling or whatever else she wants. ANYTHING!!

I can't believe what's happening. This whole arrest thing. The cop started the fight. He punched me in the gut. I was just defending myself.

I don't know what I'm going to do. They already fired me at work, and my lawyer told me I can actually go to prison for this. Anything you can to do to help with this situation, I'd be grateful for.

I'm supposed to go by the house at 3pm to pick up my clothes and other things. Am I still supposed to do that? Can you check with Rach?

Please tell her how sorry I am. I will do anything to make it up to her.

Thank you!!

Email to Sam

I'm happy you're willing to meet with me. Ronnie is my friend, and I want to do whatever I can to help.

As far as you picking up your stuff today, I tried calling and texting her, but she's not responding. She might be at the gym. I'll keep trying. I don't know any of the details regarding the pick up. I suggest you do whatever they told you to do so you don't get in trouble.

Ronnie isn't the one pressing the charges for what happened between you and that police officer, but I know the prosecutor office has been in contact with her about it. Your lawyer should know what's going on there.

Ronnie is willing to postpone the court hearing next week on the restraining order to see if you guys can work something out. Obviously, it's going to require some significant changes in your attitude, and a lot of compromise on your part. I'm up on everything that's been going on (or not going on) between you guys sexually. I know that's been a source of continuing frustration for her, and I'm sure for you also, but we can talk more about that tomorrow.

Meet me at the _____ Cafe, on _____. I'll be there at 11am.

22.

Updates

1. My date with Tinder Bull No. 2 went well last night. Not a particularly bright guy, but oh well... at least he looks good naked, ha ha. Things started out kind of slow. He was actually kind of shy, so after a while, I pretty much took the initiative. We had sex, and it was good, but he came way too fast. We fell asleep for a bit, and then he flipped me over and hit it again. The second time was better. After I left his place, I stopped over at Chad's house and spend the night with him. I really like how smooth things have been lately between Chad and I; it's like we almost got our old thing back. When i got into bed with him, he didn't ask where I had been... he just knew. When he moved under the sheets to go down on me, I put my hand on his shoulder, kissed him, and complimented him on what a good PussyBoy he was. In the morning, in the shower, I gave him a nice handjob and let him ejaculate.
2. The property pick up yesterday at Ronnie's house went well. Marc did exactly as I asked. He said Sam looked at him like he wanted to kill him, but didn't say a word. There were four police officers there to keep the peace. Two of the cops were laughing and made a comment about the "new boyfriend", and wondered if the girl was "hot".

3. My meeting with Sam this morning went a lot better than I thought it would. He was extremely subdued and mostly listened to what I had to tell him. I was very direct with him. He's going to digest what I had to say; we've agreed to meet up again on Tuesday.

More details later when I have more time...

I've had sex with a wide variety of different men... pretty much all ages, shapes, sizes, races, etc. Sexually, I prefer dark-skinned, muscled-up, dominant black men, but I'm not exclusive that way. The guy I hooked up with last night was white, with dark hair, green eyes, and Irish.

Email to Chad

So... I'm thinking it's time to step things up a bit, to see just how dedicated and focused you are on pleasing me.

I'd like you to go to a sporting goods store today and buy a pair of knee pads, and a box of three golf balls. Please make sure they are the Titleist Pro V1 brand.

I'll give you further instructions tomorrow.

I hope your day is great!

Texts with Chad

Hi sweetie... what time are you getting off work?

I was planning to leave here about 7pm.

Good. Okay. I'll drop by around 9pm. Can I spend the night with you?

Of course. Always. You don't need to ask.

I feel like I need to, still. But I appreciate that.

You're welcome back home anytime, you know.

I know you've said that, but I really want my own place. It's a privacy thing. I've been kind of dating, and living with you would be hard to explain, obviously.

Have you thought about my other proposition?

Yes. And that's very generous of you. But I don't think it's fair that you should have to move into the pool house while Ronnie and I live in the main house. That feels awkward to me. Ronnie likes the idea, though, ha ha. She's ready to move in tomorrow.

I'm serious. I wouldn't mind at all. I'd love to have you near. You can date or see whoever you want, or do whatever, I wouldn't mind. I understand you like your freedom. I'm not going to interfere.

What if it was the three of us, including Tina? Would that be too awkward? I know you two don't always get along so well.

I'm sure things would be fine. I'd like to get along better with her. I'm sorry we had that blowup back in November.

She was really upset with you. You were very rude and dismissive of her.

I know. It was my fault.

Have you told her that?

No. I've never really had the opportunity to talk with her much since then.

Maybe you should apologize to her, I'm sure she would appreciate it.

I'd be happy to do that. Should I write her a note?

No. I think you need to do that in person.

Okay. I'll defer to your judgment on that.

I'll talk to her, and get her thoughts.

Okay.

So tonight... you know what night it is, right?

Yes.

Are you ready?

I will be.

Good. Get yourself nice and clean for mommy.

I will.

Make sure you pen it in your schedule. From now on, every Monday night will be Bad Dragon Night.

Yes, ma'am.

Are you going to be a good PussyBoy for me tonight?

Yes.

Are you going to take the knot for mommy?

I'll try.

You better do more than try. Did you buy the knee pads and the golf balls like I instructed?

I was going to get them after I leave work.

Good. I want you to keep the knee pads in your brief case so you always have them available during the day or night.

Yes, ma'am.

I hope you're ready for a good fucking tonight. You've tightened up on me since last spring. We need to open you up.

Yes, ma'am.

If you're a really good PussyBoy for me tonight... like really extra good... maybe I'll give you another handjob after. And let you cum.

Or a blowjob, maybe?

Oh, I seriously doubt that, ha ha. I don't think your little penis will ever be in my mouth again. Those days are gone. You get my hand, or nothing.

I'm sorry I asked.

You should be.

Have you been touching yourself this week?

Honestly?

Yes. Honestly.

Yes.

How many times have you jacked off this week?

Five, or six.

Did you this morning?

Yes.

In the shower?

Yes.

We're going to need to have a conversation about that.

Yes, ma'am.

Masturbation is a filthy habit. Among other things, it diminishes your sex drive, and your motivation to please me.

I don't think it does.

I don't think I asked for your opinion, did I?

No, ma'am. I'm sorry.

I'll be there at 9pm. Please be ready when I get there, freshly showed and in position, wearing your pretty panties for me.

Yes, ma'am.

Email to Chad

Remember, you're all mine Friday night. I'll let you know where to meet me, but it won't be until about midnight. Those items I asked you to purchase and keep with you at all times, please make sure you bring them with you. And just so you know, Tina will be joining us.

Also, please remember you have an appointment at the salon to be waxed Saturday morning. I'm going to need you to go on your own this time.

And just so you can plan, Tina will be joining me on Bad Dragon Night this coming Monday at your house. You'll have an opportunity to apologize to her at that time for your inappropriate behavior towards her last October/November. I expect your apology to be sincere, that it will be properly and contritely expressed, and that you won't embarrass or disappoint me.

Talk soon,

22

Updates

I'm scheduled to meet up with Sam again tomorrow after work to have another talk with him about the situation with Ronnie.

Another conversation with Tinder Man today. I explained that I wouldn't be able to see him until after next week. He was disappointed, which is exactly how I want him to feel.

I have a little game planned for PussyBoy Friday night; we'll see how he does. My friend Tina is going to help you out.

Ronnie and Tina and I have decided to get away from all the recent drama, and go to Las Vegas for a few days next week, to relax and just have fun.

Email to Chad

I know you're nervous about tonight, and honestly, considering how wickedly devious your ex-wife can be, you should be. ha ha.

In addition to your kneepads and the three golf balls, there are two more things I need you to bring with you: A small bottle of mouthwash, and a brand-new toothbrush.

Please get there at exactly 12 midnight.

I expect that you will be on your best behavior.

See you soon!

e-mail to Chad

I haven't heard from you today, and wanted to follow-up regarding what happened on Friday night.

I'm very, very proud of you. Tina was convinced that you were going to safe word on us. I, on the other hand, had total confidence that you wouldn't. When she came back to the table, after speaking with you, and leaving you in the bathroom, she told me, *"He'll be back in five minutes. You watch."* Thank you for proving her wrong.

I know that was an unexpected and very intense experience for you, but you did very well; exactly as I expected you would.

What I really appreciate, though, was how obedient and respectful you were with Tina. You minded your manners, and did what you were told. Tina was surprised by that; I wasn't. I've always told her what a good PussyBoy you are.

I'd like to speak with you later this week about your offer that Ronnie and Tina and I can move into the main house, and that you would move in the pool house. Maybe we can have dinner.

Both Ronnie and Tina are ready to move in tomorrow, but I still have a few concerns. I want to make sure that if we decide to accept your offer, that we're not going to have a problem with you changing your mind and then kicking us out. I also need to make sure that your expectations are appropriate.

I talked to my lawyer about my concerns. He suggested that we enter into an agreement, whereby you would lease the main house to me for one dollar a month, for like maybe 24 months. So, I'd like to talk you about this. If I decide to accept your offer, we would need to have some of the rooms redecorated, and some of the furniture replaced. Any furniture in the house that Emma ever sat on, or slept on, I want gone.

Call me later tonight, please.

22

Sam's Choice

Unfortunately, Sam has decided that he's not interested in being Ronnie's cuckold... even in a dominant role. Which is too bad. He had a chance to try to save his relationship with her. She's very disappointed, and now more determined than ever to have him prosecuted for what he did to her. She's going to meet with her lawyer (actually, my lawyer, who I introduced her to) tomorrow.

Email to Sam

You need to please stop calling and texting Ronnie. You're in violation of the restraining order. And besides that, she doesn't really want to talk with you. Don't make us call the police again.

22

Texts with Sam

Please 22, I need to talk with her. Please!!

So now you're going to start bothering me?

I just need to talk with her. Can you please tell her?

She doesn't want to talk to you, Sam. Go away.

Where is she? Is she with you?

She's in the other room.

Could you please just let her know?

She's busy Sam.

Doing what?

She's busy.

Please just tell her.

Her door is closed. I'm not going to interrupt her.

What is she doing?

Do you really want to know, Sam? Do you want the play by play?

Can you please just tell her I'd like to talk with her?

Oh, I'm pretty sure she doesn't want to be interrupted right now

Why? Was she doing?

Do you want me to tell you the truth, Sam? Or do you want me to lie to you?

Just tell her I'm on the phone. Please.

I'm not going to interrupt her.

What is she doing?

My guess is... they're probably still fucking. He hasn't been here that long.

Who's she with??

I think you met him last week, didn't you?

That nigger at my house?

He's African-American, Sam. Don't be crude.

Are you fucking kidding me?? Are you serious?

This conversation is over. Stop texting me.

PUT HER ON THE FUCKING PHONE!!!!!

I'm calling 911. Have fun in jail.

FUCK YOU 22_!! FUCK YOU!!!!

Sam is in jail again

Sam's back in jail again, this time for violating the restraining order that Ronnie took out against him.

His criminal charges so far... battery on a police officer (for when he got into a fight the police when they tried to serve him with the restraining order), domestic battery against his wife (for when he beat the crap out of Ronnie), and two violations of the restraining order.

They put a $100,000 cash only bond on him.

Email to Chad

It was most curious to me that late Friday night, in bed with me, after you showered, you were unable to get an erection, despite my opening my legs for you to make love to me. I'm sure you can image my disappointment.

And yet last night, while I was strapping you, and you took the knot for me, and we were "joined", when I reached around, your little dick was throbbing hard, and then you immediately spewed all over the sheets.

Most curious, indeed.

Email to Chad

I have a very important date on Friday with a guy that I'm really crushing on, and I want to be ready for him. His name is unimportant.

So… I'd like you to please help me get ready. I want to be super-smooth for him, and lotioned and perfumed in all the right places. I'd also like you to please pick my panties for me, and paint my toenails.

Are you game?

Email from Chad

Of course, I'm game. I'd love to help you get ready for your date, and share that with you. Any chance I'll be able to see you afterwards?

Please know that as disappointed in me as you were Friday night, I was even more disappointed in myself. I promise I'll make it up to you.

Chad

Email to Chad

Oh wow! The way you were feasting on the pussy late last night after I dropped by… licking and slurping and sucking out all that sweet cream he left for you… I was impressed. You are very good at that, boy! I love that I can always count on you to service me that way.

Did you miss the taste of black dick on me? It's okay to admit you did. I'll keep your little secret safe.

I was thinking… maybe we need to get a big fat one back in your mouth again, so you can remind mommy what a good little cocksucker you are.

Are you ready to do that for me again?

I should probably tell you that Tina has expressed an interest in watching you do that.

Email to Ronnie and Tina

It's all done, bitches!!!

I just got a call from my lawyer. Chad went over and signed the lease. We can move in next weekend. We need to plan a huge party!!

Email to Chad

Thank you for signing the lease. My lawyer thought that was the best way to handle it. I appreciate your agreeing to it.

I told Ronnie and Tina that we could move in next weekend. Does that give you enough time? I'm perfectly okay with you keeping your office/study in the main house, as you requested. No problem.

Date tonight

Chad will be helping me get ready for my Tinder date tonight. I'm super excited!

Chapter 22

Temptations

I've been having to confront some major temptations the last week or so. I never understood the power of "triggers" until I got out of rehab. They are very real for me.

So far, I'm okay. Spending a lot of time with my sponsor and my friends. Going to counseling. And fighting the urges. It's been very difficult for me, but I'm determined not to back down that dark road.

Chad has been a major source of comfort. Just being with him, even if we're doing nothing, gives me strength. He's taken off work every day this week to be with me.

Please forgive my lack of updates.

Email to Marc

I've been missing you! Sorry I've been so busy. Things should settle down later this week. We're all moved in. Time to party!!!

Email to Chad

I'm sure you're in your office right now.

I hope you're feeling better. I know you weren't expecting that this morning. But I think you understand why your penis needs to be locked up.

Tina was perhaps a little impatient and rough with you, the way she pulled your balls through the ring, but she means well. I want you to send her a nice note this morning thanking her for doing the honors. I think it was extremely gracious of her to put it on and lock you up.

As I've explained to you, Tina is interested in exploring her dominant side, and learning more about FemDom. So, I expect you to be as respectful and obedient towards her as you are to me. I don't want to hear anything back from her that you have been anything less. In fact, what I want to hear back from her is what a good PussyBoy you are.

As I also explained, there will be occasional and random inspections at your office, and other locations, to make sure your chastity device is secure. Tina has agreed to take the lead there for now as well.

I need to give some more thought to what the rules are going to be going forward regarding your release, but one thing is certain… you will have to earn it. For the most part, it will be based on your behavior, attitude, and demeanor.

Remember… tonight is Bad Dragon Night. I want you to prepare yourself as usual, and get ready. I'd like you to be draped over the edge of the bed and waiting for me at precisely 9pm. Tina will be doing the honors tonight as well; I will be there to guide her, comfort you, and watch.

I hope you have a great day, sweetie!

22

Email to Marc

You're so awesome! Thank you for the flowers. Very nice!!! You didn't have to do that, but I'm glad you did.

I have a thing with my cuck tonight. Tina and I do, actually. But if you want to come by afterwards, that would be nice. Just you and me and that big ole dick of yours, ha ha. It's been too long, baby. You're going to need to remind me why you're on my speed dial…

I'm serious about what I told you on Saturday. You should fuck him for me. I know how much you like a tight ass, ha ha.

Don't worry… fucking a cuck doesn't make you gay. Or at least make him suck your dick. He has lots of experience doing that already. Who knows, you might like it, ha ha

If you do that for me, I'll go dance for you at the club and take you back to the VIP room like I used to. I know you've been wanting that. I know the owner, so I can pretty much go dance whenever I want.

Get back to me about tonight, so I know if it's going to be you, or some other nigga hitting it, ha ha.

22

Email to Tina

I think tomorrow morning would be a good time for you to conduct a surprise inspection at Chad's office. He won't be expecting it.

Make it extremely humiliating for the little faggot. I want him to know his place. Let me know if you get any resistance.

22

Email to Chad

I was disappointed to hear about what happened this morning at your office when Tina dropped by. Obviously, there will be consequences.

Making her wait for 45 minutes out in the reception area until you finished a staff meeting you were in is not acceptable.

I'm going to have her address this with you on Sunday.

Email to Marvis

So, I think this is how I'd like to reintroduce him to your cock...

There's a fetish party that Chad and I have gone to many times. They have it once a month at the home of couple who put them on. It's up in West LA. They always have a certain theme for the party. It's a mixed group, but all very upscale. It's mostly couples, but there are also single women and men, as long as they're sponsored by one of the member couples, so I can get you an invite.

We haven't been to one in almost a year, but I'm thinking of taking Chad to the next one (on Saturday, March 26). My friend Tina also wants to go.

I'd love it if you were there, and we "just happened" to run into you.

I can give your more details later.

Are you game?

Tinder Bull No. 3

... hit the Golden Snatch last night. Tore. It. The. Fuck. Up. Nigga style.

And then he surprised me.

Afterwards as we lay in bed, I told him how much I love it when a guy goes down on me after I've been fucked, when it's all creamy wet. I told him my ex-husband always did that for me.

And then... he did it! I was totally not expecting that! I've never known a black guy to do that. Ever.

I was like, "That's it... clean it up! Taste that whore pussy! You like that, don't you?"

I had so much fun with him!

I'm really loving my Bull rotation now. Seven of them... five black, two white... and at least one is always available when I need him.

Email from Marvis

You know I'm game for that! Just tell me what the rules are.

Texts with Chad

Marc just left. My pussy is filthy with his cum, and needs cleaning. Why don't you come up here and remind me what you're good for?

Yes, ma'am. I'll be right there.

If you please me, maybe next time I'll let you secretly watch him fuck me... from the closet.

I'd like that.

Good. Get up here, boy!

Email to Chad

I was going to just surprise you, but then I thought it would be better to give you a heads up, so you can plan.

I've been wanting to go to one of the fetish parties for quite a while now, but things of been kind of busy and crazy.

And Tina and Ronnie have been wanting to attend one.

The next one is this Saturday, so I thought we would all go together.

I'm still undecided about whether your penis will be locked up or not. Obviously, there are pros and cons.

Email to Chad

A few ground rules for the party tomorrow night:

You will wear your business tux.

You will be introduced to everyone as my PussyBoy.

Your penis will be locked up in chastity, and you will wear your pink lace thong panties underneath your tux.

Your bitch hole will be plugged.

You will be on your best behavior, obey both Tina and I at all times, and do exactly as you're tell.

You will be differential and respectful towards everyone who engages you in conversation.

Your oral services will be available to anyone at the party who wants them, as long as Tina or I are present. That includes both men and women.

If you're a good boy at the party, I will unlock your penis the next morning, and permit you to remain free all-day Sunday, and reward you with a nice foot job, and let you cum all over my feet, the way you like.

Email to Marvis

So… we're all set for tonight.

We need to be careful to play it cool when we "accidentally" run into you at the party tonight. Chad is going to be extremely nervous, so you need to go slow with him, help him relax, etc.

I'd like you to take him to one of the private rooms upstairs and fuck him really good. Remind him what his little bitch hole is for, ha ha. Then tie the used condom around his nuts when you're done.

I'm excited, are you??

Texts with Chad

I'm starting to get nervous about the party tonight. I don't have a good feeling about it. I'm not very comfortable with Tina being so involved. Do you think it could just be us tonight?

Relax Chad. You'll be okay.

But I don't trust her like I do you.

We're all going to have a good time. Don't worry. I've talked to her about your limits. She knows.

I don't want her to embarrass me.

She's not going to do that. Don't worry. You'll be fine.

Can you please promise that you won't leave me alone with her?

I can't really promise you that, Chad... especially if I meet someone I want to hang out with for a while.

Would you be mad if I used my safe word to not go tonight?

I'd be disappointed. But not mad. I told you before, you can use your safe word anytime, without any negative consequence. Is that what you want to do?

I'm not sure.

I love how manly and decisive you are sometimes. It's very attractive.

I'm sorry. I just don't have a good feeling about tonight.

Because of Tina?

Mostly, yes.

It sounds to me like maybe you just need another disciplinary session. Is that it?

No. It's not that.

I think it is. I don't appreciate your negative attitude towards Tina.

I'm sorry I brought it up.

Are you sure? I don't need a PussyBoy with attitude tonight.

I'm just nervous, that's all. There are going to be people there tonight, other couples that we know. From before.

I'm sure there will be. And tonight, they'll see you in a new role. Not as my husband, but as my PussyBoy. Is that why you're so nervous?

Partly, yes.

You'll be fine. Don't worry. It's not like any of them ever saw or thought of you as the big stud or anything.

I know.

I expect you to be on your best behavior tonight. And do what you're told.

I will.

Because you want to? Or because you're being forced to?

Because I love you, and I want to make you happy.

Good. That's better. Do you remember the rules for tonight?

Yes.

Are you prepared to follow them?

Yes.

I'd love nothing more than to reward you tomorrow morning for being a good PussyBoy. Are you going to make me proud of you?

Yes, ma'am.

Good boy!

Chapter 23

Email to Chad

I was going to remind you to send Marvis a note today, thanking him for giving you the long-over-due-fucking you needed last night at the party, but then I thought of a better idea.

Instead, I'd like you to go thank him in person, with your mouth. I'm sure he could use a really nice, relaxing blowjob this afternoon.

I think you remember where he lives. I told him you'd be there at 5:30pm to express your appreciation.

When you get back home, I have a nice surprise for you. I think you're really going to like it!

Please text me when you leave, and get back.

22

PS: Tina really enjoyed watching that last night. She was quite impressed by how obedient you were, and doubly impressed the way you took every inch of Marvis's cock, and backed up on it like he told you to. Good boy! I'm very proud of you!

Email to Marvis

Thank you so much for everything last night. I thought everything went perfectly! Tina said Chad totally freaked out when he saw you there, and started to hyperventilate, ha ha. I appreciate the way you talked to him, and calmed him down. The way you gently put your hand on his ass, like he was your bitch, and pulled him towards you... I LOVED THAT!

I also loved how you casually left the door open to the room when you took him up there, and the way you handled him when he asked you to close it. That was perfect!

So... as we discussed, he'll be there tonight at 5:30pm. He knows he's there to thank you, and suck your cock, but, of course, you can do whatever else you want with him. Your house, your rules. He knows that I expect his obedience.

Be good to him, and let me know how he does...

Email to Tina

I got your message. No problem. Feel free to communicate with him about whatever you want, and do whatever you want with him. He's so busy all the time, I tend to communicate with him by email quite a bit, and he does with me... particularly when I just need to inform him of something, or don't want to deal with his whining or questions.

Keep him on his toes! He hates it when you call him "the little faggot", and is still totally stressing that you saw Marvis fuck him. Use that to ratchet up his angst. Make him feel it.

Please copy me on all of your communications with him. I'll start copying you on mine to him, and vice versa. Thanks!

Texts with Chad

Tina sent me two emails this morning that I noticed she copied you on. I haven't yet responded.

I expect you to do what you're told. And stop whining about it Chad.

I'm not comfortable with her becoming so involved, particularly just on her own like that.

I understand. I'll let her know you obviously need another disciplinary session tonight when you get home.

It's not that.

How late are you going to work tonight?

I don't know. Pretty late. We have several deadlines we have to meet.

Make it not so late. Please be home by 8pm. I'll let Tina know you need a reminder.

Can I just think about this longer?

You don't need to think, Chad. And this isn't a negotiation. You just need to obey and do what you're told.

When it's you, yes, I know. But with Tina, that's very uncomfortable for me. I don't feel like I can trust her. Not like I trust you.

I understand. We can talk about that tonight. Please be home by 8pm.

So, we can just talk about it then?

Yes. We can talk about whatever you like. You are always free to express yourself. I've told you that before.

I know. Thank you. Just you and I, then?

At first, yes. Then we obviously need to bring Tina into the conversation.

Can't she just meet someone on her own? And have her own relationship?

I'm sure she will someday. But for now, we both have you. You're the house PussyBoy.

I just want a relationship with you.

Well, we can talk about that tonight.

Thank you.

Don't be late, boy.

I won't.

Email to Chad

Make sure you don't eat anything before you come home tonight. I need you nice and hungry. I'm going to prepare a special dinner for you…

Texts with Chad

I gather that we're not going to have any more attitude problems with you after last night?

No, ma'am.

Good. It's annoying.

I'm sorry.

The golden shower on your face after you finished your dinner... that was unexpected. I didn't know she was going to do that. But I thought it was a nice touch.

Yes, ma'am.

Was it nice and warm, ha ha?

Yes.

Did you enjoy that?

It was difficult for me.

She felt that you needed something to drink after your meal.

Yes, ma'am.

I appreciate that you didn't pussy out and safe word on us last night.

Yes' ma'am.

I can tell how motivated you are to be obedient. And I appreciate that.

Yes' ma'am.

Please make sure you send Tina a nice note today, thanking her.

I will.

And flowers would be nice. She likes pink roses.

Okay.

I feel like I've been neglecting my Bulls this week. So, I might be kind of busy this weekend.

I understand.

Are you going to be okay if we don't speak for a few days?

Yes.

You can always call me if something important comes up. But otherwise I expect you to quietly stay in your little box if I'm entertaining. I'll text you whenever I have company, so you'll know.

Yes, ma'am.

Good. We'll talk soon. Be a good boy for Tina. Just as you would for me.

I will.

Wait. One more thing. I need you to please have your friend at the DA's office check on the status of Sam's case. I'd like to know the details before I go see him.

In jail?

Yes.

Why are you going to do that?

Because Ronnie wants me to. And she can't.

That's probably not a good idea.

She wants me to talk with him again.

Why?

In her own crazy way, she still loves him, and feels very guilty about what's happened. She wants to me to try to help her fix things with him.

I'm not sure that's possible. It's not just what he did to her. The bigger problem is getting into that fight with the cops. They want him prosecuted. They could have shot him.

I know. I just want to talk with him again. Kind of see where he's at. Feel him out. He's been in jail for over a month now.

Okay. I'll find out what's going on.

Thank you, sweetie.

Email to Chad

I think you like the discomfort of having your little dick locked up.

I think you like the frustration of not being able to get an erection.

I think you like the angst and anguish of knowing that I frequently and openly fuck other men.

I think you like being denied the pussy because you realize you don't deserve it.

I think you know how pathetic and worthless your little dick is.

I think you like the fear and anxiety that other people might find out you're just a PussyBoy.

I think you like that Tina is getting more involved, and keeping you on your toes.

I think you like the taste of cock and cum in your mouth, despite your protestations otherwise.

I think you know what a good little cocksucker you are, and it scares you.

I think you like the pain of being fucked in the ass.

I think you know what a sweet, tight little ass you have.

I think the reason you don't like Tina calling you a little faggot is because you know that's exactly what you are.

I think you like being my bitch.

Email to Tina

I thought the "Aunt Tina" idea was awesome. I love it!

Have fun with our little bitch boy this weekend. Put him through his paces. Remember, he has "panty washing" duty tomorrow morning.

Email to Chad

So... there's this guy who was at the fetish party last week who I've exchanged a few text messages with. I don't remember meeting him, but he got my number from Janey. His name is Garland.

He was there with his girlfriend who he said is from Thailand. Her, I do remember; she's that young girl who was wearing that beautiful red sequin minidress and was dancing in the cage when we got there.

He said she spent most of the evening in the Bang Room, and joked that she has the "tiger pussy" ... which he described as "aggressive, voracious, and likes to eat dick".

Anyway... he heard about the fucking you got from Marvis, and was asking me about you. I told him you were my PussyBoy, and that Tina and I were training you. He asked me if you were "available". I told him, "He might be. It depends on what you want him for."

We then had a conversation about how much you like to suck cock, and what a good little bitch you are. Then I told him the story of how Marco took your cherry ass and turned it into a bitch hole.

I hope you don't mind me being proud of you...

Email to Creed

It's been too long, baby... I'm looking forward to Sunday! They'll have your name at the gate. I'll expect you at 7pm.

I love black men...

I love how black men are so tall.
I love how black men are so muscular.
I love how black men are so masculine.

I love how black men are so well hung.
I love the swagger of black men.
I love the confidence of black men.
I love the charisma of black men.
I love the style of black men.
I love the aggression of black men.
I love the passion of black men.
I love the way a black man touches me.
I love the way a black man holds me.
I love the way a black man grabs my breasts.
I love the way a black man pinches and pulls on my nipples.
I love the way a black man bites my tits.
I love the way a black man kisses my lips.
I love the way a black man nibbles on my neck and shoulders.
I love the way a black man hugs my hips.
I love the way a black man grabs my ass.
I love it when a black man pulls out his cock.
I love it when a black man makes me call it a "nigger dick".
I love it when a black man makes me hold and stroke it.
I love it when a black man tells me to take the head in my mouth.
I love it when a black man makes me suck it for him.
I love the way a black man fingers my pussy.
I love the way a black man licks my pussy.
I love the way a black man gets me wet.
I love the way a black man gets long, hard, and thick.
I love the way a black man uses that dick.
I love the way a black man stretches me out.
I love the way a black man opens me up.
I love the way a black man turns me out.
I love the way black men fuck.
I love the way a black man makes me feel.
I love that feeling when a black man busts his nut inside me.
I love it when a black man soaks his cock inside me after he cums.
I love how black men stay hard even after they cum.
I love it when a black man flips me over and takes my ass.
I love it when a black man makes it hurt.
I love the way a black man owns it.
I love the way a black man makes me cum.
I love the way a black man makes me serve him.
I love the way a black man makes me love him.
I love the way a black man calls me up when he wants pussy.
I love the way a black man tells his friends about me.
I love it when a black man shares me.

I LOVE MY BLACK MEN!

Email to Chad

I've had time to think things through.

I'd like you to please contact your lawyer today. Tell him that you and I have agreed to extend the filing of the final entry of divorce for six months, but that the property settlement portion of our agreement will be permanent.

I will call my lawyer today to confirm the same.

I'd like us to go away somewhere this weekend to spend some time together, just you and I. I can take off work Friday and Monday, before my business trip to Dallas next week. Why don't you plan something for us? Cabo or Napa would be nice.

Last Night Was Perfect

A good PussyBoy is truly worth his weight in gold.

Chad was so perfectly obedient and loving last night, I'm so incredibly proud of him. I swear, I don't deserve this guy.

After Creed left last night... he was great, but not really the subject of this post... I sent Chad a text to come up. He was in my bedroom within 3 minutes. He had been anxiously waiting in the pool house for the Batgirl Signal.

I didn't need to remind him what he was there for. He got naked, climbed into bed with me, and immediately got his face between my legs and started doing his thing... getting after it with his mouth and tongue, licking me out, cleaning me up. Not having used a condom... I don't make him wear them anymore... Creed had left a wet spermy mess for him.

In that situation, Chad knows exactly what I expect of him... he needs to clean front and back, both cunt and asshole, and down to my toes if necessary... if the cum has dripped down my legs... until all evidence of my

Bull's sauce is gone. Chad knows I hate going to bed with a dirty, cummy pussy.

He had watched it happen, or at least saw the beginning of my encounter with Creed, outside next to the pool, on the grass, before Creed picked me up like I was a little rag doll and took me upstairs to finish what he started.

"Did you like watching that tonight, boy?"

"Yes."

"We're going to need to get you up here in the closet so you can watch it all next time like a dirty pervert. Would you like that?"

"Yes."

"Do you think you could stay quiet as a mouse, so my Bull doesn't know you're there? I could put some music on to help hide you."

"Yes, ma'am."

"Oh yes! Like that! Do you like the taste of that, boy?"

"Yes."

"Do you like the taste of whore pussy after it's been filled up with cream?"

"Yes, ma'am."

"You like watching me fuck other men, don't you?"

"Yes."

"Watching me get nasty with them, huh?"

"Yes."

"Mmmmmm... Yes! Yes! Right there! You're going to make me cum again!!"

As I talked to him, Chad just kept after it, tongue gently and then more fiercely swirling around my clit, two fingers inside me, touching my g-spot. He knows how much I like that! I just laid back and enjoyed it.

"You're such a good little cuck. What did you think of Creed? He's huge, huh? He's like 6-5 or something; used to be a linebacker in college. He likes the white pussy. He knows it's his whenever he wants it."

Chad didn't say anything. He was still busy eating.

"You don't mind that, do you? That other men get to fuck me, and you don't?"

"No, ma'am."

"Seriously, you don't mind?"

"I just love being with you. I don't mind flowing your rules and waiting."

"You know they fuck me better, don't you?"

"Yes."

"And that your little penis doesn't really do anything for me."

Chad was quiet.

"I have like five Bulls now. Do you think that's too many?"

"No."

"Five black stallions. And a white one. From age 23 to 56. All with big, thick bull cocks. All of them taking turns fucking your wife."

Chad was quiet. Focused. Just doing his thing.

"Except, actually, I'm not your wife anymore, am I. You made me divorce you."

"I didn't make you do that. I didn't want you to do that."

"But you cheated on me Chad. You picked that fat cow over me. And even got her pregnant. What else was I supposed to do? I didn't trust you anymore."

Chad stopped, and looked up at me. "I never picked her over you, 22. I never stopped loving you."

"I didn't tell you to stop, boy! Get your mouth back on it. You're not done yet."

"I'm sorry." Chad got back on task.

"You fell in love with her. That's what you told me. It was just supposed to be a sex thing, just a fun thing... and you let yourself get manipulated by her. I was very disappointed in you."

"I know."

"It still feels like you're my husband, though... even though you're not anymore."

"I still am, technically, until the 12th. It's not final until then. We don't have to go through with it."

"I know. Did I make a mistake?"

Chad knew better than to stop eating me, but I could tell he wanted to talk. He paused for just a second, and then said. "We don't have to go through with it. We can still stop it." Then he got his mouth back on me.

"But you already gave me all the money, put it all in the trust for me. I'd have to give it all back to you. And then I'd be vulnerable again, like before."

"No, you wouldn't. It's yours. You can keep everything. I don't want any of it back. I just want you."

"Did you know that your lawyer tried to hit on me when I ran into him that day during lunch. He's such a creep."

"I remember you told me. I can get another lawyer. We can stop it. We still have time."

Chad's tongue stopped licking. He was looking up at me now, with that pleading puppy dog look. I let it go.

"I don't know. I'm not sure I can totally trust you. I need more time. And I like my freedom. I don't want you trying to control me again."

"I don't want to control you, 22. I just want you to be happy and healthy. That's all I want. That's all I've ever wanted."

"You've always tried to control me with money. And you know it."

"Only when I was trying to help you."

"I know. And I appreciate what you did for me. I hate to think where I'd be now if you didn't intervene the way you did."

"I've just always wanted to love you, 22."

"Maybe... we can agree to postpone it. To give me more time to think about it. To see if I can trust you again."

"We can do that. I'd like that."

"Do you like being my hubby?"

"Yes. And I love having you as my wife. That's all I've ever wanted."

"Even if you can't control me with your money? Like you have before?"

"I don't want to control you, 22. You can't honestly look at the relationship we've had and conclude that I controlled you. You always did whatever you wanted. And I've always been fine with that."

"Do you want to be my cuckold hubby again?"

"Yes."

"And my PussyBoy?"

"Yes."

"Are you sure? That hasn't always been so easy for you."

"I'm sure. I love you, 22. I'll do anything for you."

"Anything?"

"Yes."

"I love you too, Chad. I always have. I was upset with you, and extremely hurt by what you did, but I never stopped loving you. I feel like we're made for each other."

"We are. I think we're perfect together."

"Okay... so... I have a question; a serious question."

"What?"

"This is serious."

"Okay."

"What if one of my Bulls accidentally gets me pregnant? Or... what if I decide to go off the pill? And I have a black baby? Are you still going to want me? And stay with me? And support me emotionally, and financially as my loyal, loving husband?"

Chad was quiet for a moment. He needed to think about that one. Then he answered. Quietly. "Yes."

"That wouldn't change things for you, if your wife had another man's baby?"

"Not if you still loved me."

"What if I also loved him, my baby daddy?"

"Would you?"

"I don't know. I could. Maybe. I was in love with Marco. You remember what that was like. I don't know. What if I did?"

"That could get complicated."

"I know. I'm just trying to be honest with you. Because I think about that. What if I loved both of you?"

Chad was quiet. I let him think to himself.

"If that happened, the whole 'torn between two lovers' thing, would you stay with me so we could try to work things out? Or would you just dump me?"

"I would never just dump you. 22."

"So, you'd stay with me so we could work through it?"

"Yes."

"Would you help me raise my baby?"

"Yes."

"Would you raise my baby as your own?"

"Yes."

"And love my baby as if it was your own child?"

"Yes."

"I don't know if I believe you."

"I would, 22."

"How would we explain it to people? To your family, and our friends? The people you work with? If my baby had dark skin?"

"If it happens, we'll deal with it."

"People would know my baby daddy was black. That wouldn't bother you?"

"We could deal with it."

"Sometimes you just melt my heart, and make me want to cry. You're such a good man. You know I love you to death, don't you?"

"Yes."

By this time, Chad had climbed up next to me; we were face to face, talking.
I motioned him down, and opened my legs for him. And teased him. "You're not finished yet, mister. I'm still kind of revved up. I need you to make me cum again, so I can sleep. Did you want to spend the night with me?"

"Yes. If that's okay."

Chad got back to doing his thing. I was still extremely wet for him, and getting wetter. I lay on my back, my head and shoulders propped up on the pillows, my legs spread wide for him. He was feasting.

After a while, I moved my right foot down, underneath him, and rubbed his balls with the tops of my toes, kind of flicking them. They felt warm and tight.

"Is your little dick trying to get hard in your cage?"

"Yes."

"I love keeping you locked up until you're desperate to cum. I love controlling you that way."

Chad kept doing his thing... more intensely now.

"Tina thinks I should have your balls removed. She thinks that's where your attitude comes from, when you resist us."

Chad didn't say anything.

"But I think they're cute. I like playing with them. I love sucking on them for you when you're locked up."

Chad was basically ignoring me.

"I told Marvis he can fuck you whenever he wants. Any night he wants. As often as he wants."

Chad was still ignoring me, enjoying what he was tasting.

"He really loves your mouth, the way you suck him. The way you take your time and work his balls. And your ass. He told me it was nice and tight. He was joking around that your ass hasn't been blown out like a lot of bottoms."

Chad just kept doing his thing. I could feel him getting me closer.

"Are you going to be a good little faggot for mommy, and suck his cock, and put your ass up for him, whenever he wants?"

Chad continued to ignore me, like I wasn't even there. He was at one with the pussy. Feasting, tongue getting all up in it, with his thumb in my ass.

I gently tapped his balls with the top of my foot. Once. And then again, harder, not quite kicking them, but almost. And then again, trying to get his attention. He yelped after the fourth not-so-gentle tap.

"I asked you a question, boy."

"Yes, ma'am"

"Yes, ma'am, what?"

"I'll do what you want me to."

"That's better."

Then I motioned Chad to get on his back, underneath me, and I rolled over on top, sitting on his face. Looking down at him, I could feel more of Creed's semen oozing out of me, from deep inside where he put it... nine inches deep inside me. Chad was catching it on his tongue. It looked like white foam.

"Swallow it. Taste it. Taste my Bull's cum. Lick it all out of me."

Slowly, I started to ride his face. Sliding back and forth, smearing my juices all over, from chin to forehead. And back again. His face was glistening in the candle light. He looked so handsome!

And then I felt it starting to happen.

Whenever I'm getting ready to cum, it always starts in my legs; my quads and my glutes tighten. My abs tighten, and I start to spasm between my legs.

If Chad's penis was inside me, it would have felt to him like my pussy was suddenly gripping his dick, and squeezing, letting go, and then squeezing it again. But he didn't feel that because his little dick was locked up in chastity.

I screamed out. "That's it... that's it... oh fuckkkkk... yessssssss!! Uhhh... uhhhh... Mmmmmm... yeahhhhhsssss!!"

I started kind of bucking and thrashing on his face, like I was riding a wild bull.

And then I exploded on his face. It was super intense. Creed had already made me cum twice that night, once outside on the grass with his hand before he penetrated me, and then again upstairs while he was fucking me.

Part of me was disappointed that Creed didn't finish fucking me out there on the grass, so Chad could have seen the whole thing, rather than just part of

it. I play-acted for Chad (who I knew was hiding and watching in the dark from the pool house) when Creed picked me up and tossed me over his shoulder, "No, no! Put me down! You're just going to want my ass again! I'm not that kind of girl! Your cock is too big for me. It hurts me."

But of course, even Creed knew I was just messing around with him; as he made clear when he smacked my ass a few times and told me to be quiet. "We both know what you need, little girl."

I was going crazy with Chad's mouth on me.

Unlike with Creed, this orgasm, with Chad, was different. It was more like the slow-moving train that gets closer and closer and closer... and then suddenly crashes into the wall and explodes.

I squeezed his head between my legs, almost crushing it. And then in the next moment my legs turned to jelly and I collapsed on his face with my full weight, nearly suffocating him.

My whole body was shaking. I lost control of... everything. I could feel the urge to release, but held it. I suddenly needed to go really bad, like I had been drinking beer all night or something. I kept trying to hold it. Until I couldn't any more. Or didn't want to.

In an instant, Chad knew what was happening. He knew it I wasn't just cumming. I was peeing on him. It felt like all this pent-up pressure was leaving my body. I could feel the wet heat. The golden stream. It was a lot. It felt like a high-pressure hose suddenly opened. I lifted myself up on my knees, hovering over Chad, and sprayed all over his face. Not caring what he thought. Not caring about the mattress. I was just feeling myself in the moment.

Why is pee always so warm, almost hot coming out?

Oh God, it felt good just to release like that. It was like, "ahhhhhhhhh."

Chad was kind of shocked at first. He kept his face there, not that he had much choice since I was sitting on his face. His mouth closed, he was moving his head from side to side. I reached down and grabbed him by the hair, and pulled his head up off the bed, to make sure he didn't try to get away.

"Open your mouth, boy. Don't be shy. Open it! Show me what a good PussyBoy you are. Taste it! Drink it! You earned it." He did as he was told.

And then, I just kind of collapsed and passed out from exhaustion. I don't even remember falling asleep after that, although obviously we did.

Sometime, in the middle of the night, I woke up and realized where I was. Chad was lying next to me, sleeping, spooning me, holding me. I felt sore between my legs, but it was a sweet kind of sore, the kind that makes my toes curl and warms my heart, remembering how it got that way.

Underneath us, the bed was cold and wet. But I didn't care.

I pulled the covers over us. And just lay there, feeling him, hearing him breathe, and loved him.

To Be Continued…..

Made in the USA
Middletown, DE
27 September 2022